KEEPER of the Light

DAUGHTER OF DESTINY

Keira F. Jacobs

Cover art by Dar Albert, Wicked Smart Designs

Published by Oliver-Heber Books

0 9 8 7 6 5 4 3 2 1

CHAPTER ONE

Le'Gar's skyline had once been a silhouette of cathedrals and stone towers. It had been magnificent, but quite usual. Then the gargoyles came, and the pointy tips of horns and the sharp edges of rocky wings overtook the rooftops. Now the city was flecked with stone beasts and ghoulish grins.

On the peak of the king's cathedral sat a griffin, his wings outstretched toward the drizzly morning sky. Being permanently bound to the highest spot in the city, the griffin could see Naomi coming up the street below before the stone angel or the goblin below each of his wings had a chance to spot her.

"Here she comes," purred the griffin.

The angel shifted, attempting to peer down the dark, stone street that dumped into Center Square.

"I don't see her," the goblin grunted, a gravelly sound.

The griffin shook his stiff, solid feathers. "It's because you're so puny down there."

"Might I remind you *again*," the goblin shook his fist, "that I did not choose to be below you. I was built here, you magnificent idiot."

The angel darted her round, one-toned eyes to them. "Will you two *hush*? She may hear us."

"From all the way up here?" the griffin doubted. "She'd have to have big ears."

"Shhhh," the angel spat.

The gargoyles looked down again at Center Square. The cobblestone was a grayish blue in the early morning hours. No one in Le'Gar was awake yet.

No one except Naomi Smyth.

She brisked through the city with a cloak drawn around her tattered blouse and linen trousers, snuffing out street lanterns that hadn't faded during the night. That was her job—as strange as it may seem—but someone had to do it. Every evening, lantern-lighters would rush around Le'Gar to illuminate the city with flames that created menacing shadows within the towering stone alleyways. Then, in the dark of the morning, lantern-snuffers would move about and smother them. Only those desperate for a job would inquire about being a lighter or a snuffer, and Naomi had been a snuffer for two years now.

The goblin watched Naomi move about below. "You think *she* could be another?" he doubted. "She's an eighteen-year-old snuffer who has been in Le'Gar for eleven years now. We would have seen her do something extravagant by now if she were who you assume she is."

"No." The angel shook her head, making a grinding noise. "That's just the thing. She is not who she says she is."

The goblin glared. "Why does she lie about who she is?"

"She doesn't lie," the griffin defended. "Not with ill intent, anyway. She doesn't know who she is."

The goblin pondered this. "What does the old man think?"

"Old Man Magnificent has been suspicious of her since the

day she arrived in Le'Gar," the angel explained. "Why do you think he has stayed in Le'Gar all this time?"

The gargoyles sat in silence, watching Naomi finish dousing the black poled lanterns in Center Square. She looked up, staring right at them. Her brown hair was tousled and held back loosely with a tie. Looking at her, anyone could tell she was not a native to Le'Gar. Her skin was too tan to be from this chilly, gray mountain city. She had grown up in Beezus: a seaside peninsula three months south of Le'Gar on the Desarian Sea.

Naomi looked back down and kicked at something on the street. Aimless. Bored. Tired. Then she moved on to continue her task.

The goblin's stone chest had tensed when she looked at him. "If she is who you suspect her to be, doesn't that mean she's in danger?"

The angel nodded. "Yes."

"We all know Naomi," said the griffin. "She's too innocent to be anyone but who she says she is. Shouldn't we just leave her be? Let her live the life she's living? If she doesn't know, then King Tal doesn't know."

"That is not necessarily true," the angel countered. "King Tal Demar was born into a dangerous game and acquired knowledge he shouldn't have. If he discovers her secret before she does, she may not have enough time to get away."

CHAPTER TWO
BEEZUS: TWELVE YEARS AGO

"I'm going to find you!" Naomi's mother taunted in a sing-song voice.

Naomi giggled and wriggled her six-year-old body deeper into her parents' wardrobe. She faded behind one of her father's cloaks and slunk to a sitting position. Her knees met her chest and she rested her chin on them. Her long, brown hair draped over her arms like a form of protection. Her heart pounded, awaiting the wardrobe door to fly open and for her mother to shout, "Got you!"

Hide and seek was their favorite game to play. They played it every day. Even when Naomi didn't want to. Sometimes Naomi was tired, especially at the end of a long day trailing her mother at the market. But even on those days, her mother forced a game.

"You want to be the best hider in Beezus," her mother would say. "Remember: no crying and no moving."

Thinking of her mother's instructions now, deep inside the wardrobe, Naomi practiced steadying her breaths. In, out. In, out. Breathing through her nose was a lot trickier when her heart thudded so hard, but her lungs weren't weak. Chase was another game her mother liked to play. She would take Naomi to the wildflower fields on the cliff tops overlooking the Desarian Sea and send her off in a sprint.

"Run, Omi!" Her mother would always laugh when she said it, setting off to catch her. "Run like your life depends on it!"

Naomi's lungs were strong. Her muscles were conditioned. She was only six and she could do what most teenage boys could. The only thing she could do better than a teenage boy was hide, and she was proud of that. Her mother and father made sure she knew that was something to be proud of.

"I'm the best hider in Beezus," Naomi whispered to herself.

The wardrobe stifled her small voice and she looked up at the cloak towering over her on the hook and rod. It loomed in a menacing sag like a drooping ghost. She knew her parents were right outside the wardrobe, but she suddenly wished they would find her already. A trickle of fear invaded her mind that maybe she was too good at hiding. Maybe her parents wouldn't find her and she would be here forever. Her mother always said, "Don't leave your hiding spot. *No matter what.*"

Just when Naomi grabbed her necklace to nervously twist it between her fingers, the wardrobe doors flew open. She screamed, then laughed.

"Good job, darling," her father said, reaching into the hanging cloaks.

Naomi stretched toward him and he pulled her out, twirling her into the bedroom.

Her mother stood by the bed, adjusting the single quilt. "You're getting better, love."

Naomi's father set her down by the stone hearth that kicked heat into the damp room. Beezus was a seaside town full of dingy white, dome structures that were always wet from the salty, humid air. The hearth was lit every night, even in the summer, just to dry out the place. Naomi never minded it though. It made the evenings relaxing and comforting. She didn't have a hearth in her own bedroom, just a soggy window. Many nights she would crawl into bed with her parents after they fell asleep. It was warmer that way. Safer. Not that Naomi knew of any impending danger that could snatch her away in the night. She'd only imagined those kinds of things.

Her father motioned to the wood floor in front of the hearth. "Sit here and get warm now."

Naomi sat, crossing her legs and tucking her nightgown around her knees.

Her father pulled a wooden chair away from the wall and sat. Leaning forward, he looked down at her. His black beard moved with his soft smile. "I'm going to tell you a story, is that all right?"

Naomi giggled, her brown eyes glittering. "Of course it's all right, Papa. I love your bedtime stories."

The wrinkles in his forehead deepened. "This one isn't a bedtime story, love. This one is real."

Naomi noticed her mother shift and cross her arms. But her father looked up and nodded at her mother. Some sort of silent acknowledgement passed between them and her mother sat on the bed, folding her hands in her lap.

"You already know some of the story." Her father reached up and grabbed a marble from the hearth's mantle. The marble was a pearly sphere swirling with wisps of blue. It had always sat on the mantle, never removed until now. "This. Do you know what this is?"

Naomi shook her head. She knew it was a marble, but she also knew that was not what her father was asking.

He placed the marble in his right palm, facing up. "This represents our world."

"Thãen," Naomi said.

"Yes, love." Her father's eyes became weary. "A world is rather heavy to hold. Have you ever imagined that?"

Naomi frowned. "How can you hold a world?"

"You can't." He smiled then. "And neither can I. Or your mama."

"So does Thãen float?"

"Oh no, no it does not." He rolled the marble around in his palm in little circular motions. "See how my hand cups this marble?"

She nodded.

"That is how The Hand of Protection holds Thãen."

"So there *is* a hand that can hold the world?" Naomi's mouth hung open. "You just said there wasn't!"

He leaned forward and shook his head. "Not a human hand, but a very powerful hand. One that is not of this world. As you see, the hand is outside of our world, holding it. There is a different realm that surrounds our world. A space for higher, immortal beings. We call it the Outer Void."

Naomi squinted, trying to follow.

Then her father reached into his pocket and drew out four tarnished, gold coins. Probably all he had. He held the coins in his left palm, also facing upward. "What do you think these coins represent?"

"Another world?"

He smiled at her tan nose. "Good guess. But no."

She huffed.

"These coins represent people. People within Thãen."

"Why are they outside of Thãen, then?" She pointed to the marble. "Shouldn't they be in that hand?"

"They should be." Her father's voice lowered. "But they aren't."

A thump of fear beat with Naomi's heart. "Oh. What happened to them?"

Her father pressed his lips together. The quiet that passed between them allowed the cracks of the logs in the hearth to command the room. "They don't belong to Thãen anymore," he murmured. "They belong to The Hand of Calamity."

Rain began to smack the bedroom window, making Naomi jump. Her mother jumped, too.

Naomi shivered. "What is The Hand of Camamity?"

"It's Calamity, dear," her mother softly corrected.

"It's another hand outside of our world," her father explained. "It also resides in the Outer Void. Only it doesn't hold our world like The Hand of Protection does. But it wants to."

"Shouldn't The Hand of Protection share?" Naomi suggested. "It's nice to take turns."

Her parents smiled at each other, amused.

"It's nice to take turns when both parties' intentions are of merit," her father agreed, shaking the coins in his left hand. "The Hand of Calamity doesn't want to hold Thãen with care and safety. It wants it out of greed, power and control."

"Oh." Naomi frowned. "Then why is it holding people from Thãen? Are those people okay?"

Now her father dropped his head, closing his eyes momentarily. "That's the sad part, Omi. The Hand of Calamity can't have Thãen, so it's plucking Thãen's *people*. Eventually, The Hand of Calamity will hold more people in its palm than Thãen itself holds. That's when the scale will tip and the world will roll from The Hand of Protection into The Hand of Calamity."

Naomi imagined Thãen rolling like the marble from palm to palm. She couldn't picture what that would feel like or even how that was possible. If she was still in the world when it happened, would she turn head over heels like she did when she rolled down the wildflower hills? A part of her was waiting for her father to tell her he was just joking. That this was all a bedtime story. But he did not. And her mother grew more forlorn the longer her father talked.

"You see, Naomi," her father went on, "Thãen may not always exist as you know it. One day…"

Her mother bit her lip, but nodded, urging him on.

"One day Thãen may fall into Calamity's possession." He reached out and touched her distraught face. "And there may be no turning back once it happens."

Naomi shook with what she learned. The city of Beezus had always been a place of happy memories and safety for her. The Desarian Sea was a crystal aqua, and blue and pink wildflowers covered the surrounding fields. Nothing was wrong with Beezus. Until now. But it wasn't just Beezus that had been tainted. Her whole world had.

Her mother rose from the bed and strode to her. She bent down so she was eye level. "But there is something else you should know. You can fight to remain true and loyal to The Hand of Protection."

"I will, Mama." She meant it.

Her mother grabbed Naomi's miniature hands.

"Calamity has disciples here in Thãen," she revealed. "They're people Calamity has taken a hold of, but has spared their lives in exchange for service to itself. They walk among us. You must stay away from those in the world who have fallen into The Dark Hand's service. They can trick you and trap you, stealing you to be one of them. Or they can deliver you to Calamity itself and you would be gone from this world. Forever."

Her father gave her mother a shadowed look. "Now, wait—"

"No." Her mother snapped her eyes up to her father. "We cannot soften the blow. She must know it all. At least everything that will help keep her safe."

Her father clamped his lips.

Naomi took turns looking back and forth between her parents, confused.

"You stay away from them," her mother repeated.

"How will I know who is bad and who is good?" Naomi asked.

Her mother pointed at Naomi's heart. "Right here. You can *feel* their desolate souls and lust for glory."

Her eyes widened. "I can?"

"Yes," her father confirmed. "If you are in tune with what is true, honest, and just, then you will be able to detect those who have fallen into The Hand of Calamity."

Naomi squeezed the fabric of her nightgown. "What if… what if I do get taken by The Hand of Calamity?"

Her mother grew stern. "If you ever see the shadow of a hand creeping out of the darkness, you hide. And if that shadow finds you, you run."

CHAPTER THREE

It was a year later when The Dark Hand found Beezus. Naomi had just gone to bed, burrowing deep under her quilt. Rain hit her window in a constant pattern. Her toes were cold. For some reason this spring has been the least pleasant one yet. It rained almost every day and the sky was always gray. Naomi found comfort beside her parents' bedroom hearth most nights and dreaded when it was time to go to her own room. Not only because it lacked warmth, but she had gone to bed afraid every night since her father revealed to her the story of The Hand of Calamity. She would often think herself into seeing shadows and convince her mind that long fingers of masked light stretched across her bedroom.

Which is why she almost missed the real thing.

A single movement of shadows glided atop her quilt. They started on one side of her bed and rippled across her legs, disappearing once more.

When Naomi saw it, she froze, holding the blanket under her chin. It was just her imagination. It was always her imagination.

Her window waned darker as another shadow passed by it.

Then the shady movement was gone again. This time Naomi sat up in bed, knowing it wasn't just her eyes playing tricks. The air had chilled, even more so than it typically was in her bedroom. She squeezed her blanket, heart pounding. An eerie swoosh flooded past her ears and she flung around, catching sight of five shadow fingers creeping up her wall. She flew out of bed and charged for her bedroom door. Her hand touched the doorknob but it swung open before she could do it herself.

Her mother was on the other side, her face drained of color. "Come, Omi. Now!"

Naomi fell into her mother's arms. Her mother guided her into the kitchen where her father was quickly shoving food into a raggedy cloth. Naomi assumed they were going somewhere. Leaving this house of shadows. And she was thankful for it. She'd never be able to sleep in her bedroom again.

Her father honed in on her mother. "Where is her bag?"

Her mother slung a bag onto the kitchen table. "Here."

The bag had sat in the back of her parents' wardrobe for years. Naomi had never questioned why.

Her father stuffed the food sack inside and said, "Come, Omi. Put this on."

Naomi let her father slide the straps over her shoulders. "Papa, where are we going? Is it because Calamity found us?"

"Yes, love." He kissed her head.

She looked over her shoulder toward her room.

Her mother grabbed her face and aimed it forward. "Don't."

She stared into her mother's blazing eyes. "Where are we going?"

"Somewhere far." She swallowed. "You are going to meet us there."

Her parents shared a look.

A crash came from Naomi's room.

Her father grabbed Naomi's arm. "She has to leave *now*."

Her mother hugged her tight, kissing her six times. Then she removed Naomi's necklace.

"Mama, no," Naomi fought. She had worn that necklace since her father gave it to her on her fourth birthday.

"We have to keep it for now," her father settled. "You know how to get to the docks, Omi, my love?"

Naomi nodded.

He pulled her toward the front door. "Go to the docks and board the tall ship with all the other children."

"The other children?" She stumbled out the front door. The streets were thick with darkness but she spotted a boy running toward the Desarian Sea with a backpack of his own.

"Inside your backpack are papers," her father went on. "They are your identification papers. Look at me." He grabbed her shoulders.

She stared back, trembling.

"You are Naomi Smyth." Her father was stern. Scary even.

"No I'm not, I'm Naomi M–"

He gripped her shoulders even harder. "No. From now on you are Naomi Smyth. Your papers say so."

Her mother had tears in her eyes. "Listen to your father."

A scream erupted from the house next door.

Her father hugged her. "I love you. May the sun cover you with light, the moon guide you when you tread in dark places, and the stars protect you with their numbers as an army."

"Don't send me alone," Naomi begged.

"We will meet you," her mother reassured, pulling her little body close. "I promise."

Naomi didn't believe her. She knew in her heart that something about this parting was final. She couldn't bear it. To live without her parents was something she never imagined even in her most dangerous nightmares. Her parents were always there to save her from the nightmares. Now she was leaving them.

And she had nothing to remember them by. Naomi couldn't leave without having a piece of them.

As her mother hugged her goodbye, Naomi slipped her tiny hand into her mother's pocket and snatched the necklace back. The theft went unnoticed, and Naomi slid the jewelry into her own jacket pocket.

A window in the kitchen shattered.

Her mother shoved her toward the street. "Run, Omi."

Naomi hesitated.

Her mother leaned forward. "Omi, RUN!"

Startled, Naomi took off.

"Go, my love!" her mother continued to shout in the distance. "Run like your life depends on it!"

And as Naomi tore for the Desarian Sea, all those years of playing chase suddenly made sense. It all made horrifyingly, perfect sense.

CHAPTER FOUR

It took three months for the tall ship to reach the mountain that held the city of Le'Gar. Naomi cried for the first seven days of the sea fare. She couldn't explain what happened after that, only that her mind fought to make sense and comfort out of the situation. No matter how devastated she was about being ripped away from her parents along with all the other children of Beezus, her mind decided to embrace her lot. Her parents had trained her to be strong, so she would be. She vowed to make them proud. Even when one of the sailors found a young girl speaking to a black snake below deck two months into the trip, Naomi didn't cave to fear. Not even when that young girl mysteriously vanished from the ship the next day. She decided that numbness was better than fear. Strength was better than hysteria.

The ship unloaded on the docks at the base of the mountain. These docks were nothing like the ones in Beezus. Yes, they were wooden, but they were sleek and had very little rot. Where Beezus' docks were narrow and rickety, Le'Gar's were wide and stable. And Naomi had never seen a mountain before. This mountain had lush trees that were dark green and damp. The entire mountain was covered with the color, except for one spot farther up. When she craned her neck, she could see peaks of gray structures poking through the vegetation. She didn't expect this place to look so different from Beezus. She had hoped that, at the least, the city would have white domes like her seaside hometown. But Le'Gar was gray. Cold. Unwelcoming. It was haunting, the way the city hid within the trees, and Naomi found her fear surface. Her chest tightened at the thought of living here alone. She suddenly wanted to jump back on the tall ship and beg the crew to return her home. She wanted to scream at them, force them to send her back. But as a group of men in thick gray cloaks and white ruffled sleeves emerged from the mountain, she swallowed her hysteria. There were four of them and they all held the same blank expression.

With all the children off the ship, the dock was crowded. Naomi bumped shoulders with kids around her own age, all of which she knew now. In the beginning of the voyage, Naomi learned that one ship couldn't hold all of the children of Beezus. Another tall ship had left Beezus on the same night to travel to a place called Ode to deliver the rest of Beezus' children. Now, standing in a sea of Beezus's offspring, staring up at the mountain and the mysterious gray peaks of Le'Gar, Naomi wondered if Ode was warmer than here. More welcoming.

One of the men in cloaks and ruffles waded through the children to reach one of the sailors. "How many?" he demanded as his ruffles, well, ruffled in the breeze.

The sailor, Jeb, who Naomi particularly liked, looked down at the heads below his elbows. "Thirty, sir."

Ruffles looked directly at Naomi then back to Jeb. "Only thirty?"

Jeb lowered his voice. "The Hand was silent when it came. Only the homes closest to the sea made it out."

Naomi's throat closed. *Made it out.* What had happened to

those who were left behind? Dead? Were they *dead*? Her father had said that The Hand of Calamity stole people, not that it killed them. But maybe where they were taken to was equivalent to death. Or worse.

"We will need to see everyone's papers," Ruffles told Jeb. "No one enters Le'Gar without identification. Once we have recorded everyone, they will be sorted into their houses."

Naomi's spirits rose. *Houses.* Thank goodness. Maybe her house would have a hearth like her parents' bedroom.

Jeb nodded. "Right." He turned in a circle, grabbing all the children's attention. "Papers! Get out your papers!"

The sound of sifting and searching fluttered through the crowd as the children retrieved their identification. Naomi's fingers shook as she unbuckled her bag. *I am Naomi Smyth, I am Naomi Smyth,* she recited over and over in her head. Her palms sweat as she clutched the papers. The front page said Naomi Smyth, daughter of Vincent Smyth and Emilia Smyth. Their first names were right, at least.

All the men who had arrived from Le'Gar's city waded between the children, grabbing papers to inspect them. Conversations buzzed above Naomi's head as she waited for a pair of ruffled arms to snag her own papers. Her stomach squeezed. *I am Naomi Smyth, I am Naomi Smyth.* Panic rose beneath her skin. She fought it off, knowing it could give her false identity away. Her father's words sang in her mind, soothing her: *May the sun cover you with light, the moon guide you when you tread in dark places, and the stars protect you with their numbers as an army.*

"Papers?" a voice spoke down at her.

She opened her eyes, not even realizing she had closed them. The man standing above her did not wear ruffles. He wore a gray robe and simple brown boots. His hair was also gray and hung past his shoulders, almost blending with his beard. Was everything in Le'Gar gray?

"Papers," he said again.

She lifted her hands, offering what he desired. He smiled at her, then took them and examined the first page.

She trembled. He was looking much longer than she thought he should. It was simple. Her name was right at the top, why was he staring so long?

"Naomi Smyth," the old man read.

She nodded, sweating.

He mumbled. "Smyth." Turning the parchment to have a look at the second page, he lost his grip and dropped them both. They fluttered to the ground and clung to the soggy wooden dock. "Ah." He was slow to retrieve them.

Naomi didn't say anything, but her heart lurched. He was going to ruin her proof of identification. This mean, old man. How could he do such a thing? She wouldn't get placed in a house if she didn't have legible papers!

"Oh, dear." The old man shook the soggy sheets. They were crusted with dirt and sea salt. He gripped them hard, crumpling them even further. "Sorry about that, Miss Smyth." He handed them back. "You'll be in the Chamber Home For Girls on Fanning Street. It's a wonderful establishment. You'll be well looked after."

She seized the papers from him. Her important documents were now soiled. And a home for girls? Did that mean a home without parents? Without a hearth in the bedroom?

"Stay safe, Naomi Smyth." The old man tipped his head at her and turned away.

She glowered after him.

A firm hand gripped her arm. "Papers."

She yanked her arm away.

The man with ruffled sleeves raised his eyebrows. "I said papers, young one. Quickly."

She obeyed, but argued. "I've already been placed into my house."

The man frowned as he looked at her papers, but he returned them to her with haste. He didn't spend time staring like the old man had. "You have? And what house were you told?"

"The Chamber Home For Girls," Naomi said.

"Oh." The man looked over her head. "Who placed you?"

"The old man." She scanned the docks. "He was...I don't see him now."

"We're all old to you." The man winked at her. "All right, off you go then. Follow that gentleman there with the red feather quill in his hand. You see him, don't you?"

She nodded, but she kept searching for the old man. He had vanished.

"I see the red feather, yes."

"Go on." The man nudged her.

She jostled her way across the dock. The children around her split this way and that as they headed to their designated chaperones. A commotion to her left made her stop.

Ruffles was standing in front of a boy, Simon, waving Simon's papers around to flag down another man in ruffles. "Here. See here."

Jeb looked up from his place among his passengers. "What is it, sir? Is there a problem with Simon's papers?"

"Yes," ruffles admitted. "They look brand new." Ruffles gave Simon a quizzical look. "Son, are these your original papers?"

"Yes, sir, I swear it," Simon pleaded. "My mother loves to organize. She keeps things tidy. I promise, sir."

Jeb faced ruffles with a hand on Simon's shoulders. "I can vouch for him."

Ruffles offered a weary smile. "I'm sure it's nothing, but you must understand, we have to be diligent about who we let into

Le'Gar. There are certain...bloodlines that we must tread carefully with."

Jeb frowned. "I'm afraid I don't understand."

Ruffles removed Simon from Jeb's grasp and led him away toward the mountain scape. "Come with me, son. We will get this sorted out."

Naomi watched Simon drag his feet, reluctant to follow, and she prayed for his safety. But now she felt sick. There was a possibility she wasn't supposed to be here. Or, more so, allowed to be here. This new knowledge sunk in and she no longer felt she could keep her fears at bay. She wanted to be strong and find comfort in Le'Gar as she had in Beezus but that didn't seem possible anymore. She was lying about who she was, and if anyone found out, she would be dragged away with Simon. Only Simon would get off okay. His mother really *was* obsessed with organizing. Naomi, on the other hand, could be found out.

Because she wasn't Naomi Smyth.

The wet identification papers were still in her hands, wrinkled from the old man's grip. Before the old man got ahold of them, they had been as neat as Simon's, if not neater. Because they were not her original papers. They were new. Just as the man in ruffles suspected Simon's to be. She had scowled at the old man as he left her, angry that he was so careless with her documents. But now she had an inkling that maybe she should have thanked him instead.

CHAPTER FIVE
LE'GAR: PRESENT DAY

Naomi's dwelling sat above Le'Gar in the midst of the gargoyles. To access it, she had to climb a flight of stairs hidden behind a wall in an abandoned steeple then cross a catwalk that connected the roof of the steeple to the library roof. The dwelling was just one room and had sat empty for years until Naomi took it over.

When she had turned sixteen, she no longer had a place in the Chamber Home For Girls and was turned onto the streets. Lucky for her, she had a bond with the librarian, Deirdre, who jokingly offered for her to stay in the abandoned room. Deirdre figured Naomi would decline the offer, having to live so close to the mysterious gargoyles. Not to mention the roof of the room had several leaks and the catwalk had no railing. Nonetheless, Naomi preferred it over the streets and found it to be quite peaceful.

It had been two years since she left the Chamber Home For Girls and now she was able to give Deirdre a small amount for rent. The librarian refused her offer the first few times, but Naomi was persistent. She couldn't allow herself to mooch. Even if the room only had window access.

The sun wasn't up yet when Naomi returned home from snuffing lanterns. She strode onto the catwalk and stopped in the middle to peer down over the stone ledge. It was such a long way down that her vision warped and her heart jumped. She leaned back and steadied herself. It frightened her every time she dared to look down, but she could never stop doing so. Something about being up there, so close to the sky, so far from the rest of the people of Le'Gar was thrilling. Thrilling for her, at least. She never desired to seek adrenaline beyond a limit she could handle. She had adopted that characteristic when she decided being Naomi Smyth meant going unnoticed and drawing no attention. It had worked for eleven years, too.

She lifted the hinged window within the library's roof, slipped inside, then shut it behind her. Per routine, she grabbed the dark brown, glass bottle of clove oil that sat on the windowsill and tipped it upside down to make a line of drops on the planked floor. A snake barrier. She lived high up enough that it shouldn't be an issue, but snake sightings had increased the last few months. Black snakes, specifically. And black snakes were rumored to have a direct relation to Calamity.

The room's wooden rafters exposed the underside of the roof, and as Naomi clunked across the floor, she glanced up to check the sticky fly trap that hung from a rafter. There were only three flies. A huge relief. Because fly swarms were also being reported lately. Unnatural amounts of them. Another hint that The Dark Hand may be closing in.

Naomi dropped onto her metal-framed bed to remove her shoes from her aching feet. Her shoes had holes on the underside. They'd been that way for eight months now.

Grabbing the handheld mirror from the bedside table, she examined herself. Her hair was a mess and the skin under her eyes were dark smudges. "I'll get new shoes soon," she told herself. "As soon as I can justify it." She laughed a bit. Her own voice sounded foreign. "Ha-ha-ha," she said slowly, purposefully listening to the sounds she made. "It's funny," she went on, "how I can go days without talking." Studying herself in the mirror one last time, she touched a spot on her tan face that was pale. "And it's also funny how long it takes for a cut to heal."

A rumble of thunder in the distance rolled across the rooftops of Le'Gar. She turned to stare at the dark clouds moving in.

"Another thunderstorm? How fun."

She skipped to the window because no one was around to judge her. She knew she must look silly, but she had to find joy in life somehow.

Swinging the window back open, Naomi slid back out onto the roof. The oncoming storm clouds hadn't reached Le'Gar's gargoyles yet and the morning hours were still dark enough for the full moon to be visible. Naomi was glad for it. She was high enough up and the moon was so massive that it sat directly in front of her eyes. She hung her feet over the roof's ledge, positioned right beside a beastly gargoyle. The moon's glow illuminated the loose hairs floating around her face. She thought of her father's words on the night she was sent away on the tall ship. Somehow, she never forgot them...*The moon guide you when you tread in dark places...*

"I don't know where it could guide me," Naomi said to the sky. "I've never set foot outside of Le'Gar. Sorry Papa, I'm not as adventurous as you thought I would be."

She smiled, picturing her father laughing at her remark, but her smile was short. Her father's face wasn't clear in her mind anymore. Every year she forgot more and more.

At one time in her life, she plotted a return trip to Beezus because she had missed her father and mother so intensely. She was especially close to following through when Ms. Chambers at the Home For Girls forgot her birthday. Ms. Chambers was apologetic, but not sympathetic. Of course, there was no way for Naomi to actually return to Beezus. Not unless she learned to sail. And not unless she dared face what The Hand of Calamity had done to the home she left behind.

Naomi eavesdropped often in The Chamber Home. It was the only way for her to piece together what had happened to Beezus and the people who were left there. From what she gathered throughout the years, The Hand of Calamity had captured those remaining and Beezus fell.

"No survivors," Ms. Chambers had sighed, speaking to the cook one night.

Naomi had been on all fours, hidden behind the doorframe of the kitchen.

The cook stirred a pot of soup. "A tragedy."

Ms. Chambers nodded. "The children are lucky to be alive."

Naomi had sobbed that night. Knowing her parents were never going to meet her in Le'Gar like they said.

Now, Naomi hugged her knees, gazing over the top of the city. Steeples and pointed roofs spread out like a thorny thicket. Gargoyles silhouetted the skyline. Some were gnarled. Some were angelic. But all were important. Naomi knew they protected the city and she assumed they were protection from The Dark Hand. But the gargoyles weren't allowed to move. Their spell forbade it. That part, she didn't understand. How were they to protect Le'Gar if they couldn't move? She had tried to ask the beast gargoyle—the one she sat by now—about it one night, but it communicated nothing. Another forbidden action, she learned.

Naomi reached inside her pocket and drew out a necklace. It had a gold chain with a circular pendant that was open in the center. A pearl sat lodged between a golden half-moon in the middle of the circle. She held it up to the moonlight. "I'm sorry for stealing it back, Mum," she mumbled. The moon glinted off the pearl. "I just needed a part of home with me."

The beast sitting beside Naomi didn't move its head, but its stone eye rolled slowly to look at her.

Her skin crawled as she stared back.

They studied each other.

"Stop gawking at me," Naomi whispered. "You know I think out loud."

It eyed the necklace, then looked forward again.

She frowned. "You're kind of creepy, you know that?"

The beast didn't budge.

"But I don't mind your company." She sighed. "At least I have company."

The distant thunder almost drowned out the sound of hooves against the streets below, but she heard it. She stood, creeping closer to the beast now. She stuffed the necklace back in her pocket and peered over the ledge. A trail of horses and riders darted through the city, looking narrow and small as a piece of grain from all the way up on the roof. Yet even in the dim light and far distance, Naomi knew who and what they were. They rode in pairs; twelve Riders in total. The Riders of Le'Gar. King Tal's faithful watchmen and Le'Gar's law enforcement. Not a cruel bunch, but Naomi always steered clear of them. No need to get stuck in any sort of business that could reveal she'd been lying for eleven years.

The Riders were heading to King Tal's cathedral. The home of his throne room and his royal dwelling. Naomi always admired how grand the cathedral's stone architecture was. Especially the griffin that towered high above in the center, as if ruling over the king himself. There were secret passageways within the walls, too. Naomi discovered them in her younger years when she would go out seeking fun as children do. She'd played in them, unnoticed, because she, of course, was a great hider. Until one day she found a passage that led to a room overlooking the cathedral hall itself. The space resembled an attic, but one entire wall was green and red stained glass. When her nine-year-old self peered through it, she was positioned behind the king's throne and she had a bird's eye view of the royal hall. Through the glass, it looked warbled in green and red, but she could hear clearly. And she heard King Tal talking to himself. She thought it was humorous at first, until she realized he was distraught. His hands were shaking and all he kept saying over and over was *no no no no no*. It frightened her. King Tal was their leader. She saw him as a protector of Le'Gar. But after that day, Naomi feared that even Le'Gar wasn't as safe as she thought it was. And she never returned to that hidden passageway again.

Tonight was different, though. She clung to the beast's right horn and leaned out over the ledge to make sure the Riders were truly heading to the cathedral. There could be a formal reason for their urgent re-entry into Le'Gar from their watch in the mountains, but Naomi had been a lantern snuffer long enough to know the Riders of Le'Gar didn't return from night duty until after the sun came up.

Not unless something had happened.

"That's not normal, right?" she asked the beast.

The beast only gazed downward.

She squinted. "I'm going down there."

Now the beast crunched his head her way. He cast a long, hard glare.

"Don't you dare look at me like that," she said slightly threateningly. She let go of his horn and scurried back across the roof. "There could be something dangerous happening. Wouldn't it be better if we knew about it?"

The beast couldn't answer even if he wanted to, but his continued stare was enough of a response. Thunder growled and she turned away from the gargoyle. She always feared that The Hand of Calamity would reach Le'Gar. The memory of a shadowed hand wavering over her quilt in Beezus had never left her. Even after all this time. To either become enslaved or lose her life to a power so crushing and desperate for control was terrifying.

"I have to know." She leapt onto the catwalk and moved swiftly. "I want to be ready to run."

CHAPTER SIX

Startled crows zipped out from their nooks within the city's arches as Naomi ran through the streets. The moon neared the horizon and the first pale haze of morning crept onto the city's peaks. The king's cathedral loomed ahead, its dome silhouetted against the sky. Naomi darted across the center square, avoiding looking up at the griffin atop the bell tower. She knew he was watching her. No need to feel even more guilty about being an eavesdrop.

In the graveyard beside the cathedral, the secret passage entrance she knew of was a square, wooden door sunken into the mossy ground behind a gravestone that only said, *Death too, shall pass*. The moss had grown over the door since the last time Naomi had been here, which was years ago. She had to claw it away with her fingers. Dirt lodged under her nails but she didn't bother picking it out. The door was exposed again, and by now the Riders of Le'Gar had been in the cathedral for over ten minutes. She was losing time to listen in.

Beneath the graveyard, the inside passage wound in crumbling stone and falling dirt. It twisted in an illogical, non-linear path, avoiding the places in which bodies lay buried. Though so much time had passed, Naomi was still able to follow the twists and turns. When the tunnel ended at another wooden door—this one standing upright like a normal door—Naomi stepped through it into a dumbwaiter. She had to sit cross-legged and hunch her shoulders with her head low to fit inside, but she managed. She grabbed one of the ropes and pulled hand over hand as the pulley system lifted her upward. Her heart raced when the dumbwaiter jerked to a stop, reaching its destination: a cavernous hole in the wall leading to a stone, attic-like space with rotting planks securing the roof's rocky angles.

For a moment Naomi hesitated. Her guilty conscience nagged at her, telling her how inappropriate it was to snoop. And to snoop on the king at that. But she was inside the attic before she could decide to turn back. She took to her hands and knees. The brown trousers she wore were already covered in lamp oil and soot, so scraping against dust covered planks was no bother. What was a bother was how the walls around her were narrower than she remembered. They were solid stone, muffling any outside noise.

Green glass glowed ahead. Naomi steadied her crawl, making sure to keep her knees from thudding. The stained-glass spread out in front of her like a mural, covering the entire length of the far wall. When she looked through, she had a bird's eye view, positioned behind King Tal's throne, of the entire hall. The same view she had when she had come here as a child.

Voices floated upward and seeped through the glass. She leaned closer to take in the scene. The Riders of Le'Gar were without their horses now, but still in their positions, lined up two by two on the navy runner that ran from the hall's entrance to the throne. One Rider was out of rank in front. King Tal stood face to face with him.

The Rider was rigid. "It was found in the city of Ode, sir."

King Tal was not in his formal attire. It felt odd to Naomi, watching him address his Riders in some sort of second choice robe. His sleepwear was probably underneath it. She never imagined King Tal wearing pajamas and the thought made her grin. A brief grin, because then King Tal spoke.

"But Ode was destroyed a full month ago." Tal's voice was strong. A true leader's imperial tone. It matched his firm physique and tough, middle-aged face.

"Yes, sir," the Rider agreed, "but it survived the destruction."

Tal paced. "Of course it did." He stopped and frowned. "Who recovered it?"

The Rider cleared his throat. "Word from the other side of the mountain is that Riders of Raina set out on a quest to retrieve it. A man by the name of Hux led four others into Ode's territory. Or what's left of Ode."

"So Raina is in possession of it now?" Tal said, sharp.

The Rider hesitated. "No, sir."

Naomi held her breath. She had no idea what item they were referring to, but she could feel the importance behind it. The tension in the king's hall settled in her own stomach.

King Tal sighed. "Why? Why can this never be that easy? Who has it, then?"

"The man, Hux, sir." The Rider seemed taught. Even more so than he was before. "He disobeyed orders and didn't return to Raina after the quest. He is said to be the only survivor. The rest of his men were lost to Calamity in Ode."

Naomi's heart jolted. *Calamity.* Had The Hand of Calamity claimed another city? Ode was nearer to Le'Gar than Beezus. Beezus was across the Desarian Sea. Ode was—if she remembered her geography correctly—only a month's trip across the mountains. Half the children of Beezus were sent on a tall ship to Ode. She blanched at the knowledge that some of her own people had escaped, only to meet the fate of those left behind eleven years later.

She focused back onto the conversation in the hall, desperate to know more.

"If Hux is the only survivor and he didn't return to Raina, how do we know he did survive?" Tal interrogated. "And more importantly, how do we know he has it?"

The Rider looked uncomfortable.

"Well?" Tal snapped.

"A golden witch, sir." The Rider looked down.

"A *golden witch*?" Tal boomed.

"She entered my mind, Tal."

Naomi frowned at the Rider's casual language with the king. It had the feeling of old friends rather than superior and wage-earner.

King Tal relaxed. "You know golden witches aren't on our side. Whatever the witch told you is trying to lead you astray."

"Not this one," he argued. "She's different. She's...I trust her."

King Tal was inches from the Rider's nose now. "Listen to me, Saul."

Saul didn't flinch.

"Golden witches want there to be all out war. They don't fear the death that will come." The king's face was red. Naomi could tell even through the stained-glass. "If a golden witch came across the quill, she would do everything in her power to get it into the hands of a Massoud."

Naomi's veins went cold. *Massoud.* Her throat constricted. She hadn't heard that name since she left Beezus. All these years she had recited the phrase, *I am Naomi Smyth,* over and over until she believed it. Since she stepped foot onto the docks of Le'Gar she had never again been true to herself. She had never once said, *I am Naomi Massoud.*

Saul's voice rose. "This witch wants to get rid of the quill."

King Tal said through clenched teeth, "The quill cannot be destroyed. Leaders have tried for ages."

"Then what do you propose we do?" Saul held his palms up. "Say the quill is with this man, Hux. How do we know Hux won't seek out someone from the Massoud bloodline?"

"Hux risks putting his home territory in danger if he gives the quill to a Massoud. The quill makes a Massoud very power-ful." Tal pinched his nose with his thumb and finger. "But his territory wouldn't be the only one in danger, ours would be, too. If Calamity is provoked by a powerful Massoud, it won't target one city, it will target every city. Calamity wants all people. Le'Gar could end up falling."

Saul bore into the king. "Have you ever wondered if a Massoud resides in Le'Gar?"

Naomi held her hand over her mouth, suppressing panic.

The king began to pace. "We have kept detailed records for years of those entering and passing through Le'Gar. We would know."

Saul shook his head.

Tal lowered his chin. "What do you know?"

"I know that half the children of Beezus were sent to Ode eleven years ago."

Tal laced his fingers. "Go on."

Saul shifted. "And half came here. First The Hand of Calamity consumes Beezus, now Ode? What if The Dark Hands now knows of a Massoud who used to reside in Beezus but escaped on a tall ship all those years ago and is hunting them down? Isn't there a possibility that a Massoud is in Le'Gar?"

The panic in Naomi's chest surfaced. Her breathing labored and she swore she might pass out.

"But the quill," King Tal pointed out. "Why was it in Ode? It has been missing for centuries."

"Maybe it wasn't missing," Saul offered. "It's possible someone was keeping it hidden."

"Ridiculous," Tal roared. "Why would someone hide such a powerful weapon?"

"To save it for the perfect time," Saul said. "Sir, you *have* to follow this lead."

The king whipped around and towered over Saul. "You may be my closest confidante, but *I* give the orders and make executive decisions. If I want to seek out Hux and confirm this rumor, then I will command it."

Saul shrunk. "Yes, sir."

The hall grew quiet.

Naomi backed away from the stained-glass but she could still hear King Tal's voice. "If the quill unites with a Massoud, Le'Gar will not stand," he said.

"Yes, sir," Saul recited.

"And all of the territories outside of Le'Gar won't survive either."

"Yes, sir."

The king spoke louder now to all the Riders standing quietly in the hall. "I want to know if a Massoud is in Le'Gar."

A tingle of hysteria spread under Naomi's skin.

"Search the city," Tal commanded. "Interrogate if you have to. Anyone found living under an alias will be delivered to me. We will decide what to do with them then."

Naomi didn't need to hear any more. She crawled through the attic space and dragged herself back into the dumbwaiter. Her hands shook as she leveraged down. She ran, stumbling through the tunnel beneath the graveyard. When she burst into the open air, the sun had risen and the grass surrounding the tombstones glinted with dew. Her feet made wet imprints as she darted from the graveyard. The damp air clung to her skin. Tears fell from her eyes as she tore home. She had lived a lie for eleven years only to face repercussions now, for reasons she didn't understand. *I was forced to live this lie!*

When she scurried into her room under the library's rafters, she paced at a frantic speed. Should she stay? Should she go? *Where* would she go? Did she have any friends who could help her? Or did everyone she ever trusted feel the same about the name Massoud? Should she be afraid of herself? *What was she?*

The thunderstorm broke loose over Le'Gar.

The Riders took to the streets.

Naomi waited to be found.

CHAPTER SEVEN

Ode lay desolate before Hux. What once was a village of colorful, clay buildings on the rocky side of the mountains was now washed in dust and darkness. There was no evidence of what Ode had been. Its history was lost. Its people gone. Yet King Leeland of Raina had sent Hux and four other Riders of Raina to inspect Ode's damage. King Leeland had heard of the quill and he believed The Dark Hand knew of it, too. Leeland had one mission: find the quill and defeat Calamity.

It sounded heroic. And if Hux thought about it at an angle, it could sound selfless. But he knew his king. Leeland only sought glory and honor. Every territory, king, and queen would answer to him after he saved Thãen from The Hand of Calamity.

Being the newly appointed Lead Rider of Raina, Hux had bit his tongue when Leeland ordered they travel to Ode. Hux had heard of the quill in stories and believed it to be made up. Seeking it was like chasing after the wind. But he had kept quiet when King Leeland sent him off. He knew he was lucky to be Lead Rider in the first place.

Since birth, Hux was told he would become nothing. Not

because his parents didn't love him, or because his teachers saw an educational lack, but because he was physically different. He was born with paralysis in his right arm from the elbow down. His forearm and fingers curled in toward his body in a limp arch. Never knowing any different, physical tasks weren't much more difficult for him than they were for the next person. The way Hux executed them was unique, but there were very few things he couldn't do. Even now, riding on the back of his dapple-gray horse, he held the reins with his left hand while his shield was strapped to his right bicep instead of his forearm. King Leeland had a smith create an extra wide shield for him, to cover the extra distance. Though Hux didn't particularly agree with Leeland's commanded task of going to Ode, there were things about Leeland that were good, and because of that good Hux could overlook the King's ignorance.

The charcoal sky swirled with thick clouds as Hux's horse stepped into the remnants of Ode. Hux's team followed silently behind him. Ode had been made from mountain rock. This side of the mountains had few trees and harsh sunlight—usually. Now the mountain looked bare. The debris of Ode blended in with the natural scape, and the sun was gone.

Hux's adrenaline peaked as he listened to the sound of his horse's hooves clop against the rock. Where had all the people gone? Did they simply vanish when The Dark Hand came to take them? Or was the ultimate result death? Did they now sit trapped in the Outer Void?

The Riders passed by an intact well, which meant they had reached the center of Ode. Hux peered into the stone hole in the ground and frowned. No water. The Dark Hand couldn't even leave that. But what really haunted him was the evidence left of Ode's people. A book flopped open on a pile of rubble, a single shoe, a pan.

"Sir." The Rider on Hux's left shoulder pointed ahead. "That building stands."

Hux looked where the Rider pointed. A building *did* stand. Part of it, at least. The stone structure looked as if it had been cut in half. By examining the half that stood, Hux deducted that it used to be a house. The chimney still remained, though leaning, and a lace curtain blew out of a shattered glass window.

"The only building left to stand, it seems," Hux mumbled. "I suppose this is promising enough." He pulled the reins and headed toward the house. His four men followed. But he knew that there weren't four riders following behind him.

There were five.

On the edge of Ode's territory lines, a figure rode out of the misty woods atop a black horse to watch Hux and his Riders enter Ode. This figure hung back, making sure to stay out of the Riders' eyesight. It would seem threatening, had Hux not known of this figure's arrival. But he had invited this rider. As soon as Leeland ordered this quest, Hux sent a messenger, sworn to secrecy, to tell the rider where to be and when.

Hux reached the half-house and dismounted. The Rider directly behind him followed his lead and strode to his side. If something should happen to Hux, this Rider, Geoff, would lead the crew back home.

Geoff stood shoulder to shoulder with Hux, staring straight ahead. "Sir, have you noticed the rider trailing us?"

Hux continued to examine the house. "Oh?"

Geoff nodded. "Been stalking close behind since we entered the city."

"Really?" He wandered from Geoff to the gaping side of the house.

Geoff followed. "You don't seem too interested, or concerned, rather."

Hux stepped into the crumbling house. Bits of rock covered

the ground and demolished, wooden furniture stuck out of the rubble like spikes. "I'm not."

Geoff was right behind. "Sir?"

"The rider is a friend." He wandered through what used to be the living space.

"A friend." Geoff stopped. "What kind of friend?"

"A trusted one. You never know when you may need a friend close by. Why wait until it's too late?"

Geoff kicked aside the leg of a wooden chair. "That's why you have us riding with you. A little unnecessary to call backup for your backup."

"Unnecessary or wise?" He smiled over his shoulder.

"Does Leeland know?"

Hux lifted his head from watching his footing and zoned in on an open bedroom door. He felt a tug in his chest. A calling of sorts. "No." He stepped toward the room.

"You called backup against King Leeland's orders?" Geoff scoffed. "You're testing thin ice, if I may say so, sir."

"You may say whatever you wish."

Hux entered the bedroom. Every single piece of furniture remained standing and looking as if it was just as it had been when the house was whole.

Geoff squinted at him. "What do you see?"

"Nothing." He scanned the furniture. "I just *feel*."

"Feel what?"

But he didn't have time to answer. Screams sounded from outside where the other Riders stood watch.

Hux darted from the room, Geoff following. They flew through the open walled side of the house to the outside again, only to find the horses fleeing, all absent of their Riders.

"Where did they go?" Hux thrashed his head around. "Geoff! Where did they go?"

Geoff drew his sword. "They've vanished, sir!"

Hux stayed close to him. "Nobody just vanishes. Unless this is the work of The Hand of Calamity."

Suddenly, a monstrous cloud of flies came bursting forth from the ground. They funneled upward and swooped toward the two men. The sound of their collective wings thrummed in Hux's ear with the strength of a roaring sea. He backpedaled into the house, tripped against the broken foundation and fell onto his back onto the living room rubble. But the flies came too fast. And Geoff didn't react quickly enough.

"Hux!" was the last thing Geoff managed to scream. Then the flies took him. Like in a locust storm. Geoff simply disappeared in their swarm.

Hux gagged and staggered up. Through his trauma, he managed to run. The swarm soared into the home, but Hux was already in the bedroom again. He threw the bed covers aside, flipped the side table, yanked open a dresser drawer. His body jolted to a stop. This was it. It was *right here*. Untouched. Intact.

The golden quill.

The sound of the flies drummed closer.

He grabbed the quill.

The flies entered the room.

Lifting his shield, he prepared for the worst. The swarm dove for him as he closed his eyes. Then a flash of light exploded around him. When he looked again, the flies were dropping to the floor like a heavy snowfall. Dead.

In the bedroom doorway, the rider whom he had invited lowered a cloak hood. Her eyes pierced into his with dark green ferociousness.

"I knew I needed you, Vira." He let out a relieved sigh.

She waved him toward her. "Come. That's not the only swarm. Ditch the quest. It's not worth it. There will be another chance."

He lifted his left hand, revealing the quill.

Vira's pointed nose and chin dropped in awe. "You found it."

"How?" he asked. "It might as well have been sitting out in the open. The Dark Hand could have just swiped it."

"But it didn't, and now you have it," she said. "You know what this means, right?"

His shoulders dropped, but he wandered over to her.

She placed a hand on his arm. "I'm sorry."

He touched her hand, but didn't let it linger. "I'm not."

She raised an eyebrow. "King Leeland is not as nice as I remember him?"

He smiled. Vira had left Raina on ill terms eleven years ago. Mostly on account of the king.

"I question his intentions, yes," he confessed. "Not returning to Raina feels like the better decision."

"Maybe King Leeland will think you're dead." Her eyes dimmed. "You are the only survivor."

Hux envisioned Geoff disappearing into the cloud of flies. "What happens to them? Where do they go?"

She shrugged, looking off. "The Dark Hand has them now. They are no longer of this world."

He studied her, a woman he had known since they were children together in Raina. "Can I come with you?"

She almost laughed. "Of course, you're coming with me." Her smile cut short when a buzz erupted in the distance. "We need to get out of Ode."

He nodded, following her through the house and out into the gray skies. He didn't pause to look where his Riders had stood only a few moments ago. No use in growing queasy all over again.

He climbed up behind Vira on her horse. His own horse had fled with the others, which was a shame, because his horse had been with him since he first became a Rider of Raina. But he would rather be with Vira at this moment, though he hadn't seen her but once in the last eleven years. And she could offer him safety. King Leeland would not take his mutiny lightly. That is, if Leeland found out about it.

Vira nudged the horse and they were off, out of Ode. Hux held tight to her, but slipped his strong hand under his breast plate and let the quill rest there for safekeeping. He prayed that The Hand of Protection would remain sturdy in the coming days. Or maybe The Hand of Protection would smite The Hand of Calamity, crushing it between its fingers in a death grip. But he knew the powers outside of this world weren't as logical or cut and dry as humanity thought they should be. There was so much he didn't know, and so much to be afraid of.

Vira looked back at him, sensing his contemplation. "You know I've been living in Zul."

He nodded. "I know."

"We should be safe there. Everyone in Zul is there for an obscure reason." She quieted, knowing even she fell under that category. "No one will ask about anything."

He stared at the back of her head. Her long, black hair flowed silky down her back against her cloak, but only from the top and midsection of her head. The sides of her head were shaved, keeping the hair away from her ears. It was strange for him to see her like that. So warrior-like. So independent and fierce. Yes, she had always been strong-willed and unafraid, but now she embodied those qualities like a beast.

He held her a little tighter as the horse skirted out of Ode and toward the village of Zul. If King Leeland found out he survived and had the quill, his head would end up on a stake. Lead Rider or not.

CHAPTER EIGHT

"News from the cherub in the cathedral!" the goblin called up to the griffin.

In the distance, Le'Gar's cathedral bells chimed the first tone to signal morning.

The griffin tilted his neck, his stone crunching as he faced the goblin. "What is it?"

The angel perked up. "Did he say news?"

"Yes, news!" the goblin said. "The quill has been found."

"*The* quill?" the griffin doubted.

The goblin sighed. "Yes, *the* quill."

"Oh no." The angel sagged. "What has King Tal done with it?"

"Tal doesn't have it," the goblin reported. "But he's afraid. He's sent out his Riders to search Le'Gar for a Massoud."

The griffin held back a roar. "Our Naomi."

"No," the angel cried through a gasp. "We must do something."

"We can't do something," the griffin ordered. "It's forbidden that we speak to humanity, witch, or Magnificent. And we don't even know for sure if Naomi is a Massoud."

"We've watched her long enough to know she is hiding something. What else could it be?" the angel argued. "And Old Man Magnificent has watched her just as much."

The goblin nodded, his stone thunking with the motion. "If she *is* a Massoud, Tal will do to her what has been done before. We mustn't let that happen."

The angel faced the griffin. "He's right, she may be the last weapon Thãen has."

The griffin kept quiet.

"We are to protect," the goblin strained. "And I will protect her even if it means my demolition."

The griffin tensed. "It will mean your demolition. We are bound by the laws of the spell. Break them and the spell will no longer apply to you."

"I will do it," the goblin dared. "Send me."

For once, the griffin looked at the goblin with awe, then paused before saying, "I have wings. Let me."

"No." The angel stretched out her own wings. "You will be too noticeable if you're gone. Let me. I'm less significant."

The griffin and the goblin stared at her with sorrow in their cold eyes.

"I will not let another being fall victim to Tal's long line of evil doings," the angel gritted. "We will save Naomi Massoud."

Silence rippled between the three.

The griffin bowed. "It has been a pleasure residing with you all these years."

"Don't be afraid," the goblin comforted.

The angel looked off into the brightening sky. "I am not afraid." She leaned forward. The base of her solid dress cracked and tore away from the cathedral. Her wings groaned up and down as she fell toward Center Square before she shot up again, caught the wind, and soared past the griffin and over the goblin.

A tremor ran through Le'Gar. All the gargoyles looked upward. They saw the angel, and they knew the tides were about to change. The angel knew it, too. Her own tide was about to turn for the worst. But she kept her wings steady and her focus in check as she sailed to the room above the library.

The beast gargoyle that sat perched outside of Naomi's window jolted when the angel landed on the roof. "What have you done?" the beast hissed.

"I will not let her be killed," the angel spat right back.

———

From inside her dwelling, Naomi saw the angel drop in front of her window. Her first thought was a Rider of Le'Gar was coming to capture her, but then she saw this being was clearly stone. And breaking the law.

Naomi stepped forward. Her tears hadn't had time to dry and her whole body still shook. She shoved open the window. "Go away!"

"No, please." The angel held her hand up.

Naomi froze. She had never heard a gargoyle speak. No matter how hard she tried to get the beast to converse with her he wouldn't, and she knew he shouldn't. But this angel was defiant, and a little distressed.

"What do you want?" Naomi's voice trembled.

"Run, Naomi," the angel warned in a hushed voice. "Get out of Le'Gar."

Chills shot down her neck. "Wh—what? Where am I to go?"

Right in front of her eyes, the angel's face began to crack like old porcelain. "*Run*," the gargoyle whispered again. "Go, Naomi Massoud. Get out of here."

A crack shot up the angel's solid dress, breaking her in two.

"Oh no, no." Naomi reached forward. "You poor thing, no."

The angel's face began to fall to pieces. "Go."

Naomi scrambled out her window and tried to catch the pieces of the angel that slowly fell apart. "No!" She felt the tears again. She didn't know why she felt sorry for the angel or why she felt the need to save her. The angel had defied the spell, and now she was a pile of rubble at her feet. "I'm so sorry." She dropped to her knees and gently touched the pile of stone. She shut her eyes, hot tears pressing against her lids. "Thank you."

The beast stared at the scene in somber shock. Even through his solid eyes, Naomi could see his emotion. She feared that he too might jump from his place.

"Don't move," Naomi whispered. "I'm leaving. I'll go."

He turned away.

Muffled shouts rumbled from the streets below. She knew she had little time. The only place she could flee to was the mountains, and she knew they were cold even in the spring.

The shouts in the streets grew closer now.

She jumped back through her window and pulled on her worn leather boots, her brown trousers and buttoned shirt. She grabbed her cloak and slung it over her shoulders. That was all she had. Except for one other thing.

The side table by her bed held three items. Her lantern, her mirror, and the necklace she had stolen from her mother. She slipped it into her pocket and vanished through the window once more.

The cathedral bells sang their morning melody as Naomi fled over the rooftops of Le'Gar. She pretended the bells were bidding her farewell. A melodious goodbye. A prayer to keep her safe.

CHAPTER NINE

Naomi didn't run through the streets. She strode. Brisk, but casual.

More people trickled into the streets as the day began. It was easy to blend in. It was just her. No one would expect her to be on the run. She had no bag. No horse.

There was a proper entrance to the city of Le'Gar: a stone walkway and two columns with gargoyles perched on the top of each. But that was too obvious of an escape. No one left Le'Gar unless on business. Usually miners, hunters, or Riders. That was pretty much the sum of who left on a daily basis. But Naomi knew of an alleyway that transitioned from stone to dirt and dumped into the base of the mountain. Riders often guarded the perimeter of Le'Gar, passing the alleyway's exit, but she was fast. As soon as there was a clear opening, she bolted from the alleyway into the forested mountains, never looking back.

When her feet hit the wet, compact dirt and spongy moss, the tamaracks and cedar trees swallowed her up. A twig cracked under her foot. She heard a shout from behind. But she knew how to run. Her mother had made sure of it. The crisp air penetrated her lungs. A chill stung her face. Tree trunks swished by her peripherals as she sprinted further into the dark foliage. For a moment, her heart soared with freedom, then crashed in pain as the toll of running uphill caught up to her. She gasped for air but kept going. She couldn't get far enough away. The image of the angel crumbling to bits and the urgency in her grave, dry voice clung to the forefront of Naomi's mind. There was danger in Le'Gar. Danger meant for her.

She slowed and listened. The air was thick with quiet. Peaceful. No matter which direction she turned, there was nature. Behind her the ground sloped down with jutting rocks, dark soil and thick moss. The cedar trees clung to the dirt, standing strong on the slant. Le'Gar was no longer visible, buried within the mountain's misty scape. She had never been so deep within the mountain before. When she was a child, Ms. Chambers had taken the girls from the home on a field trip to the outskirts of the mountain. They had learned the importance of the wet climate on the moss and what kind of woodland creatures inhabited the area. Naomi specifically remembered one of the girls asking if golden witches lived on the mountain in huts. Ms. Chambers had laughed and said, *"Golden witches aren't creatures, they're people."*

Naomi smiled at the memory.

The sun was higher now and the forest wasn't as menacing. She allowed herself to enjoy the moment. She stopped walking and turned slowly in a full circle. Birds chirped. Branches waved. And that was all. No clacking of hooves on stone, no cathedral bells, no voices. She had never known such serenity. But the serenity was momentary when she remembered she had nowhere to go from here. If she'd paid attention in her history classes, maybe she would have remembered where the other cities lay outside of Le'Gar. Different cities crossed her mind: Raina, Ode, Litzen, Zul. Ode was out of the question for obvious reasons. She knew next to nothing about Raina. Litzen was ruled by a militaristic queen who did not welcome visitors well—so Naomi was told—and Zul was known to be the outpost for outcasts and troubled characters. Raina could be a safe bet, but how to get to Raina was the next problem.

Moss squelched to Naomi's right. The sound of something approaching.

She shot her head in the direction of the sound and gasped. A black horse and a black-hooded rider stood still within the trees. Naomi stared for a beat, then darted.

Her thighs burned, lungs fighting. The mountain sped past her. Hooves followed behind. She cursed herself as she ran. Why had she bolted? Two legs out-running four? She was an idiot. An *idiot, idiot, IDIOT!*

The horse and rider leapt over a log next to her. A mass of black equine muscle and bony knees blocked her vision and cut her off. The horse's hooves spewed dirt in her face. She swiped at her eyes, stumbling to a stop. The rider flew from the horse's back and landed inches from her.

Naomi backed up, gasping. "Get away from me!"

The rider said nothing, the black hood shadowing the face beneath. "Relax." The voice was deep and gruff.

"I'll relax when you leave me alone," Naomi panted, continuing to back up.

"Stop." The man reached forward and grabbed her wrist.

She tried wrenching it away. "Let go! I'm innocent!"

He didn't let go. But he lowered his hood with his free hand to reveal tousled black hair and dark green eyes. Naomi's body calmed. He wasn't much older than her.

"If you're innocent, why do you run?" he challenged.

Naomi's mind flipped through lie after lie. She couldn't tell this man the situation. He may be just as dangerous as Le'Gar.

"I was scared when I saw you. That's all."

"Unlikely." The rider narrowed his eyes. "Who are you?"

"Would you *let go*?" Naomi successfully yanked her wrist from his grasp.

He didn't reach for it again.

"I'm Naomi Smyth. And I'm leaving Le'Gar."

The rider's face fell for a fraction of a second. "You're traveling like that?"

Naomi looked down at herself. "What do you mean?"

He almost smiled. "You won't last a day out here. The mountain still gets frost most nights. And where is your bag? No food or water? Are you on a suicide mission?"

Naomi ran her hands through her hair. "I'll be fine." But her lips trembled.

The rider watched her with curious eyes. "Let me guide you back to Le'Gar."

"No!" Naomi was the one to grip his arm now.

He shook her off. "Tell me your real business then."

She glared. "My business is my own. What authority do you have over my comings and goings?"

"I'm a ranger of the mountain, keeping the peace between cities and territories for the good of everyone." He said it with no emotion. "So, tell me your business or I'll have to handle you like I do the criminals I come upon."

"But I'm not a criminal." She fought away tears. "Can't you help me?"

He sighed, glaring. "I can't help you if I don't know your situation."

"Would you help me if you knew?"

"Probably not."

She scoffed. "Leave me be then, ranger." She was shocked at her own voice. Her spit-fire.

Again, he almost smiled. "What's so bad in Le'Gar that makes you want to leave so hastily? Controlling husband? Pestering children? Distasteful profession?"

"None of the above. I've always wanted children." Why she chose to highlight that, she had no idea.

He stared, steady. "Where are you headed, then?"

She hung her head. "Oh, I don't know." Her decision suddenly felt foolish. She never should have left. There was no way the Riders of Le'Gar would have found out she was a Massoud. Her papers said Smyth. What other evidence did she possess that would give away her true identity? In fact, fleeing the city was more damning than helpful.

"You'll freeze overnight in the mountains." The rider snapped his fingers for his horse to come near. The stallion nudged his shoulder and the rider gave the horse's nuzzle a single stroke. "Let me take you back. I have the feeling you really shouldn't be out here."

She agreed and disagreed all at the same time. Going back to Le'Gar felt so, so wrong. But remaining in the mountains felt dangerous, too.

"If you take me back, I need you to tell the guards that I got lost on a walk," she ordered.

"Oh, I'm not going into the city." The rider pulled himself up onto his horse. "I'm taking you to the territory lines and leaving you there."

Leaving you there. As if she were baggage.

"A lot of help you are," she mumbled.

He didn't look at her but lowered his hand to help her onto his horse. "Coming or not?"

She almost said no, but she truly had nowhere to go, so she accepted his hand. It was clumsy the way he pulled her up, and she nearly fell as she situated herself behind him.

"You never told me your name," she pried.

"So?" The rider nudged the horse forward. They moved at no urgent pace.

"So I'd like to know the stranger I'm riding with."

He was quiet. Naomi thought he really wasn't going to tell her. Then he pulled his hood back up over his head. "Ferrin."

"Okay." Knowing made her a tad more comfortable. "Well thank you, Ferrin, for your semi-abrasive and rude gesture of help."

She couldn't see his face, but his tone held a hint of amusement. "Anything to keep the mountains clear of crazies."

CHAPTER TEN

Pointy peaks from Le'Gar's skyline appeared again behind the mountain's treetops. The closer Ferrin and Naomi got to the city, the more anxiety welled in her chest. She couldn't help but hear the angel's warning over and over in her mind. *Run, Naomi. Leave Le'Gar.* Three times Naomi almost told Ferrin to turn around, to take her back into the mountains, even if it meant brutal survival. But she couldn't bring herself to say it. Because then she would have to tell him why she was running and he might harm her if he found out. At least, that's what she assumed the Riders of Le'Gar would do to her. Why would Ferrin's response be any different?

He stopped the horse. "This is as far as I take you."

"Oh." She didn't move. "Okay."

He turned to look at her. "You do know how to get back from here, don't you? It's literally right down there."

"Of course, I do," Naomi grunted. She slid from the horse and landed on the ground with a spry thud. She looked up to thank him one more time, but he wasn't looking back at her. His eyes pierced into the forest in the direction of Le'Gar. "Uh," Naomi hummed. "What are you–"

"I hear Riders." Ferrin pulled his horse around to leave her.

Then she heard them too. Shouting. Hooves. They sounded far enough in the distance, but they were definitely out there.

"You'll be alright," Ferrin said. "Do me a favor and don't tell them you were with me."

"Wait, what?" She frowned. "Why?"

"I'm a friend to many, but not to all. Farewell, Miss Smyth."

Panic almost killed her. He really was going to leave. And the Riders were going to find her. She scrambled to find a way to make Ferrin stay. He suddenly felt way safer than Le'Gar. Perhaps because he, too, didn't want anything to do with the Riders.

"No, Ferrin, please. You have to help me."

He glared hard, a knowledge coming over his eyes. "They're after you, aren't they?"

"Yes, but I can explain," she begged with her hands in a prayer clasp. "Just don't leave me here. *Please.*"

Then he was off his horse. Before she knew what was happening, he had a knife at her throat. "Tell me now." He breathed in her face. "Tell me what they want you for."

Tears spiked behind her eyes. "I *can't.*"

He grabbed her arm and dug his fingers in. She winced and squirmed.

"Tell me." His actions were fierce and harsh, but his eyes said something different. At least for a moment anyway. "Or I'll leave you to them."

She began to cry. All the years of hiding who she was came out in a sob. "I'm Naomi Massoud." As if that was enough of an explanation.

And apparently it was. Because Ferrin dropped the knife and drew his hand away from her arm. "You...a *Massoud?*"

"Please don't kill me," she begged. "I don't know what's

happening to me or why they want me. I'm just trying to live. Oh please help me!"

Without another word, Ferrin swung back onto his horse. He reached down to her. "Get up."

She gazed up at him with tear glistening cheeks. "Are you going to hurt me?"

The sound of the Riders was closer now.

"No." Ferrin gripped her hand and pulled her up. "I'm going to help you."

She slung her leg over the horse and clenched the back of his cloak. "You are?"

"You're a Massoud."

"What does that mean?"

He took one extra moment to peer at her. "You really don't know?"

She shook her head. "Why would you help a Massoud when everyone else seems to want me captured?"

The horse jolted forward. He didn't reply.

"Ferrin?"

"You're lucky I found you, Miss Massoud."

Miss Massoud. The name flooded Naomi's heart with a burning fullness.

"Would the Riders have killed me?" she asked in a whisper.

"As soon as they could have," he affirmed.

"But you won't?" She just had to make sure.

"No."

She believed him.

CHAPTER ELEVEN

Zul had a specific smell. Tobacco, hay, and mud. At least that's what Hux was able to pull from the stench that met his nose. The establishment lay in a crevasse where two mountains met. Runoff water made the ground constantly muddy so the residents of Zul laid hay around their tents to make traveling cleaner. He realized as he and Vira rode through why Zul had such a nomadic reputation: it was built entirely of tents.

A circular, closed off tent stood larger than the rest in the center of the establishment. Its peak loomed into the night sky, towering over the town in obvious importance. Lanterns were held in place by rope to the tent's supporting lumber.

"The Hub Tent," Vira explained as they rode past. "That's where all trade happens, rations are sorted, and any sort of militaristic situation is addressed. Zul has no royalty, but Simeon has gained the unofficial title of leader. In a way. He's good with decision-making and keeping order."

"Don't people fight over being in charge?" Hux couldn't imagine what would happen if Raina had no king. It'd be chaos.

"Not really." She gave a single wave to another young

woman standing outside a triangular tent. "Everything here is loose. Unspoken. No one is under any rule or law. It's just the way of Zul. Everyone is here because they have nowhere else to go. You treat people differently when you realize all you have left is each other."

His heart clenched. It hurt him to know she had been here alone for the last eleven years, thinking she had no one left. The day she left Raina was still a painful memory for him, though no one knew how much he still berated himself for that day. Ever since she left, he had regretted not doing something to alter what had happened. When he ran into her seven years ago on a voyage to Litzen where rations of rice and cornmeal were being handed out during a year of drought, she looked so different. But what always struck him was the way she didn't act bitter toward him. She had every right, and yet she never let a vile comment fly his way.

"How do you acquire a tent?" he asked, scanning the over-crowded landmass of tattered fabric.

"You either bring one, buy one, or rent one." She pulled the horse up to a round tent that had a flap in the front to enter. It sat on the end of a row with other tents of different shapes and sizes.

"I suppose I should rent one," he said.

She slid off the horse and waited for him to join her on the ground. "I don't think that's a smart idea. Better to stay laid low. We don't need King Leeland getting wind of your whereabouts."

"Oh." He frowned and shifted. "Well, what should I do, then?"

She parted the tent flap. "You can stay with me. If you're okay with that."

Hux felt his face flush, but held his mouth steady. He nodded and followed her in. A single cot sat to the right. A wooden pole held the center of the tent up while a table and two chairs claimed the left side of the home. Barrels of clothes, fruit, and grains sat crowded around the table. Tiny stones and gems hung from the ceiling, tethered to the ends of strings. When Hux looked up, they reminded him of stars, only different colors and not as bright.

Vira finished lighting the lanterns which sat on the dirt floor in four evenly spaced places.

"I still collect stones," she said.

"I see that." He looked back down. "Is this...all you have?"

She slid her cloak off and tossed it into one of the barrels. "Yes. And I'm okay with that."

"I didn't mean it in a negative way." He held his arm up, warding her off.

She smiled with half her mouth. "I'm not offended. Just making sure you know I'm alright."

His shoulders relaxed.

She stepped forward and pointed to the shield that was strapped to his back. "Custom made."

"It is," he nodded. "King Leeland's doing."

She looked surprised, but pressed her lips together. "Good. He was smart to choose you as his lead Rider."

He removed the shield, resting it against one of Vira's clothing barrels, then shrugged his cloak off his left arm. She reached out to help him slide his right arm free but he slipped it out with ease. She backed off.

"I've gotten quicker with things," he chuckled. "Feels normal now that my body has stopped growing in length."

"As it should." She sounded relieved. "Because to you, it is normal."

He stared at her. Oh, how he had missed her honest eyes and kind tone. Again, he found himself reliving the day she left Raina when they were both nineteen years old.

"I should have done something to protect you," he said.

Her dark eyes drew in. "What?"

"When you were exiled from Raina."

"Hux," she softened, "that was long ago."

"But I stood back and did nothing. Said nothing."

"You were training to be a Rider of Raina for King Leeland. I didn't expect you to say anything against him or his decisions."

"But I should have." He clenched his jaw. "I was afraid. And I let you be thrown out."

She shook her head. "I was in the wrong."

"But for a reason."

She remained quiet.

"Right, Vira?"

She crossed her arms. "Yes, of course, for a reason. I would never steal money from the king if I didn't desperately need it."

"He would have given you an ear if you would have told him you were a golden witch."

She held a finger to her lips.

He raised an eyebrow. "You're still not telling people?"

"If I expose myself, I could be putting myself in danger. I have an important task to fulfill." She wandered away from him to nowhere in particular.

"We were inseparable as kids and close still as adolescents." He stared at her back. "I'd like to think that even after years of separation, we've remained friends."

She faced him. "Of course we have. I trust you just as much as I did then."

"So tell me why you stole from King Leeland."

"Hux, I—"

"Vira."

She looked down. "I suppose if I were to ever tell you, it would be now."

His spirit rose. "And why is that?"

"Because you just found the item that completes my purpose."

His breast plate was still on, holding the quill against his body. He slid his hand under the plate and pulled out the golden feather. It was the length of his forearm. Each part of the feathered end was a miniscule hair of real gold, able to move with ease like a real feather would.

She marveled at the find. "I can't believe I'm looking at it."

"What's it for?" He turned it over in his hands. "Doesn't a quill require ink? Is something missing?"

She touched the tip of the quill with one finger. "Possibly."

He studied her intense expression. "You aren't planning on going up against The Dark Hand with the quill, are you?"

"Oh." She looked up. "I can't."

"But it's the one weapon that stands a chance against The Hand of Calamity, and now we have it. You could start a war if you wanted to."

"No." She shook her head with vigor. "*I* can't."

Hux squinted. "It doesn't answer to everyone, does it?"

"No," Vira said.

"So even if King Leeland did get his hands on it, it would be of no use to him?"

"It's no use to anyone who isn't from a certain bloodline," she explained. "And King Leeland is not of the chosen bloodline."

"Which bloodline?"

She leaned in, dropping to a whisper. "The name is Massoud."

"Massoud?" His heart rate picked up even just saying the name. "Are they royalty?"

"Not of royalty." The lanterns created leaping shadows on the material walls. Her black hair almost blended with them.

"They're a bloodline originating in the warmer parts of the Desarian Sea. A bloodline with few descendants."

The knowledge gave him chills. "How do you know this?"

"I'm a golden witch. It was revealed to me in a dream when I was eighteen. I dreamt of a scroll with a written genealogy list. It was a list of the Massoud descendants. The very last name on the list was the only one not crossed out, but it was blurred."

"And you never told me?"

"If you knew, you would have been in danger." She took the quill from his palm and held it up. "This quill, when in the right hands, means defeat for The Hand of Calamity. The Dark Hand will do anything in its power to destroy those of the Massoud bloodline."

"But I'm not a Massoud. Doesn't that mean I'm safe?"

"Not anymore." She sighed, seeming apologetic. "Now that you know, Calamity will seek you, too. So will its disciples in Thãen. It will do anything to prevent this quill from falling into the hands of a Massoud. That means killing anyone who may aid in that happening."

He paced. "Is that why Ode was destroyed?"

"Yes. The Dark Hand must have known someone had the quill in Ode. It can't destroy the quill, so it must have sought out the quill's possessor."

"But shouldn't the quill in the hands of a Massoud be near invincible?"

"A Massoud must not have been in possession of the quill in Ode," she clarified.

He understood. "Just a carrier."

"Which is what we are now." She placed the quill in a leather bag lying under her cot.

"Calamity will come for us. We should go somewhere else. Away from people." He thought about Geoff being swallowed up by flies. He didn't want to see that happen to everyone in Zul. Geoff was haunting enough.

She sat on her cot and unlaced her shoes. "It will have to find us first. And don't forget about The Hand of Protection."

He had forgotten. Or rather, believed in The Hand of Protection a little less. The Hand of Protection was a quiet subject compared to the Dark Hand. Hux believed the Hand of Protection held Thãen, but he never understood why it hadn't wiped out Calamity, which led him to assume that The Hand of Protection was not as powerful as Calamity.

"What about it?" he asked.

"It's still holding us." She moved to create a sleeping spot on the ground for him, draping an older cloak over the dirt. "And though we may not see it, it's still protecting us. Protecting Thãen. We have to believe that."

He nodded, but he struggled to blindly side with her. "What next?" He lowered himself to the ground bed, unbuckling his chest plate.

She tossed him a lumpy pillow from her cot. "What's next is what I've been trying to do since I stole from King Leeland."

He caught the pillow in his left hand. "Which is?"

"Find the last remaining Massoud."

He got chills again. "How do you know there is only one more?"

She smirked. "Hux, I'm a golden witch. Remember? The dream."

"Right. I'm sorry, I just—it's hard to piece it all together."

"I know." She laid down on the cot. "But it was revealed to me eleven years ago that the last Massoud showed up on our side of the world."

"The year you were exiled from Raina," Hux said with a raised eyebrow.

"Yes. As soon as I had that knowledge, I knew I needed to

find that person. But I was broke, as you know, and there was no way I would be able to make a cross terrain search with no money in my pockets." She looked down. "So I did what I thought I had to do."

He finally had clarity. "You stole from the king to seek out this Massoud."

She stared up at the tent's ceiling. "Yes."

"Why didn't you just ask me for money?" He gazed up at her cot from the floor, waiting.

"It's in the past, Hux." She turned over, facing away from him. "All that matters is I never found a Massoud, and I learned about the quill eight years ago. That's when my focus shifted. Finding the quill became step number one and finding a Massoud step number two."

"I want to help you find them."

"I want you to help me, too." Her voice sounded far away. Sad.

"Just promise me," he begged. "No more secrets."

She rolled back over to see him. "No more secrets."

CHAPTER TWELVE

King Tal was pacing the cathedral hall when his lead Rider, Saul, burst in. Saul held a woman by both her arms, arms which he had wrenched behind her back.

"Deirdre Lloyd?" Tal strode to them. "A Massoud?"

"No, sir." Saul shoved Deirdre forward. "But hiding something."

Deirdre's hair had fallen from her updo, leaving whisps floating around her panicked face. "Sir, I swear I know nothing!"

Tal lifted his hand, telling Saul to step back. "Ms. Lloyd," he coaxed her down, "I'm sorry for your brash summoning today but you must know, we are dealing with a very serious matter."

"Which has nothing to do with me." She glared back at Saul. "You had no right to drag me from my library in front of all those scholars. Do you know how humiliating that was? I'm just doing my job and you come and snatch me away like a criminal!"

"Ms. Lloyd," Tal tried again, "I ordered the Riders to search Le'Gar for someone in particular."

"Well, it's not me you're looking for." She struggled to remain respectful. "I own a library. How sinister."

"And a rooftop loft," Saul interjected. "One that has clearly been recently vacated."

Tal raised an eyebrow. "Is this true, Ms. Lloyd?"

"If it even qualifies as a loft, yes," she complied. "I rented it out to a young woman named Naomi Smyth. If she's fled, I've no knowledge of when or why."

"Smyth." The king frowned. "Naomi Smyth. I don't know the name."

"She's a nobody." Deirdre winced. "In the most respectful way. Keeps to herself. She's a lantern snuffer."

"And you believe she fled recently?" he asked Saul.

"A witness claims he saw someone crossing the catwalk at daybreak," Saul confirmed. "The catwalk only leads to the loft. Upon searching the dwelling it seemed previously occupied, but it's empty now."

"She doesn't own a lot of things," Deirdre defended. "She's poor. She's been on her own since she left the Chamber Home for Girls."

Tal perked up. "The Home for Girls. Is she an orphan of Le'Gar?"

"She's one of the children that arrived here from Beezus."

Saul and Tal made eye contact.

"All the papers were checked upon arrival." Saul shook his head. "*Thoroughly.*"

"Maybe not thoroughly enough," Tal pondered. "Thank you, Ms. Lloyd, for your information. You are free to go."

She stayed put. "You aren't going to hurt her, sir, are you?"

His face flashed with heat, though he tried to repress it. "Thank you, Ms. Lloyd, I said you are dismissed."

Muffled shouts and shrieks made it through the stone walls from Center Square outside. Saul caught King Tal's eyes and they took off across the cathedral hall, Deirdre at their heels.

Center Square was filled with people, more trickling in from the surrounding streets every second. They all looked up to the cathedral roof. Some people pointed, some stared blankly. King Tal studied their postures and picked up on subtle whispers throughout the crowd.

"She's gone."

"The gargoyle?"

"No it's not. The griffin is right there."

"Not the griffin, the angel."

"The angel is gone."

Tal arched his head back and looked to the skyline. His chest heaved. "Saul."

Saul stood next to him. "Have the gargoyles been released of their spell?"

"No." He was almost shaking. "The angel defied the law."

Those around King Tal grew quiet, hearing his preposterous suggestion.

"How do you know for certain?" Saul brought his voice down. "Maybe the one who can release them has made a move?"

"No," he said, sharper this time. "If that were so, all the gargoyles would have up and moved. This is one gargoyle. The question is, where did she go?"

"Maybe she—" Saul stopped, cutting eyes at him. "I mean isn't it possible that this has something to do with our unnamed Massoud?"

Tal rubbed his eyes. More people were watching him now. "How?" he whispered to Saul. "How could a Massoud have lived under my watch for all these years and I didn't know it? I've failed."

Saul seemed to decipher the emotion behind Tal's expression before responding. "If the girl who fled Deirdre's loft was a Massoud, aren't we in the clear? Isn't Le'Gar better off without her? Safer?"

His cheeks flared red. "It's bigger than just Le'Gar. If a Massoud finds the quill, all territories risk war, not just Le'Gar."

"Then align with the other kings and queens," Saul suggested. "Make a pact to find her. Come up with a plan to eliminate her."

He considered it, but his shoulders dropped. "Not all royalty feels the same. Some believe in a greater good."

"Through war?"

"They think war can fix the oppression of The Dark Hand. What they don't know is that we don't stand a chance. The best way to avoid death to all is to keep The Dark Hand at bay and *never* make the first move."

Saul nodded, Tal's loyal servant dog. "So, what now then?"

Tal glanced up to the empty space where the angel had been. "Take the Riders into the mountains. If this Naomi Smyth fled on foot, she should be easy to track down. Find her and bring her back to me."

"Yes, sir." Saul straightened, then left to gather the rest of the Riders, pushing through the thickening crowds.

———

On the perimeter of Center Square, an old man hung close, blending with the panic-stricken masses. Those who knew of this man's powers referred to him as Old Man Magnificent. Those who merely knew he existed in the world knew him as Eli. But no matter the name he answered to, he had the same life mission.

Old Man Magnificent zeroed in on King Tal, focusing. When he closed his eyes, he could pick up bits and pieces of Tal's conversation. They seeped into his mind in a telepathic whisper: *Dierdre's loft. Naomi Smyth. Fled. Take the Riders. Bring her back to me.*

The old man's eyes flung open. It was as he feared. What had happened before was going to happen again.

Saul had turned on his heels and was heading toward him. Quickly, the old man stepped back down the side street, pushed on the stone wall, and disappeared behind a secret door. He'd lived in the secret tunnels of Le'Gar all these years for this exact moment. He would not fail again.

CHAPTER THIRTEEN

Naomi and Ferrin traveled all day, on an incline the entire time. Though she had spent hours sitting directly behind him on his obedient horse, he had said very few words.

"Do you know where we are?" she asked. Her voice sounded louder than it really was in the quiet of the forest as night fell. There were fewer cedar trees and more pines now. Less moss and more rock.

"Yes." His tone was flat. Uninterested. The opposite of friendly.

She sighed. "Aren't you going to tell me where we're going? Or what you're planning? Or what's wrong with me?"

"I'm still not convinced you know nothing about your bloodline." Ferrin slowed the horse and looked around, as if searching for a landmark.

"How can I convince you?" She would rather argue than sit in silence.

Ferrin nudged the horse left. "You can't."

"So I lose either way."

"You don't lose. You're still alive, aren't you?"

"I suppose," she mumbled.

The horse trudged up to a cavernous opening in a rock formation that lumped up from the ground. It was black as midnight inside. The thought of going into the cave made Naomi's heart race. She had come to accept that she was afraid of the dark. Or shadows, rather.

"We'll stay here through the night." He slid off the horse and helped her down.

She played with her fingers. "In the cave?"

He whistled, drew an apple from beneath his cloak, then tossed it to his horse. "Yes, in the cave." He walked to the entrance.

"How do you know it's safe?"

He paused in the mouth of the cavern and turned to her. "I live here." Then he disappeared into the dark.

She ran after him, not wanting to be alone at all. She'd rather be trapped in a cave with a stranger than alone in the night-laden forest. "Ferrin?" her voice caught.

A lantern appeared in front of her face. She screamed.

"Shhhhh!" Ferrin cursed. "You'll spook my horse."

She covered her mouth. "Sorry."

He turned away. "Follow me and watch your step. The ground is jagged and the pass is curvy."

She wanted to reach out and grab onto his cloak, but she was afraid to touch him. Something about him seemed powerful. And not only that, but he seemed to dislike her presence. If her presence irked him so much, how much more would a touch?

The winding passage opened up to a domed cavern with lanterns resting on nooks in the rock, illuminating the space. A bed of clothes lay near one of the lanterns, most likely a place to sleep. A bow and a quiver of arrows, a sword, and a shield leaned against the wall of the cavern. An empty wooden bucket accompanied the weapons. A few papers were scattered about on the floor near the clothing bed: a map, hand written notes, quick sketches.

Ferrin picked up the empty bucket. "Come on. You can leave...well...never mind, you didn't bring anything."

She followed him back out of the cave where he led them to a stream running gently between a wide crack in the stone ground. He filled the bucket with water and brought it back near the cave where he started a fire. The entire time his horse moseyed around the cave entrance, picking at the weeds between the rocks.

"How did you get your horse to obey so well?" She sat by the fire, watching the animal.

Ferrin tossed grains into a cast iron pot filled with water and positioned it over the fire with a triangular support system made from what looked to be scrap metal. "He's been with me since I became a ranger."

She held her hands out to the warmth of the flames. "When was that?"

He stared at her through the wavering orange. "When I decided to leave Le'Gar."

"You used to live in Le'Gar, too? We must have been there at the same time! You're not much older than me, right? When did you leave?"

"I left a while ago." He looked down at his hands.

She tilted her head. "You started as a very young ranger then?"

"Sure."

She dug deeper. "Who appointed you to be a ranger?"

He glanced up with blank eyes. "Me."

She smiled, thinking he was joking. "That's not how it works, is it?"

He almost offered a smile back.

"Is it?" she repeated.

"I became a ranger because I saw the need for one in our mountains and surrounding territories." He clasped his hands together. "Now you. Why did you tell me your name was Naomi Smyth?"

She gave him a quizzical stare. "Because I'm a Massoud. Shouldn't that be reason enough to use another name?"

"Yes, but you said you didn't know your real name held any weight." His pupils bore into hers. "So either you're holding back on me, or someone told you to lie."

"My parents forced the name change on me," she confessed. "Before they sent me across the Desarian Sea from Beezus to Le'Gar."

"Beezus." He lifted a brow. "Were you there when The Dark Hand came?"

The image of the shadowed hand sweeping across her quilt sent a shiver through her. "Yes. That's why I was sent away. With all the other children of Beezus. Half went to Le'Gar and half went to Ode."

"Your parents were smart," he said, nodding in approval.

Pride welled in her heart and just a tad of warmth grew toward him. "I know. I think they knew The Dark Hand would come eventually."

"And they knew about your bloodline." He leaned forward. "By telling you to lie, they were trying to keep you safe."

"But what exactly can a Massoud *do*?" Naomi felt a prick of excitement. "Am I similar to a golden witch? Or a Magnificent?" She threw her hands to the side. "That would be bizarre!"

Ferrin watched her childlike excitement rise then fall again. "That's where the mystery starts," he revealed. "A Massoud has never done what it's said they can do."

"And that would be?"

"Defeat The Hand of Calamity," Ferrin said, his voice flatlining.

Her mouth dropped open. "Oh. I can't do that."

"But you've never tried," he offered.

"Yeah, because The Dark Hand is an ancient terror that has preyed on Thãen since history began." She let out a doubtful breath. "Besides, I think I need some sort of quill."

Ferrin's chin jerked upward. "A quill?"

"That's what I overheard King Tal say." She told him how she had learned of her name's importance by snooping on the king. How a man had found a quill and a golden witch revealed the quill's discovery to one of Le'Gar's Riders, Saul.

Ferrin listened intently. So much so that Naomi couldn't read if his expression was anger, fear, amazement or disbelief. "And that's when you decided to flee Le'Gar?" he finally said.

"Well, I thought about it, yes," she explained, "but I was scared to make a move. What drove me to run was a gargoyle. A stone angel, rather. She flew to my window and told me to escape then withered right in front of my eyes to a pile of crushed stone." The sadness of watching the angel crumble hit her all over again. "It was terrible. I felt so...helpless."

Ferrin stood. He paced back and forth in front of the fire. His horse watched him. "A gargoyle defied the curse for you?"

She watched him pace. "Yes..."

"Listen," he stopped. "You are going to be hunted. By a lot of people. The best way for you to survive is to forget this whole thing. Pretend you are a Smyth again. Bury the name Massoud."

She wanted to live, she really did, but for the first time in years she felt whole. Living a lie took a toll on her mental health in a way she hadn't realized until now. She was afraid, yes, and felt utterly exposed, but she was herself. Someone she hadn't been for eleven years. "What if I tried to do what a Massoud can do?"

He crossed his arms. "Then you're going to do it without me."

Her heart plummeted. She expected him to urge her on. To say he would help her. She was confused why he would offer to take her away from Le'Gar in the first place if he wasn't interested in helping her discover her power. "Are you afraid of me?"

He laughed sharply. "Absolutely not. I just don't want trouble, alright?"

"You're going to leave me all by myself?" She questioned him like a challenge, but felt like a child.

"No, I'm going to take you to Zul." He checked the grains over the fire and removed the pot with a thick piece of cloth. "It's the safest place for someone like you. I'll get you there, but then you're on your own."

She nodded, looking down. Every circumstance in her life led to her being alone. She left Beezus alone. Even in the Chamber Home for Girls she had fended for herself. Then living in Deirdre's loft, she was entirely on her own. She never found friends or family in Le'Gar. The thought came out of nowhere, but it hit her before she could stuff it down again: When was the last time she heard someone say *I love you*? Or had said it herself? She was *so alone*.

"Can't you just—" She stopped herself. What more was there to say? He was taking her to Zul. There was nothing else he could do beyond that.

He cut his mossy-colored eyes at her. "I am not your friend."

His words speared her heart and dug to her core. Of course he wasn't her friend, but did he have to put it so simply? So poisonously?

"You're not a very eloquent speaker," she grumbled.

"Oh, I'm sorry," he pretended, bowing. "Would you like me to just be on my way then?"

She rolled her eyes. "No, but it'd be nice if you—"

He held his hand up. "Shush."

"Excuse me? I—"

"No." Ferrin grabbed the water bucket and doused the fire. "Someone's coming."

The fire hissed and spat to coals, spritzing Naomi's legs as she sprang up.

He grabbed her arm. "Get in the cave."

She stumbled over the sudden dark terrain to the even darker cave mouth. "What about your horse?"

He shoved her inside. "Go."

"Aren't you coming?" she whispered.

"Just *go*."

She turned and headed into the dark and twisting tunnel. Now was as good a time as ever to face her fear of shadows.

CHAPTER FOURTEEN

Ferrin reached into the steaming pot of grains and came out with a mushy handful. He trotted over to his horse and held the grains under the animal's mouth. The horse lapped them up, happy, oblivious to the slight shake in Ferrin's hand. He steadied his breathing and closed his eyes. *Be calm. You're here alone. Act like you didn't know they were coming.*

"You!" a voice called from the dark wood. "Identify yourself."

He turned toward the voice. Eight Riders morphed out of the black night into the glow of the dying fire. "Can I help you?" He waded their way.

The Rider in the lead stared down at Ferrin. "Yes. I'm Saul, Lead Rider of Le'Gar. State your name and what order of business you have out here."

"Ferrin. Ranger."

Saul's face froze. "On your way to somewhere in particular?" He glanced around the camp.

"No. I live here."

Saul lowered his chin. "Ah. Because Le'Gar won't have you."

Heat rose up Ferrin's neck, but he kept his expression rigid as stone. "Is there anything I can help you with?"

"Yes, ranger, there is." Saul dismounted. "We're looking for a fugitive."

Ferrin sounded surprised. "From Le'Gar?"

"Fled just this morning." Saul eyed the cave. "We don't believe she could have gone far. Unless she had help."

Ferrin held his hands up. "I don't dip my hands in the messes that leak from Le'Gar."

Saul flared his nose. "You haven't always said that, have you?"

Gritting his teeth together, Ferrin fought to remain calm. This Rider seemed to know about the things he wished to be forgotten. "When you've lived as long as I have, you learn to mind yourself."

"I'm sure it would be alright then if we search the cave?" Saul hunted for a lurch in Ferrin's expression.

Ferrin didn't offer one.

"This is my home," Ferrin grumbled. "Must you trek through the entire thing?"

Saul smiled. "Dismount and enter the cave!"

Uninvited panic swelled in Ferrin's stomach. "There is nothing in there, just my personal items." He tried stepping in front of Saul, but Saul shoved him aside.

"Then we will confirm that." He leaned into Ferrin's face as the other Riders flooded into the cavern. "Or we will find what you're hiding."

———

Naomi heard the scuffling footsteps enter the cave behind her. Her breathing quickened and she moved faster. The glow of the lanterns in Ferrin's domed living space shone ahead, but she stopped. The tunnel she was in had less light. Her best shot at going unnoticed would be to remain in the dark. To hide.

The footsteps approached.

She felt around the stone walls for a crevice. A crack. A *slit*. Her hand fell into a space and she clambered toward it. It was barely large enough for her to slide into but she forced her way. The rock scraped at her back and caught parts of her face as she squeezed in as deep as she was able.

The tunnel glowed with the Riders' lanterns as they paraded closer. Their voices were clear now. She even recognized one as the Rider Saul. She held her breath as his shadow stretched toward her along the tunnel wall.

"Search the space up ahead," he ordered. "Trash his things if you have to."

Three Riders brisked passed her toward Ferrin's living space, but Saul stayed back. He was frozen two feet away from Naomi's hiding place. He seemed to be listening for something.

She held her breath.

His side profile moved into view. He was right next to her. His lantern made his face dance. The light chased away the protection of the dark. Then he turned his head and looked right at her.

CHAPTER FIFTEEN

Within the walls of Le'Gar, in an unknown passageway, Old Man Magnificient shot upright. His slumber disappeared with the jolt, but his dream did not: the face of Naomi Massoud tucked between rock. The grim outline of Saul's nose and eyes nearing her hiding place.

The old man clamped his eyes shut and pressed his fingers together. He dug deep. Deeper than he had in a long time to a place in his soul that had gone nearly dormant. Then his lips began to move.

"Be but a shadow to the eye," he whispered. "Be but a shadow to the eye."

CHAPTER SIXTEEN

Naomi's heartbeat slammed in her ears. She could see Saul's pupils shrink in the lantern light. He could see her, clear as day. She was caught. This was the end.

The other Riders emerged from Ferrin's cavern. "Nothing to report, sir."

Saul didn't move his eyes from her.

One of the Riders glanced at him. "See something?"

Saul breathed. "No."

Her body shook.

"Just a shadow." He turned away. "Move out. There's nothing here."

It didn't make sense. He couldn't have missed her contorted body within the wall's crevice. But he did, and she still shook from the adrenaline.

Ferrin's voice echoed up the way. "Are you quite finished searching my things?"

Feeling safer at the sound of his voice, she peered out just enough to spot him. Saul was inches from the ranger's nose.

"You're lucky we didn't find anything," Saul threatened.

Ferrin was quiet.

Saul's voice lowered and he leaned in. "I don't trust you. None of us do. Not after Estell."

Ferrin stepped back. "Are you through?"

Saul paused and looked him up and down. "Yeah. We're through."

The Riders flooded from the cave. Horse hooves clacked as they rode away back into the night.

Ferrin stood still for a moment longer, making sure they had truly vanished.

Naomi didn't dare move.

"Naomi?" he finally whispered.

She slid out from the rock.

He let out a breath.

She was happy to see him relieved. "Saul looked right at me."

"He obviously didn't, because you're still here." He moved toward her.

"No, he did see me. Or at least...should have."

He frowned. "He let you go unnoticed?"

"No, I think he really couldn't see me," she said. "I think I was invisible."

He stared at her too long.

Her stomach twisted. "What?"

"Did you ever meet an old man while in Le'Gar?"

"I didn't make friends in Le'Gar," she stated dully.

"Really," he doubted. "At all?"

"Acquaintances maybe, but making friends didn't feel safe." She held up her hands. "Honestly. I was afraid someone would find out I wasn't a Smyth."

He narrowed his eyes.

"There was an old man that I remember who checked my papers when I arrived in Le'Gar," she admitted. "But I never saw him again."

"Ah," he said, a knowing look on his face. "You've been in good hands during your time in Le'Gar." He brushed past her and strode toward the dome.

She turned and followed. "How do you know? What are you talking about?" He was starting to be more mysterious than her own personal unknowns.

"I used to live in Le'Gar," he reminded her. "I met people. Had relationships." His voice thinned. "I knew King Tal's great grandfather."

"Personally?" She followed him around the dome while he aimlessly picked up items the Riders had knocked over.

"Yes, personally." He sounded angry. "And you did the right thing by leaving Le'Gar. Tal is not on your side."

She played with the pockets of her pants. "How do you know so much about my bloodline?"

He stopped scuttling about. "It's a legendary name. Everyone knows it."

"No, they don't," she said, firm. "It seems only people with inside information do."

He gave her a sideways glance. "I don't know what else to tell you."

She knew of something he could tell her. "Who is Estell?"

At the mention of the name, his figure became rigid. "It doesn't matter."

"Then why did Saul bring her up?"

He stood tall and locked eyes with Naomi. "It doesn't matter. She's dead."

CHAPTER SEVENTEEN

"How did King Leeland find out?" Hux grumbled low. "I was the only one to make it out of Ode alive. Unless *you* reported my survival."

Vira gave a single laugh. "Yes, because I decided to side with the man that exiled me." She pulled the small satchel out from under her cot and checked to make sure the quill was still there. It was.

"I shouldn't stay," he said. "If you heard the rumors correctly, the Riders of Raina will be here in a few days. I am surprised that King Leeland has already assembled a new crew after losing everyone in Ode, but I think his hastiness shows just how desperate he is to get his hands on the quill. I really should leave."

"And where would you go?" She crossed her arms. "Le'Gar?"

He shrugged. "Maybe."

"Oh good, I was hoping you would say that." She flicked her long hair back.

He squinted. "Why?"

"Because that's where we're going."

He dodged a hanging crystal in Vira's tent. "Why?"

She rolled up the thin blanket on her cot and stuffed it into a backpack. "I have visions." She waved her hand around her head. "All the time. It's just part of being a golden witch. And I know the last Massoud is in Le'Gar." She paused, hovering over her backpack on the cot. "Wait."

He stood behind her, gazing at her flowing hair. "Wait? Why?"

She turned to him, pointing to her heart. "Something feels gaping here."

He furrowed his brows. "I'm not sure what you mean."

She strode to the tent's opening, making sure the flap was overlapping, blocking out as much light as possible. "This Massoud is on the move."

"How can you tell?" He ran a hand through his blond hair. Hair that needed to be washed sooner rather than later. "You'll have to explain these things to me. I haven't been around you enough to understand how you, uh, work." He grimaced a little, worried that his words might make her feel like an object.

She took no offense. "I feel things. Spiritually. It's like knowledge lives in my being."

"I suppose that makes sense," he tried. "So you feel that this Massoud is not in Le'Gar anymore? That he or she is on the move?"

"Yes."

"So..." He stood in the middle of the tent, lost. "We stay here?"

She walked back to him, hands on her hips. "For now."

"And if the Riders of Raina come?"

"They won't get to you," she thundered. "I won't let them."

He smiled downward. "If they come, I'll leave. I'm not going to drag you through the dirt with me."

She looked at him with visible confusion. "I've been living in the dirt since I left Raina. This is no different."

Guilt and hurt pounded him with the force of a thundering waterfall. "I'm sorry."

Again, Vira seemed confused. "For what?"

"For not standing up for you."

"Hux." She stood square with him. "Leave it behind you. We are here now."

They stood staring at each other. Hux tense with turmoil, Vira relaxed and poised.

"Don't let guilt destroy you." Her eyes did not waver, but her voice did.

Hux clenched a fist. "You must not know guilt like I do."

This time, her expression changed. Sorrow. Full of it. "I know guilt, Huxton. It's not worth dwelling on."

He opened his mouth to reply but a soft swishing sound caught his attention. He glanced toward the tent entrance just in time to see a shadow flit away. The shadow of a person.

She saw it too. "We need to be on guard," she whispered. "Zul is supposed to be a safe place, but I've doubted that for some time now." She lowered her voice. "Although, The Dark Hand has never swept over Zul. It seems to avoid it."

He frowned. "Any particular reason?"

"Zul is full of misfits. We aren't quality goods."

"Does the Dark Hand care about quality over quantity?"

"Wouldn't you take gold before you took silver?" she reasoned.

He shrugged. "If I only had copper, I'd take anything I could get."

"But Calamity doesn't just have copper." She shook her head. "It has kings and queens."

"In which territories?"

She shut her eyes. "It's hard to say. They're trained to stay quiet. They'd be murdered by their own people if their alliance with Calamity was found out." She gave a devilish eye. "Would you put it past King Leeland?"

He laughed once. "Leeland sent me to fetch the quill so he could defeat the Dark Hand."

"So you were told." She rested her hand on Hux's limp arm. "You can't trust everyone."

He shivered under her touch. "Am I to assume evil in everyone?"

She hesitated. Her eyes searched his with invasive longing. To have his heart. To be trusting to a fault. She wanted to be like him, but her years in Zul taught her that his heart didn't belong in this world. It was too pure. Unlike hers. Very unlike hers.

"You do what feels right," she said. "I believe you will be able to pinpoint evil when you see it." She moved away from him, roaming to the tent's wall. She put her hand against the material and breathed in.

He squinted and crossed his arms. "What are you doing?"

"Something isn't right," she murmured. "Something in Zul. I've felt it before, but I feel it even more so now."

His heart raced. "What is it that you feel?"

She turned her sharp nose to him. "Betrayal."

CHAPTER EIGHTEEN

Ferrin sat leaning against the outside of his cave. The stars glinted with elegance, the mountain black and screaming with night insects. His stomach twisted up in knots. Something he hadn't felt for years. He felt uncomfortable. Invaded. Worried?

His horse shifted in the dark to his right, meandering slowly around the sparse grass between the rocky terrain. He moved his eyes toward the animal for a moment, then back to the cave opening. The girl asleep inside had the power to change the course of Thãen's future. Naomi Massoud. Did she *really* not know what it meant to be a Massoud? He had toiled over this thought over and over but he kept coming back to her eyes. Her eyes held nothing but fear and confusion when he found her. He hated that he trusted her, but he couldn't change the discernment in his heart. Naomi Massoud had fallen into his hands and there was no way she could survive on her own.

Cursing under his breath, he ran his hands through his coarse, black hair. Out of all people, why him? It seemed like an ill fate. After his colossal, horrific, soul-sinking failure all those years ago, how had he found himself in a similar situation?

Most people of Thãen never meet a Massoud in their lifetime, and if they did, they probably didn't know the weight the name carried. But now he had met two Massouds. And the current one was even more clueless than the first. It made him sick. Near vomiting, sick. Because she was probably going to die. And he was going to have to witness it. Again.

The wind blew, sending leftover leaves that had survived the winter months toward his boots. He picked one up, brown and brittle between his fingers. It crumbled when he ground it lightly between his finger and thumb. Just like everything else he touched. At least, that's how he felt. He let the pieces fall and clenched his fingers, letting his anger flow to his fist.

Why was he still alive? Every day he suppressed his abilities so that maybe the world would decide he was no longer useful. No longer needed. Then maybe he would be able to age and eventually he would die. He *so* wanted to die.

The thought wasn't new, but for the first time in decades, he felt an ounce of pushback. It startled him and he cursed the new feeling. He wasn't useful. He was a failure. There was no reason for him to feel hopeful about his new situation. Even if this felt like a second chance. He couldn't help Naomi. Maybe someone could, but it wasn't him. He needed to get her off his hands. Fast.

———

The next morning, inside the cave Naomi sat still. She had slept rather uncomfortably on the floor of Ferrin's cluttered cavern. Her cloak added little cushion and her mind constantly rambled with thoughts. Now, sitting cross-legged, her hair fell over her shoulders in brown waves to her hips. She breathed in, calming herself, willing herself to get up and face Ferrin outside, where he told her last night he would stay to keep watch.

The events of the day before had caught up to her. Yesterday she ran on adrenaline. Today she was bogged down by reality. She had left Le'Gar with nothing but enemies at her back. Had it not been for Ferrin, she might not have survived her first night. She was thankful for him. Even if he was so openly put off by her.

His voice erupted into the cave. "Naomi!"

"Do I need to hide?" Her heart slammed back and forth.

"What?" His face appeared from within the tunnel. "No. Are you still sleeping? You need to get moving. We're heading out."

She jumped, scrambling to her feet and combed her fingers through her hair. "I'm awake. I've been awake."

He stood still, watching her gather up her cloak from the hard ground. "Did you sleep like a rock?"

"What?" Naomi frowned. "Was that a joke?"

He sighed, turning away. "Yes, Naomi, that was a joke."

She fought a smile. "You can call me Omi."

"No thank you." His back was to her, gathering up little burlap sacks of grain.

"It's what most people call me."

"I won't be with you long enough to call you by a nickname." He grabbed a backpack from behind a boulder and waved her forward. "Zul is right over the ridge then down into the ravine between this mountain and the next. We'll be there in two days." He shoved the backpack into her arms. "Here. Take this. There is food, a canteen, and an extra pair of slacks and rope inside. Put it on. You'll have to carry your weight."

She shrugged into the backpack straps. "Are we leaving now? Like, right now?"

He put a hand on her shoulder, shoving her out toward the cave's mouth. "Yes. Ever heard the phrase *we ride at dawn?*"

"We ride at dawn?" She stumbled to the cave entrance, realizing it *was* dawn. The mountain was a hazy yellow, as if Thãen had been dipped in gentle glory. It took her breath away. She had always watched the sun rise against gargoyles, never against nature. "I'm usually up before dawn." She moved aside to let Ferrin out of the cave. "I'm a lantern snuffer."

He ran his hand along his horse's neck. "A lantern snuffer? What the devil is that?"

"We snuff lanterns. Put them out. We signal the end of the night."

He looked over his shoulder at her. "I don't think we had those when I lived in Le'Gar."

She frowned. "Are you sure? They were around before I got there and I've been there for eleven years. You aren't much older than me. Right?"

"Wrong." He motioned for her to come near.

She stepped his way. "You're younger than me?"

He laced his fingers into a cup to provide an easy way for her to step up and slide onto his horse. "Try again."

Naomi put her hands on her hips, ignoring his laced fingers. "You have to be younger or older. You can't be neither."

He stared at her, almost glaring. "Get on the horse."

"Seriously, you can't be neither." She didn't budge.

"I didn't say I was neither."

"Yes, you did."

"No." He straightened, moving his hands apart. "You said I wasn't much older than you. I said you were wrong."

"Oh," she brightened. "You're the same age."

"No."

She felt a boiling irritation. "You're making no sense. Are you being difficult just for fun?"

He slung his pack around the horse's neck. "Are you having fun?"

"You," she ground her teeth, "are proving to be impossible."

That brought the slightest smile out of him. "I am older

than you, but much older." He grabbed the horse's mane and swung himself up. "Are you coming? I offered assistance, which you ignored, so now you'll have to find your own way up here."

She studied the height of the horse. "I'm not weak, you know. I'm a trained runner." She didn't add the part about being a trained hider. It felt juvenile.

"Then you may want to take the approach of a running start before you jump up here."

"Why must you be *so* unfriendly?" She threw both arms over the horse's back and jumped. Her feet hung awkwardly off the ground and she kicked and squirmed her way upward.

He glanced over his shoulder at her body draped over the horse. "Got it, warrior?"

"Oh, for grave's sake," she mumbled, grabbing the back of his cloak and using him as leverage to clamber to a sitting posting. As awkward as it felt to sit directly behind him yesterday, it felt even more so this morning. Yesterday he was a mysterious saving grace. Today he was equal parts devious and headstrong. It made him real.

"Good for you." He nudged the horse forward. "You accomplished the easiest task you'll face all day."

She didn't answer, just glared at the back of his head. She wanted to keep silent, sort of a way to let him know she was annoyed with him, but she hadn't forgotten what he said. "So how much older? Because you look young. You're lucky. Lots of people wish to look young forever."

He tensed for a moment, only noticeable to her because the horse moved quicker a few paces as his legs stiffened. "You really want to know?" He patted his horse's neck, apologizing for the accidental order to move faster.

"I've been asking, haven't I? Is your age some sort of secret?"

He paused. "To most."

Naomi frowned, wondering what in the world this ranger

was hiding. Then her fingers twitched with energy, realizing the possibility of what he could be. "Are you...are you a *Magnificent?*"

He remained silent.

Her mouth dropped. "No. No way. You're a ranger. Magnificents were kings or warriors. And they disappeared nearly two hundred years ago."

A red bird soared through the sparse pines, crossing in front of his face. "And where do you think they all went?"

"Well, that's not a hard question," she scoffed. "They were killed by Thãen's kings and queens when the Dark Hand made its first appearance in Lindemon, on the other side of the Dessarian Sea. Magnificents were the only ones who had enough power to do what the Dark Hand did then. It made sense, since the Dark Hand hadn't made itself known yet, that the destruction on Lindemon could have come from the power of Magnificents. It's just incredibly unfortunate that the Dark Hand was the identified culprit *after* the Magnificents were slaughtered."

He leaned forward, urging his horse on as the mountain transitioned to steeper rock. "History doesn't always tell the truth."

"Are you saying the Magnificents weren't murdered?" She clutched his cloak tighter as they angled sharply upward.

"Do you really believe that everyone in Thãen felt the same about Magnificents back then?" he challenged.

She shrugged. "Well, of course not. There are always outliers. But the majority were fearful of them."

"Ah." He straightened. "That's what history wants you to believe."

She shoved his insight aside for a moment. "That doesn't answer my question. Are you a Magnificent?"

He stopped the horse.

She went rigid, fearing he may lash out.

But he only shifted to face her. "There were some outliers two hundred years ago who didn't agree with the mass murdering of Magnificents. Actually, there were a lot of outliers. They were silent only because they worked behind closed doors and in secret to rescue Magnificents from death."

Naomi's eyes were wide, taking in his history lesson, believing every word. "How did they prevent Magnificents from being martyred?"

"There was a universal understanding that if you were a Magnificent you had to cease using your powers immediately," he explained. "Some Magnificents were too well known to be able to melt away into hiding. But those who used their powers very little or hadn't yet mastered their abilities had a better chance. The people of Thãen who wanted to protect Magnificents helped them escape into uncharted regions or provided them with aliases and backstories to cover up their real lives." He studied her brown eyes. "Kind of like what happened to you."

Her heart sank to her stomach. She always considered herself lonely and unfortunately placed in this life. She never knew there were others who had to hide their identity.

"So even after all these years there are still Magnificents roaming Thãen?" she said with astonishment.

Ferrin nodded.

"And you're one of them?" She took him in fully now. A young ranger, only young because Magnificents didn't age like the rest of the world. They weren't immortal, but they weren't entirely mortal either. Magnificents lived until their purpose in life was complete. Most Magnificents had multiple purposes. But their lives usually ended between 120 and 150 years. And even then they look to be over 100. "How old are you then? You can't be from the age of the slaughter."

"I'm not." He kept his eyes trained on her. "My father was. I'm one-hundred-eighty-seven years old. And I can't wait to die."

He shifted back around, clicking the horse forward again.

She let her astonishment marinate in silence. One-hundred-eighty-seven? He looked no older than thirty. Not only was he the oldest living Magnificent she had ever heard of, he was the only one she knew of who didn't physically age. But the sincerity in his voice at how desperately he wanted to die killed the last part of her heart that was still innocent. She had a twisted life, but she never wished death upon herself. He seemed hardened from life. Shut off. Beaten. She wondered what he had experienced that had shaped him into this man. Even though she didn't know a thing about him, she ached for him. She felt she had to say something. "Well," her voice cracked a little, "I'm glad you're not dead."

He kept staring ahead.

When he didn't respond, she mustered up enough strength to finish her thought. "If it weren't for you, I'd probably be caught and dead by now. So I'd say you're still here for a reason."

"You may still end up dead, Ms. Smyth," his voice was gravely. "I'm not your saving grace."

CHAPTER NINETEEN

Naomi and Ferrin crossed over the mountain's peak just before sunset. As they descended down the other side, the trees grew thicker once more. Moss replaced the rocky terrain, then eventually grass. Immaculate trunks and dark green leaves surrounded them by sundown, splashing the mountain in darkness before the sun fully disappeared.

Ferrin chose a spot near a twisted oak tree to set up for the night. He used fallen branches, dry leaves, and flint from his sack to ignite a fire. Naomi watched, following his every motion, memorizing the steps. There may come a day when she would need to accomplish this task, and she wanted to be prepared.

When he drew grain from his sack and poured it into a small bowl, Naomi stood right behind him. "Can I help?" she asked.

He shrugged, then thrust the bowl into her hands. "Pour some of the water from your canteen over the grains then rest the bowl over the fire."

She dumped the water into the dish then paused. She wasn't exactly sure how to hold the bowl over the fire, but she didn't want to ask him and risk looking useless. Instead, she scrounged the forest floor for two sticks of the same length. She held one stick in each hand and balanced the bowl on the ends of them, holding the grains over the fire like he instructed.

He watched her work and suppressed a grin. "That's one way to do it."

Her face flushed. "How would you have done it?"

"It doesn't matter; your way is working."

She remembered the wire structure he had used last night to cook the grains over the fire and thought perhaps he could make something similar with sturdy sticks and branches, tall enough to keep them from being burned. But he didn't give her a hard time about her way of doing things. Instead, he found his own two branches of similar length and mimicked her.

Once both bowls of grains were hot, the two sat side by side, eating in silence. Naomi had a mind to remain quiet, knowing by now that Ferrin didn't enjoy the sound of her voice. But to her surprise, he glanced over and broke the ice.

"What happened to your face?" He pointed with his wooden spoon.

She wiped grain from the side of her mouth before touching her cheek. "Right here?"

He nodded.

"It's from a knife."

"You got in a fight?" There was amusement in his voice.

She shook her head. "I got jumped."

"Oh. Pick pocketed. You gotta stay on guard, Ms. Smyth. Those little thieves in Le'Gar are rascals."

Her stomach sank so fast she almost gagged. "It wasn't a pick pocketer." She played with the edge of her bowl. "It was just a man. And I'm a woman. You get the picture."

He let his spoon rest inside his bowl and stared at her, but she looked away, not wanting to meet his eyes. "Oh." He cleared his throat. "I'm—I'm sorry."

"It's okay." Her hands shook and she squeezed the bowl between her fingertips to steady the tremor. "He cut my face because I put up a fight. I got away in the end. So, no harm done."

He set his grains down, suddenly not interested in eating. "It's harmful to even attempt something like that."

She looked over at him. "It's just what happens, I guess." Their eyes locked and she felt heat wash up her neck. "Let's not talk about it. It's not a pleasant memory."

"Fair." He stared into the fire. "What do you want to talk about?"

Her spirits rose. "You want to talk?"

"No. But I can tell that you do."

"Oh." Her shoulders sagged. "It's okay. I'm used to not talking."

He moved the toe of his boot around in the dirt. The fire's glow warbled over his stern face. "Well, we both don't get around people much. Might as well practice our verbal skills while we have the convenience."

She smiled a little. "Really?"

He shrugged.

"Okay." She placed her bowl in the dirt and turned to face him. "I want to know what you've done for the last 187 years. Did you do anything epic? Crazy? Worth telling?"

She could tell by the look on his face that she was treading into sensitive territory. His eyes shifted down slightly before resting on her.

"I was born in Zul," he gave in. "My mother was human and my father was a Magnificent." He paused, perhaps calculating what to say next. "My father aged quickly after he completed his purpose of getting my mother to safety during the slaughter and conceiving me. He passed away when I was very young. My mother lost her life from an infection when I was eighteen. I was alone, so when I turned twenty I left my home for Le'Gar to start a life of my own."

Naomi rested her chin on her knees, "Why did you choose Le'Gar?"

"I was drawn to the gargoyles. Their enchantment intrigued me. I thought that maybe I could figure out the gargoyle's purpose."

"Most people try to figure out why the gargoyles are forced to protect the city," she said. "They think they can find the one person who can release the gargoyles. Or they think they could be the ones to release them."

He nodded. "I guess I fell into that category. A part of me believed I could be involved. I'm a Magnificent. I had a better chance than most."

"But the gargoyles are still plastered to their places. So I guess you didn't succeed."

"Succeed." He looked off through the fire and into the black woods. "I did the opposite of succeed."

She gazed at his clenched jaw. "What do you mean?"

He picked a stick up from the ground and rolled it between his fingers. "Look, the best place for the past is in the past. I was involved in a job that got messy and I didn't get out in time."

"You said the Riders of Le'Gar aren't fond of you. Why?" She knew she was pushing limits, but he was being more open right now.

"Because of the job," he sighed.

"If the Riders despise you, doesn't that mean your task was in conflict with the king?"

He snapped the twig. "Yes."

She leaned forward, attempting to feel the fire more. He was right about spring nights still holding the potential for frost up here. "Who was on the throne when you lived in Le'Gar?"

"Tal's great grandfather." He leaned back on his palms, looking at her. "How is Tal as a king?"

"I don't know. Fine?" She shoved her hair behind her shoulder. "He always seems distraught. Or worried. And when he found out about the quill, he ordered the Riders to find anyone who could be a Massoud. So maybe he's not fine."

"Quill?" Ferrin's eyebrows scrunched. "Oh, right. The quill. I remember you mentioning it."

"Yes, the quill." Naomi squinted. "Kind of an important thing."

Ferrin rubbed his eyes. "You talked a lot on the horse and I didn't really listen to it all."

Her face sagged with sarcasm. "How gentlemanly."

"Cut me slack, I don't talk to anyone. I roam the mountains alone. I'm good at ignoring things."

"But the quill is important." Naomi hugged her knees. "At least Tal and the Riders said it was. The Dark Hand has been looking for it. That's why Ode was destroyed."

"How does Tal know this quill was in Ode?" His eyes were stern, consumed in the new information.

"Some Rider named Hux found it." She paused, glancing up at the canopy of dark leaves. "I think King Tal said he was a Rider of Raina."

"And this Rider, Hux, he reported his finding of the quill to King Tal?"

"No." She shook her head, remembering with clarity every bit of the conversation she overheard. "One of Le'Gar's Riders, Saul, said he was told about Hux's finding by a golden witch who entered his mind."

Ferrin's face faded to white before he turned away. "Do you find that strange?"

"Should I?" She studied his pale cheeks. "You seem to think so."

He looked at her again. "How much do you know about golden witches?"

"Only that it was a golden witch who enchanted the gargoyles to protect Le'Gar. Other than that, they're as mysterious to me as Magnificents."

"Golden witches." He stood, needing to pace, to fidget. "They have always been like-minded with Magnificents. And Magnificents don't trust humanity."

Naomi felt a crush in her heart. She was human. "So you think a golden witch wouldn't normally tell a Rider of a find so important?"

"I know a golden witch wouldn't do that." He walked three steps, his back to Naomi. "But I know of one. One golden witch who was a disciple of The Dark Hand."

She lifted her head, eyes wide. "No."

He paused. A long pause. "Yes."

"So it had to be her then, who spoke to Saul in his mind." She stood, joining him at his side. "Can we find her?"

He snapped his head toward her. "No. Never seek out someone under The Dark Hand's curse."

"But she could hold answers."

"She's dead," he said softly. "So it couldn't have been her."

He had said that before. *She's dead.* He had said it about someone named Estell.

"Was Estell a golden witch?" Naomi tread carefully.

"Don't speak her name." He brisked away from her, just far enough from the fire to make him fade into the trees. "To hear it roll off someone's tongue is like encountering an ear-splitting scream."

Her core squeezed. "I'm sorry."

"Don't be sorry. Just never speak of her again."

"I won't." She slid back down to sit beside the fire once more. She'd pushed him as far as he would go. He was a closed book once again.

CHAPTER TWENTY

Hux left Vira at dusk to wash the grime from his hair in the water that ran through Zul's ravine. Vira felt his absence, and it shocked her. She spent years alone. *Years*. Hux had only been with her for two days. Why did she feel his absence so heavily? She carefully calculated what she felt in her heart, never one to ignore true emotion. But it wasn't emotion. It was comfort. He was comfort to her. She knew she could trust him, and he would never hurt her. If she were to allow anyone to join in on her life mission, it would be him.

The entrance flap of her tent swished open. "My darling, Vira." A woman strode in, arms raised in pretend elegance. Her skin was gold and eyes narrow. Where Vira had long black hair, this woman had hair that was just as long, but ghostly white. They couldn't be more different—in looks *and* character.

"What do you want?" Vira sighed.

The woman took her graceful self to Vira's bed and sprawled out on it, getting rudely comfortable. "Oh, Vira. You don't usually keep the golden boys for yourself."

Vira faced her, hard as stone. "If you're talking about my visitor, he isn't that kind of visitor. He's my friend."

The woman raised an eyebrow.

"And he will remain in my company only," Vira finished with a bite.

"Since when do you have friends other than *those* types of visitors?" The woman examined her fingernails, studying a minuscule amount of dirt under her pinky.

Vira's face flushed and deep regret gripped her chest. "Those days are in my past, and I'm glad for it."

"Ohhh." The woman pouted. "You've become no fun, darling."

"I never thought it was fun." She looked away.

"Who is this friend of yours, then?" She sat up, balancing on the edge of the bed.

"Who comes and goes in my tent is no one's business but mine."

"He doesn't look like Zul's type."

Vira almost smiled. "It's because he's not. He's above us. Which is why I will personally keep him away from you."

"Why must you be so secretive, Vira?"

"Why must you be so nosey, *Estell*?"

Estell rose, tossing her feathery hair behind her. "Come now, darling, I know you have secrets."

She didn't budge. "Everyone in Zul has secrets."

Estell squinted. "Why are you being so shut off from me? We have a connection. That should be reason enough for you to tell me what you're scheming."

"I'm not scheming." She snapped her fingers toward the tent entrance. "Out. We don't work well together. We are not the same type of golden witch."

"There is only one breed." She glared.

"Physically, yes." Vira continued to point at the tent's flap. "Mentally, no."

"You're saying you are mentally stronger than me?" Estell strode up to her, almost nose to nose.

Vira stood still. "Not stronger, but more just."

A flicker of vulnerability passed over Estell's eyes. "Who says I'm not just?"

"When was the last time you used your abilities for someone other than yourself?"

"That's not injustice, that's just greed," Estell huffed.

Vira raised an eyebrow. "You know it's greed, yet you still act in it?"

"We have power, Vira." Her words slid off her tongue like venom. "Why shouldn't we use it for ourselves? Or against those who promise us harm?"

She frowned. "Have you used your powers against others?"

She gave Vira a screwed lipped sneer. "Of course I have, darling. As I know you have."

Vira wished Hux would come back already. "I've never used my powers to harm someone."

"That is a lie if I ever knew one."

"Harm for harm?" Vira exhaled. "Where is the benefit in that?"

Estell blew air in her face. "It's *justice*."

"It makes you no better than the one who harmed you."

"It isn't harmful if it's done for protection," Estell argued.

Vira glowered. "Who have you ever protected? You've never shown an ounce of interest for anyone's well-being. At least not while I've known you."

Estell gripped Vira's shoulder, smiling low. "You haven't known me all my life."

"Close to it." She tugged her shoulder away. "Now go."

Estell trailed her finger down her arm as she slunk to the

tent's exit. "Are you sure you want to keep that visitor to your-self? Isn't that greedy?"

Vira ground her teeth together. "He's not to be touched, Estell. Do you understand?"

"You're so plucky, darling." Estell grinned. "Don't let the golden boy break you. What's in your past could always surface. It's never truly gone."

Vira pointed. "*Out.*"

With a fingertip wave, Estell left.

Vira stood in the middle of her tent, hugging her core. She swallowed once, twice. It didn't work. She couldn't keep the nausea away. Holding her hand over her mouth, she ran outside. Bursting into the dimming night, she vomited onto the patchy grass. A few heads glanced her way from up the row of tents, but no one interfered. They just let her be. Everyone in Zul let everyone be. Usually. But occasionally, individuals collided. Though Zul was full of misfits, those misfits had feelings, passions, instincts. Those were the things that had ruined Vira, leaving her vomiting at the memory of her actions.

"Vira?" Hux appeared at the end at the dirt row and quickened his pace

She held her hand up, waving him away through another convulsive retch. Her hair fell forward, loose pieces hanging in the falling bile.

"What happened?" He ignored the wave of her hand and sped to her side. "Are you sick?" He gently took her hair in his calloused left fist and held it back. "Are you okay?"

She stopped puking, but remained hunched over with her hands on her knees, shaking.

He waited for her to say something, but she didn't. "Vira?"

She only shook her head, then gently pulled her hair from Hux's hand. "I need to rinse it." She straightened. "I'm sorry."

He stepped back, giving her breathing room. "Sorry for what?"

"I don't know," she whispered. "I'm going down to the ravine. Don't wait up for me."

She took a controlled breath and slunk away.

Hux stood rigid, watching her go. He ground his heels into the dirt, rocking back then forward, contemplating following her. But he spun back toward the tent instead. She needed space. And he would give it to her. He knew the feeling. Space was the only thing that calmed his mind as a child whenever someone would make a cruel remark about his arm. As an adult, the comments didn't hurt as much, but he remembered the hurt in the past. He would allow her the time she needed to collect herself. But he couldn't help but wonder when she would open up to him again. When would there no longer be space between them?

CHAPTER TWENTY-ONE

Le'Gar's damp streets became dry with the afternoon sun. The pleasant spring weather brought out the merchants and street performers. The city was lively and crowded, making it difficult for the Riders of Le'Gar to maneuver their way back to King Tal's cathedral. Their search of the mountains had offered no leads to a Massoud. No obvious leads, at least. Though to Saul, encountering Ferrin was worth a mention. King Tal knew Ferrin still resided in the mountains, but the ranger was quiet and moved like fog. He was rarely seen and sparsely talked about. But last night, he had been spotted in the open and seemed rather twitchy. Saul couldn't shake the image of Ferrin's eyes when he had realized the Riders were going to enter his cave. It wasn't a look of fear. It was barely a look at all. But Saul caught a look of *something*. Concern? Anxiousness? Ferrin had acted against the king before, who was to say he wouldn't do it again?

The Riders rode through the stone streets to the cathedral with Saul in the lead. King Tal paced the throne room, snapping his head up when Saul and the Riders marched in two by two.

Tal thundered up to Saul. "Did you find her?"

Saul shifted his helmet to the crook of his arm. "No, sir. The mountains are clear of fugitives. That's what we have concluded."

The king let out a low groan. "Where did this Naomi Smyth go?"

"Sir, she may have fled for other reasons," he suggested. "She was a lantern snuffer. Snuffers don't offer anything to society. All they do is put out light. Maybe she fled to find another life."

Tal studied Saul, boring hard into his frown lines. "Is that what you really believe?"

Saul shifted. "It's not my place to have an opinion, only suggestions, sir. If you believe Naomi Smyth is a danger, we can put a bounty out on her."

He glanced behind Saul at the other Riders standing still, at attention. "You are dismissed."

The Riders relaxed, turning to leave. Saul spun with them.

Tal grabbed his shoulder. "Not you."

"No, sir? What can I do for you?"

"Drop the sir," he mumbled. "Follow me."

Saul frowned, glanced at his Riders leaving, and followed Tal further into the throne room toward the throne itself. The curtain hanging behind the throne was crimson red with emerald stitching falling down it like a weeping willow. What lay behind the throne's curtain was a secret. Known only to the king. Of course there were speculations that circulated through the gossip of Le'Gar's citizens, but no tale had ever been proven true. For a moment, Saul thought Tal was leading him right to the edge of the curtain to slip behind it, but the king stopped short, facing the material.

"You didn't reveal all your findings to me," Tal said, hushed.

Saul stared at his back. "I did, Tal. We didn't find anything dangerous."

He turned, locking eyes with him. "But you saw something peculiar. I see it all over your face."

Saul held a strong gaze. "Ferrin," he answered without hesitation.

Tal's fingers curled into his palms. "Where did you see him?"

"Close to the mountain's ridge. He was alone."

"But seeing him bothered you."

"Of course it did," Saul scoffed. "Ferrin is not a friend of the king."

"But he isn't an enemy, either," Tal mumbled softly.

Saul frowned. "Excuse me, sir?"

"I said to drop the sir," he snapped. "This is not an authoritative conversation." He yanked his thin, twisted crown off and threw it into the throne chair. It bounced against the back then clattered to the floor.

Saul stood frozen, staring at him with shifting eyes. "Tal. Ferrin worked against your great grandfather."

The king was sweating. "Don't tell me what I already know. You don't think I received a briefing on Ferrin's history?"

"Then you know he's an enemy," Saul said through clenched teeth.

Tal stepped toward him, seething. "You don't know the half of it."

"You think what Ferrin did was noble?" Saul jeered.

"On the contrary." Tal's shoulders relaxed. "He betrayed the throne. That's treason."

Saul nodded. "And your great grandfather was only trying to contain terrorism, correct?"

Tal swished a few steps across the floor. "That's what he said."

"You don't believe him?"

He spun. "I believe him."

Saul tilted his head to the side. "Yet you seem so perplexed."

Tal paused, staring off behind Saul for a long moment. "Is the story of Ferrin's treason told without flaw?"

"You're questioning your great grandfather's character, Tal. Why would he tell an untruthful story?"

"Is there no ounce of it that bothers you?" His hair fell in matted pieces in front of his eyes. Eyes full of rage.

Saul dared to move closer, holding his hands up to calm him. "You're spiraling. Why? What's got a grip on you?"

Tal's face fell, red scruff twitching. "I am gripped by no one."

"Maybe it would clear your mind if you talked to your father about Ferrin's treason."

The king chortled. "You don't seek a man who can't even remember his own name and ask him about details of the past."

Saul lowered his head. "I apologize, sir. The state of your father's health slipped my mind."

"Although." He stood a speck taller. "Ferrin is alive and well."

"You want me to gather Ferrin, sir?"

Tal gave a slow grin. "Yes. Go back into the mountains and bring Ferrin to me."

———

The space behind the cathedral's stained-glass wall, under the wooden rafters, held Naomi only a few days ago. Today, it held Old Man Magnificent. He crouched low, crawling. Tal's voice carried up from the throne room, through the stained glass, and to the old man's ears. *Ferrin.* The name seized the old man's heart. He'd spoken good omens over Ferrin every day since the ranger departed from Le'Gar. It was a bitter parting that day and tears were shed. Angry tears from Ferrin, sorrowful ones from him.

Now, Old Man Magnificent knew what he had to do. Ferrin was victim to the king's actions before and the old man wouldn't allow that again. He slunk across the hidden rafter space to the dumbwaiter, leveraged himself down, snaked through the underground tunnel and ascended into the graveyard from the hatch in the ground. It was mid-day but the graveyard was hidden by soggy oak trees and overgrown moss.

He glided along the graveyard's stone wall and climbed over it into the back alley that wove behind the cathedral. He ran his hand along the gray bricks, feeling for the loose one. When he found it, he pushed. The wall slid to reveal a crack just large enough for the old man to slip through. Which he did. The crack shut behind him again, enclosing the space in darkness. But the old man knew his way around like a blind man knew the blueprint of his own home.

There was an iron ladder against the interior wall. It ran all the way up to the roof of the legal office, which was one of the highest peaks in the city. The peak was home to a gargoyle crow that sat with its wings spread out as if on a continuous flight, yet it never moved. The man often found himself sitting next to this crow to take in the sunrise when he felt the need to calm his mind from the visions that came crashing in uninvited, offering him gateways into places he was physically absent from.

Just like every other time, the crow didn't even twitch when the old man appeared beside him. The sun beat down on the stone bird, making him hot to the touch even though the weather was relatively pleasant.

"You're a faithful one," the old man said, his hand resting easy on the crow's head. "You never budge, yet I know you've seen."

The crow remained still.

The old man hung his head, breathing with purpose. "You were one of the few who witnessed the murder all those years ago."

A hardened feather twitched within the crow's wing.

Looking over the edge, the man could see the spot in the stone street below where a body once lay. Civilians never wandered the street wedged between the legal building and the cathedral. It didn't lead to anywhere necessary, making it the perfect place for a murder. But the crow had seen. He had seen the whole aching scheme unfold, but was cursed to sit in silence.

"It could happen again," the old man whispered. "There is another Massoud."

This time the crow rotated its head to look directly at him.

Raising an eyebrow, the old man smiled beneath a heavy beard. "You're tired of sitting idle."

A single nod from the crow.

"Ferrin is in trouble." The old man's eyes sagged. "And if my visions are correct, he's found himself with the new Massoud." He leaned into the crow. "You must defy the curse and fly into the mountains to warn Ferrin of the Riders' coming." He slipped his hand into his pocket and pulled out a rolled up piece of parchment paper. "This will be enough explanation for Ferrin. Take this. Deliver it. And know that you have done your duty."

Without hesitation, the crow broke away from his stone peak and leapt into the air. His wings outstretched, crunching and shifting with unnatural movements. Bits of cracked rock fell away at the base where his feet were once secured. He stretched out his talons, snatched the parchment from the old man and zipped downward to fly hidden in Le'Gar's shadows.

"Look invisible to prying eyes," the old man whispered.

"And good fortune to you until you reach Ferrin. *Do not crumble* until the task is complete, in Protection's name."

CHAPTER TWENTY-TWO

Naomi's heart clenched as Ferrin's horse descended into Zul. Shouts and brute laughter wafted from the community of tents, and with it came the smell of tobacco and sweat. The stench got thicker as the horse stepped carefully through boulders and loose rock to reach a narrow dirt path cutting right into the heart of Zul. She dug her fingers into the back of Ferrin's cloak, making sure she was gentle enough so he wouldn't know. Her hands trembled and a sob stuck inside her throat. The people here. They were dirty. Rough. Rogue, even. Men to their right tousled on the side of the pathway. Women stood to the side cheering on their chosen winner of the wrestling match.

Ferrin guided his horse right past the fight and toward the center tent that towered above the rest. The wrestlers didn't pay any mind to the two of them, but the women glanced up briefly, lingering longer on Ferrin. Naomi made it a point not to make eye contact with them.

Leaving the horse outside at a water trough, Ferrin guided Naomi inside the tent. Lanterns illuminated the space, making the air golden. Rectangular booths framed by dark wood and draped with cloth sat in rows. Some booths had food rations, some had herbs and glass jars of what looked like medicine, but Ferrin took her to a booth with a wooden sign reading *Room and Board*.

The man sitting inside the booth looked up from a book that had black inked names scribbled in it. One of his eyes was gone. "How many tents?" His voice sounded like gravel beneath boots.

"Two." Ferrin reached into his cloak and pulled out a burlap sack of coins.

Naomi played with the inside of her cloak at his side.

The man glanced at her with his one eye, then back at him. "Each tent is 167 neos."

"*167 neos?*" Ferrin squeezed his bag of gold. "Last I heard it was 50."

"People are fleeing more often these days." The man shrugged. "Had a wave from Ode only a few weeks ago. Demand is high, so prices are high."

"Fine," he grumbled. "We'll take one tent."

Naomi's stomach leapt and she refused to look at Ferrin, though her red face probably gave away her innocence. The man inside the booth took Ferrin's neos and gave her a smirk.

If Ferrin saw the smirk, he didn't let on. "Let's go, Ms. Smyth." He turned her around by the shoulders.

She obediently stuck with him all the way to the tent that was assigned to them. The cloth was the color of gray mud and was wedged between two tan tents that glowed from interior lamp light. Ferrin held the front flap open for her and she ducked inside. He didn't follow in after her right away, but she could hear him mumbling something to his horse who stood loyally in front of the tent.

She glanced around. The tent was dark except for a single red, metal lantern sitting on a round wooden table in the middle of the packed dirt floor. The flame made Naomi into a shadow, stretching up the wall of the tent. A cot sat empty on the right and that was it. This was the tent that cost 167 neos.

Ferrin appeared behind her. "I'll sleep outside."

She faced him. "No, it's all right. I'll sleep on the floor. You take the cot."

He almost laughed. "If anyone is taking the cot, it's you, Ms. Smyth."

"Fine." She crossed her arms, squirming. "But you sleep on the floor under the protection of the tent. I'm not so ashamed of bunking with you that I'd make you sleep outside under the open sky."

He shrugged off his backpack and tossed it to the ground. "It's not shame so much as dignity. Not that I have a massive amount of dignity to lose, but you might."

"Thãen doesn't even know who I am." She looked down at the toes of her boots. "No one would know if my dignity fell. They don't even know I have any at all."

He bent to his backpack and unbuckled the straps to rummage around inside. "What are you suggesting, then?"

"Nothing," she said too quickly. "I was just...you...I want you to feel comfortable sleeping with me." Her face exploded with red. "I meant sleeping *in* here with me. Not *with* me." She covered her mouth. "I'm sorry."

"Ms. Smyth." He stood, holding a dagger and a suppressed grin. "Relax."

She eyed the dagger. "I said I'm sorry."

He furrowed his brows before following her eyes to the dagger in his hand. "What?" He opened both palms, balancing the dagger in his open right hand. "This is for protection tonight, not to hurt you."

"Oh," she said, hushed. "Sorry."

He dropped his arms to his side, sighing. "I'm not going to harm you. I've already told you that."

Tears flecked the back of her eyes. "But you said you weren't my friend. If not a friend, then what are you? The only other option is foe."

"I'm just delivering you to a place that can keep you safe outside of Le'Gar until you figure out your next move."

"You're leaving me here." Her words were hot, like embers hidden beneath a white log.

His fist tightened around the dagger. "You were never meant to be in my care in the first place. I can't help your bloodline."

A sob made up of anger, confusion, and splicing pain welled in her chest. "You know more about my bloodline than I do. Shouldn't that mean you ought to help me?" She flung her arms out to the sides. "I've never lived my life as a Massoud. I'm a fake. I'm *lost*."

With one spry step, he was right against her. He pulled her toward him. "Don't you hear me calling you Ms. Smyth? Don't *ever* speak your real name out loud. Not here. Not anywhere." He loosened his grip. "I'm sorry, but do you understand?"

Tears dripped out of both her eyes. "You're just as bad as the rest of them." Her voice quivered.

He stepped back. "No, I'm not. The rest of them would have killed you when they met you."

"Why should I believe you?" She shook with anger. "For all I know, you'll kill me in my sleep tonight."

"If I wanted to do that, I would have done it by now."

Her voice cracked. "Don't leave me here alone."

He slid the dagger into his pocket and hung his head. When he brought his chin up again, he rested both of his palms gently against Naomi's arms. "You don't want my help."

"Yes, I do," she argued. "I'm—I'm scared."

He offered a frail smile. "You have a fighting spirit. I can see it. Sense it." Lowering his hands, he blew a long breath from his nose. "You'll be okay, Ms. Smyth. You'll figure out what to do. Not because you have to, but because you want to."

"I want to?"

"I can read you." He tilted his head. "You lost your family to the Dark Hand. Your life turned upside down when it arrived in Beezus. You hold a grudge. You want to see the Dark Hand decimated."

She swallowed, hearing the echo of her mother's cry. *Run, Omi!* And since that day she felt like she had never stopped running. Of course she wished to see The Hand of Calamity defeated, but the situation was deeper than that. People in Thãen were a part of Calamity's team. Kings, queens, regular folk. It was messy. Impossible. Naomi could never take a stand. Even being a Massoud. Whatever that meant. "I'm the wrong person," she said, airy.

He lowered his voice. "You're of the sacred bloodline."

"I don't care." She looked down, fighting more tears. "I'm the wrong candidate. The world needs to find someone else. I am nothing."

Rigid as stone, Ferrin watched her. His gaze didn't break once, even as she twitched her eyes left and right, unable to stare straight at him. "As long as you believe that, you'll be miserable." He sounded weary.

"Give me a reason not to believe it," she challenged.

He moved halfway to the entrance of the tent. "There is a ravine at the other end of the village that holds water from the east mountains' rivers. I'm going to fill up the canteens."

She blinked, holding in a fire of hurt at his refusal to answer. She was nothing. And he knew it, too.

"Don't leave the tent while I'm gone." He glanced sideways at her, then paused. "What was it that you said your profession was?"

"It's not a profession, it's just a job," she said with a shake of her shoulders.

"Right, well, what was it? A lantern snuffer?"

She nodded. "That's it."

"And you said you put out light."

"Yes," she huffed. "See? That's all I am."

He slid his hand into the tent's flap. "You signal the end of the night, Naomi. You said so yourself."

She stood still, watching his back.

"Don't you think Thãen needs someone who can bring an end to the night?" His voice was quiet, desperate.

She opened her mouth to reply, but he dipped through the opening and disappeared into Zul's walkways.

She stood in the center of the tent, hugging herself. Her windblown, matted hair lay in disarray against her shoulders and down her back. Her shoes—her only pair of shoes—were just as mangled. As for her linen pants and blouse? They were in slightly better condition, but disgraceful nonetheless. How could she have an impact on The Dark Hand's oppression? She had never known a life without its daunting presence. Even when The Dark Hand hadn't yet been explained to her, it still existed. The forces in the Outer Void had found Thãen centuries ago. *Centuries.* There was no way she could put a dent in history now.

The cot suddenly seemed welcoming, even in its barren state. She trudged forward and collapsed onto her side, causing the rickety bed to creak under her weight. Her legs throbbed with fatigue and she realized now how her stomach burned with hunger. Ferrin was kind enough to share his grains with her, but she knew she would have to start fending for herself once he left, and that thought terrified her. She didn't know the first thing about trading outside of Le'Gar. She knew where the markets were in Le'Gar and she knew exactly how many neos certain items cost. When Ferrin paid for their tent, she had seen a booth inside the main tent that said *rations*. Did that mean food was free but limited? Or did you have to pay for rations?

She squeezed her eyes shut, blocking out the questions that riddled her with anxiety. Another tear leaked out of the corner of her eye. Ferrin was stiff. Hard to read. Sometimes rude. But she didn't want him to leave. He had come to her aid for some reason. Even though he acted like she was a menace, he could have left her for dead. Yet he didn't, and that spoke volumes to her.

"Please don't let him leave," she whispered into the air. Her father had wished for the moon to guide her when she tread in dark places. In a sense, Ferrin was that moon. Her father's good fortune had held firm. Maybe if she prayed loud enough, The Hand of Protection would hear her and uphold that good fortune.

She was still lingering on that thought when her necklace—hanging awkwardly as she lay on her side—caught her attention. Pushing up onto her elbow, she grabbed the pendant. *Had the pearl inside the gold crescent moon always been this bright?* She poked it then flipped it over, examining the cream sphere that now looked white. Or maybe it looked like it was glowing?

Now she sat up. It was definitely glowing. Faint, but glowing.

She unclasped it from her neck and pressed it between her palms, hiding the glow. Ferrin's voice rang out in her mind, *"Don't you hear me calling you Ms. Smyth? Don't ever speak your real name out loud."* If her name was telling of danger, how much more was a glowing pendant? She fidgeted, hands clasped in her lap. Ferrin had to come back. She had to show him. Maybe this would make him stay. Or perhaps it would frighten him into leaving before dawn. But maybe, just maybe, it would make him stay.

CHAPTER TWENTY-THREE

A faint, luminescent hue drew Hux's eyes to the underside of Vira's cot.

The satchel.

He dove to his knees, reached under and pulled the bag out. The glow escaped from beneath the flap and he flung it open, peering inside. His throat constricted. The quill was still solid gold, but light bounced off it like a star. He had no inkling about what this could mean, only that Vira needed to see it. Now.

Standing, he flipped the satchel shut again and slung it across his body. It was snug, having been adjusted to Vira's smaller frame, and he felt as if it would snap. But he darted from the tent into the dirt walkways surrounded by the falling night and made haste to the ravine.

***

Naomi leapt from the cot. Ferrin was taking too long. The pendant in her hands glowed so noticeably now that she felt it might burn her. Her chest heaved, petrified that her destiny was creeping up on her at a dangerous pace. She wasn't ready.

Whatever a Massoud was supposed to do, she wasn't ready. Why an illuminated pearl should cause such a panic inside her, she couldn't say. But she knew necklaces didn't have a mind of their own. Not unless magic was involved.

She shoved the necklace into the pocket of her linen pants and burst from the tent into the street. Or pathway. Whatever it technically was. Tents lined the way left and right with lanterns situated outside of each dwelling. Some travelers lingered in the path chatting, sharing stories and drinking. They glanced up briefly as Naomi emerged into the night, but paid her no mind as she headed left. Ferrin had said the ravine was along the east mountains. That was easy enough. The mountains towered into mist that was thick enough to be visible in the early dark. She jogged, gaining a few questionable looks from the people she passed. The pendant weighed heavily in her pocket. Not physically, but mentally. What did it mean? Was it a sign of danger? Of purpose?

The ravine came into view, narrow and glistening with slow-running water. The shores were less crowded than Zul's streets, but even so, it took her a few moments to spot Ferrin. His forearms were submerged in the water, holding one of the canteens beneath the surface, his head bent.

She teetered down the embankment. "Ferrin," she hissed.

He snapped his head up and spun around. "What are you —" He stood, lowering his voice. "What are you doing? I said not to leave."

She reached him, standing close so only he could hear. "My necklace. You have to see it. It's glowing."

He put his hands on her shoulders and gently moved her away from the water. A few heads had turned their way. "Go back to the tent," he whispered.

She grabbed his arms. "*No*, Ferrin, it means something."

"Would you keep your voice down?" He leaned into her ear. "That woman over there is looking at us."

She hesitated a beat before snatching a quick glance at a woman a few feet up the ravine's shore. He was right. The woman's black hair hung over her shoulder, wet from being washed. Her eyes were an emerald green and Naomi couldn't help but feel drawn to her.

"Let's go." He linked elbows with her. "You should have waited for me."

She let him guide her back up the embankment. "I did wait. You were taking ages."

"I've been here for five minutes. Maybe ten." He dragged her along on the dusty road. "You need to learn how to be cautious. Especially when I'm not around."

She yanked her arm away from him. "If you're leaving in the morning, you have no authority to tell me what to do. We're either partners or we're not."

He faced her in the middle of the street. Tents surrounded them on all sides, but it was fully dark now, hiding their distraught faces from any lingering people.

"We were never partners." He seemed to sink his teeth into her heart on purpose. "I brought you here to help you find safety. That's all." He glared. "If you don't want to listen to me, fine. I won't stop you from exposing yourself."

A man sidestepped them, keeping his head low. Naomi shifted out of his way just as the man stepped in the same direction. Her shoulder collided with his. At the sudden jolt, his arm fell limp at his side. Naomi drew in an empathetic gasp when she saw the withered muscles in his hand and forearm. "I'm sorry, sir." She stepped away from him. "I'm sorry."

Ferrin nearly leapt to her side as Hux looked up and made eye contact with her.

"It's all right." Hux smiled. "Look." He lifted his arm. "No harm done."

She matched his easy tone. "Good. I'm—I'm sorry.."

Ferrin gave her a gentle push forward. "Have a good night, sir," he said with a nod.

Hux nodded back and went to continue on toward the ravine, but he stopped, waving to someone. "Oh, Vira. I was coming to find you."

Naomi glanced over her shoulder and spotted the woman. Vira was the same woman who had stared heavily at them at the ravine. "Ferrin," she whispered. "That woman is—"

"Shh!" Ferrin yanked her arm forward. "Go faster."

Vira began to jog toward them. "Excuse me!"

Naomi tripped over her own feet as Ferrin picked up the pace. "Ferrin, she's talking to us."

"That's why you weren't supposed to leave the tent." His breathing was labored. Mildly panicked.

Vira's voice sounded closer. "Ranger, stop."

"Vira?" Hux followed behind her. "What are you doing? They're just passing through the street."

Ferrin didn't stop, only tightened his grip around Naomi's wrist. Her skin burned beneath his grasp. She could sense that he was terrified. Terrified of the woman who was now only inches away.

"Please." Vira grabbed Naomi's shoulder. "Stop."

Ferrin slung around and stepped in front of Naomi, breaking her from Vira's grasp. "Get away. We don't want your friendship or acquaintance or whatever else you're about to offer."

Hux slowed at Vira's side. "Who are they?" he asked through a frown, looking at the two like they could be dangerous.

Vira moved back, holding her palms up to show compliance. "You're a ranger."

Naomi cowered behind Ferrin, staring at Vira with wide eyes.

"I am a ranger," Ferrin disclosed. "I don't know how you know that, but if you're going to ask me to complete a job for you, I won't. Not now. I have no time."

Vira pointed to Naomi. "Because she's your job."

He gave Vira a nasty set of eyes. "What she is to me is none of your concern. Keep moving. And don't seek us out again."

"You." Vira looked past him to Naomi. "How long have you been in hiding?"

Ferrin moved an arm across Naomi. "Don't speak to her, witch."

Vira raised a slow eyebrow. "You call me witch with such hate. That's interesting, coming from a Magnificent."

Naomi watched his face drain of menace and take on the look of terror instead.

Hux's mouth parted slightly. "A Magnificent?"

The four stood staring at each other in silence. The sounds of Zul suddenly became noticeable. A crow cawed in the mountainous distance.

"Yes, Hux." Vira side-eyed him. "Though I feel he is suppressing that title."

Ferrin spoke through clenched teeth. "How dare you read me. But then again, I expect nothing less from a golden witch."

"Wait." Naomi stepped in front of him. "Hux?"

Hux gripped the strap of the satchel draped across his body. "Yes?"

Vira tilted her head. "You know him?"

Naomi nodded. "I know of him."

"Naomi," Ferrin whispered. "*Don't.*"

"What is your poison, ranger?" Vira scoffed. "Let the girl speak. She is capable."

But Naomi held her tongue. Ferrin was right. Hux could be the most dangerous man to walk Thãen. She had overheard Saul say a man by the name of Hux had retrieved a quill of some sort. The quill obviously had significance, and Hux had failed to deliver his find to his king.

"My king spoke of you," she said carefully. "He mentioned a mission you were a part of."

Vira and Hux shared a look. Naomi could tell Hux was lost.

"And," Naomi continued, "he spoke of your treason."

Ferrin narrowed his gaze on Hux. "Treason, huh? I remember my partner telling me your story now."

Naomi felt a small stomach flutter. *Partner.*

Hux had regained his composure. "Who is your king?"

She saw no reason to lie. "King Tal."

"Of Le'Gar?" Vira gasped.

"Yes." She breathed slowly, fighting for calm.

There was silence between the four of them again.

"Come on, Ms. Smyth." Ferrin gently took her wrist again. "We don't need to associate with treasoners."

"Says the treasoner himself," Vira said, hushed.

Ferrin hesitated, fists clenched.

"I sense it on you," she continued. "But it's not a bitter treason. There is morality in your decision."

"*Don't read me.*" Ferrin's chest rose and fell like ocean swells.

Naomi stared at Vira. "You're a golden witch."

Vira smiled. "What gave it away?"

Naomi didn't return the smile. "You gave Hux away."

Hux cut his eyes to Vira. "What?"

Ferrin tilted his chin toward Naomi. "Don't make things worse."

"I'm not making things worse," she argued. "I'm making

things clear. Vira is a witch. She gave Hux away to one of Le'Gar's Riders, Saul. Saul said a golden witch entered his mind and told him of a man by the name of Hux who found a quill on a mission ordered by the king of Raina and retreated as a sole survivor, taking the quill with him."

Hux took one step back from Vira. "You...you *betrayed* me? Vira, why?"

"Hux." She shut her eyes. "It wasn't me."

"Another golden witch then?" He laughed once. "Highly impossible. There aren't that many anymore."

She set a cold stare on him. "You have to trust me." Her glare softened. "Please. This is bigger than you. Than me." She pointed to Naomi. "She's right there. The one."

Naomi's heart sped, threatening to escape. "I'm nobody. I'm Naomi Smyth. Lantern snuffer of Le'Gar. End of introduction."

"So why are you here?" Vira quizzed.

Naomi mindlessly fumbled with the necklace still sitting in her pocket. "I'm here on business." She looked at Ferrin. "Right?"

He nodded, half shrugging. "Right."

"No." Vira shook her head. "I feel it right here." She dug her finger into her own chest. "You have no idea the connection I've felt with you. It's you. *It's you.*"

Ferrin challenged Vira with death in his eyes. "Leave her alone. She's just here for sanctuary."

Vira's gaze rested softly on Ferrin. "I admire your concern, but I'm not here to cause harm to her. I've been called to help her."

Though Naomi knew Vira could be twisting the truth, her spirits rose nonetheless. "Help me how?" If Ferrin was going to leave her in the morning, maybe he would leave her in Vira's hands. A woman who wanted to help her.

Vira dropped her voice to just below a whisper. "You're of the sacred bloodline, yes?"

Hux shook his head. "The ranger called her Miss Smyth."

"An alias." Vira bore her emerald irises into Naomi's brown ones. "Right, Miss Massoud?"

Ferrin stepped forward, covering Vira's view of Naomi. "Get away from here. *Now.* You speak the name as if it holds no weight. You're putting her in danger."

Vira straightened. "You're right. My excitement has clouded my judgment." She waved her hand up the row a little ways. "Can we all meet in my tent? Let's smooth out the pieces we have here."

Ferrin turned halfway, considering Naomi. "I can't force you to do anything. You said so yourself."

She squinted. "But?"

"But if you go with them," he dropped his chin, "you could be opening the door to something you can't turn back from."

She watched the way his lips moved, slow and careful, and the way his eyes pleaded, deep and honest. "If I go, will you come with me?" she dared.

For a moment, he was still. Then he nodded.

She faced Vira. "Yes. We'll meet. But we meet in our tent."

"Fair." Vira bowed her head. "Lead the way."

CHAPTER TWENTY-FOUR

The four stood in the center of Naomi and Ferrin's tent. The lanterns inside created enough of a glow to make everyone's expressions readable. Naomi could see bewilderment in Hux, a hint of anger in Ferrin, and awe in Vira. She felt all of those things.

Vira held a hand over her heart. "I'm Vira, as you've already gathered. This is Hux."

Hux raised his left arm in a silent greeting. He didn't seem to Naomi like he belonged in Zul. Which was probably because he wasn't from here. She knew he was from Raina, a city far enough from Le'Gar that she had never given it much thought.

"Why are the two of you together?" Ferrin cut to the chase.

Vira's rigid eyes narrowed. "Your name, ranger."

He ground his teeth. "Ferrin."

She nodded, satisfied, then turned her attention to Naomi.

Naomi looked to Ferrin, searching for help. He let her search. Then he nodded.

"I'm Naomi," she wavered. "Naomi Massoud."

Vira exhaled. "I knew it was you. How long were you in Le'Gar?"

"Eleven years."

"Of course. It makes perfect sense." Vira let out a relieved breath. "Eleven years ago I had a vision of a young Massoud crossing the Dessarian Sea to reach this side of Thãen."

Naomi nodded, intrigued. "I did cross the Dessarian Sea. I'm from Beezus."

"Beezus," Hux said in awe. "Were you part of the exodus of children who fled Calamity?"

"Yes. My mother and father prepared me to run my whole life. I only figured out why when I fled to the docks that night."

Ferrin studied her with easy eyes, intently listening to the details of her escape. He had never asked her about that day. "How old were you?" he asked softly.

"Seven."

He glanced across the circle to Vira. "And you had a vision of Naomi?"

"Of a young Massoud," she confirmed. "Naomi's face wasn't fully given to me. Probably for safety reasons."

"So what have you been doing for eleven years?" Ferrin accused. "Plotting?"

She nodded. "Yes."

He straightened. "To kill?"

"Of course not." Vira remained calm. "I've already made you aware that I am not seeking to harm her. I'm meant to help her." She tilted her head. "You of all people should understand the weight of purpose. Magnificents live off of purpose."

"I don't need to hear how a Magnificent survives," he grumbled. "I've lived long enough to know."

"You're an old Magnificent?" Hux raised an eyebrow. "You don't appear so."

Ferrin tried to suppress a glare. "I know."

"You haven't completed your purpose," Vira said, matter of

fact. "You've found yourself with a Massoud. That holds purpose."

"I'm here because she needed help escaping Le'Gar," he clarified. "I didn't commit to being her ally."

Vira narrowed her eyes. "By helping, you became an ally. Why do you wish to get rid of her so quickly?"

He tore his attention away from Vira and back to Naomi. "I don't wish to drop you like a package, Naomi."

Naomi felt a flicker of warmth toward him. "I know." And that wasn't a lie. She could read the torment and confusion all over his face since she revealed to him who she was. He was fighting to detest her. He wanted to leave her. But something held him back. She could sense it. See it.

"You're just better off without me." He glanced down.

"I don't think that's true." She dipped her chin down, attempting to meet his eyes. "You got me here. The Riders of Le'Gar would have found me if it weren't for you."

"I'll ruin you in the end." He shook his head, staring at the group now. "It happened before."

Vira crossed her arms. "What happened before?"

He pointed at her. "You'd be the last to know."

"Pardon?" She drew back.

Hux stepped forward. "Why are you talking to her like that?"

"Hux." Vira put a hand against his chest, keeping him back.

Hux didn't attempt to break through her barrier, but he barked in Ferrin's direction. "You called her a witch like it was a sin. You yourself are a Magnificent. There should be trust between you two."

"And yet there's not," Ferrin spat. "My life was ruined by a golden witch. Excuse me for not being tender."

Now it was Naomi's turn to study Ferrin. "But it wasn't Vira, right?" She made sure to keep her voice level. He seemed like he would snap at the slightest off tone.

He and Vira shared a duel of glares.

"It wasn't Vira," he admitted, jaw tense. "But I won't lower my guard until I know she won't do the same."

Naomi nudged him. "Okay, she understands. Just try to be civil. For me."

He looked at her, a sag in his shoulders. "Why would I have to do anything for you?"

"You don't have to. But I'm a Massoud. And I need to do something with that knowledge." She squeezed her pocket again, feeling the necklace. "You told me Thãen needed someone who can put an end to the night. Help me figure out how I can do that."

He stared at her, unwavering. Seconds passed before she realized he wasn't going to say anything more.

Vira broke the suffocating silence. "You don't know how to defeat The Hand of Calamity?"

Naomi shook her head, shrinking back. "No. Do you?"

"No." She let out an exasperated breath. "I only know I'm supposed to help you. I assumed *you* would have the answers."

"I have no answers." She held her palms up. "Ferrin?"

He shrugged once. "I only know royalty will want you dead."

All eyes turned to Hux.

"I was only sent by my king to retrieve a quill," Hux said, as lost as the rest.

"The quill is a good place to start," Naomi suggested. "I've never heard of it, but King Tal seemed petrified when he discovered it was found by Hux."

"Which," Hux tipped his head toward Vira, "is strange. Why would a golden witch slip into the mind of a Rider of Le'Gar to give me away?"

"Because they're filthy," Ferrin mumbled, barely audible.

Vira plastered on a thin smile. "Thank you for making your view of us so clear."

Without thinking, Naomi smacked Ferrin's arm. "Stop it."

He raised an eyebrow at her.

She pretended not to notice then turned to Hux. "Do you have the quill now?"

Hux touched the flap of the satchel. "Actually, that's what I was running to the ravine about."

Vira spun toward him. "Why? What happened?"

"This." He reached into the satchel and drew out a glowing, golden feather. "It started to illuminate."

Vira snatched the quill away from him. She laid it across both her palms, studying it from pointy tip to feathered end. It was laden in gold, but a glow similar to the hue of the moon shone around it. "Naomi, have you ever been taught about a quill? Anything in your family lineage that mentions something like this?"

With a shaky hand, Naomi plunged her hand into her pocket and pulled out her necklace. "I was running to the ravine, too. To show Ferrin this." She offered it to him. "It happened while you were gone."

The golden chain hung from her hand, allowing the crescent moon and pearl to swing in the air below her fist. The pearl still glowed. The same hue as the quill.

Ferrin took the necklace in his hand. "Where did you get this?"

"My father gave it to me when I was a child," she said. "When The Dark Hand came to Beezus, my mother took it from me." She chewed her lip. "I didn't understand why she would take it back. It was so important to me. I couldn't leave Beezus without it, so I stole it out of my mother's pocket before I fled. I don't know if she ever found out."

Ferrin stared at the jewelry. Something in his eyes seemed far away.

A breeze whipped through the opening of the tent, sending the lantern flames bobbing.

"You should keep this hidden." He pressed the necklace back into her hand. He looked up at Hux, not menacing, for once. "You, too. Keep the quill hidden. All of this is a mystery to us, but it may not be a mystery to someone else."

Vira nodded, agreeing. "We need time to search for answers."

"Our time may be limited." Ferrin motioned to Naomi. "The Riders of Le'Gar are out searching for a Massoud. The only upper hand we have is they don't know it's Naomi."

"And a bounty on me is out," Hux grumbled. "There was talk around Zul this morning that King Leeland sent out a group of new Riders into the mountains. Zul may be the first place they search. It makes the most sense that I would flee here."

"Are you sure they were sent out to find you?" Naomi rubbed her arms. The air was suddenly chillier. Or she was more aware of it.

Hux crossed his arms across his taught chest. "King Leeland was obsessed with finding the quill. He said it could bring an end to Calamity. He will do anything to find it."

Naomi frowned. "If King Leeland wants to end the terror of The Dark Hand, shouldn't you let him? Shouldn't you hand over the quill?"

Ferrin put a gentle hand between her shoulder blades. "Not everyone wants to end Calamity's oppression for the good of Thãen."

His touch sent an unknown tingle through her skin. "Why would King Leeland want to end it?" she asked.

"For power," Hux grunted. "Fame. Glory. Honor. All of it. It's a selfish desire to rid Thãen of pain and claim victory for himself."

"But so what?" she said. "The Dark Hand would be gone."

"But who's to say King Leeland would be better?" Vira pointed out. "In fact, his reign could mean wars amongst our own peoples, mistreatment of other clans. The grass isn't always greener, Naomi."

Naomi nodded, understanding, then gave a half smile. "You can call me Omi. Anyone who was ever a friend to me called me that."

Vira mimicked her small smile. "All right. I'm glad you consider me a friend."

She felt Ferrin's heavy gaze. He had refused to call her Omi, yet in this circle, he was visibly on her side. She and Ferrin against Vira and Hux. But now what was it? Her with Vira and Hux while Ferrin slunk away in the morning back to the mountains?

"We shouldn't discuss business in the heart of Zul." Vira drew her cloak around her body, preparing to leave. "Tomorrow, let's retreat to the eastern mountains. We can discuss both the quill and the necklace there." She allowed herself one more wholesome look at Naomi. "And we can discuss you."

Naomi squirmed under her stare. "Okay, but I'm not much." She motioned to herself. "This is the best of it."

Hux grinned amid the lantern haze. "Looks can be deceiving." He tilted his head toward his different arm. "I was the lead Rider in Raina."

"The *lead*?" Her eyes widened. "That's an accomplishment. Your king must have had a lot of faith in you."

"Yes." He darted his eyes away, seeming lost in conflict. Probably for deliberately throwing away his rank. "He had a lot of faith, despite my deformity. I owe him a lot." He sighed, giving Vira's shoulder a single pat. "But I owe you more."

Naomi watched the two, attempting to decipher their relationship. Their history. They looked to be the same age, but definitely not related. Vira was older than she was, probably ten years, maybe twelve. That would land her and Hux at around thirty or more. Vira didn't have a marriage piercing on the upper cartilage of her ear and Hux didn't have an infinity symbol tattooed on his collar bone. At least not that she could see. Thirty and unwed was rare. It made sense for Hux, being a lead Rider. Most leads never married. But Vira was a dark mystery. Between the golden witch's cold, green eyes and raven black hair, Naomi couldn't imagine why she would still be single. Surely it wasn't because she had spent her whole life preparing to help her. That couldn't be true. No way did Vira take her that seriously. Yet here the four stood, an unspoken agreement to join forces, all because she was a Massoud. No one knew what her purpose was, but it mattered enough to bring about this meeting. This alliance.

"We meet at dawn," Vira said. "In the eastern mountains. Ferrin, do you know the landmark known as the Rooted Lady?"

He nodded.

She tried to give him a pleasant gaze. "We'll meet there." She trailed her eyes around the tent once. "Are you both staying here?"

Naomi willed her face not to flush. "Yes. Rent was expensive. Right, Ferrin?"

"Mhm." He smiled a little, seeming tickled at the way she squirmed with innocence under a circumstance that didn't look horrible to most.

Vira acknowledged Naomi's anxiousness. "People in Zul don't care. But it's a fresh sight to see someone who wishes to uphold morals."

Naomi blushed, looking left and right, having no safe place to gaze.

"You're embarrassing her." Hux took Vira's arm and turned to give Naomi a quick wink. "Goodnight. See you at dawn."

"Dawn," Ferrin echoed.

Vira and Hux disappeared from the tent.

Naomi and Ferrin stood shoulder to shoulder, taught with awkwardness.

"Are you hungry?" he asked.

She brought her eyes up from the ground. "I am."

"Good." He reached into his cloak and pulled out two apricots from an inner pocket. "I have something other than grain."

She stared at the fruit with hesitation. "Where did you get these?"

He sat on the ground, leaning against the cot. "I traded my flint for them at the ravine."

She dropped next to him. "Your flint? That wasn't smart. We may need it." She bit her lip. "I mean, you may need it. When you leave tomorrow."

He held the apricot out to her. She stared into his eyes, which were sunken with fatigue, before gently taking the apricot from him. He smiled when she took it.

"Oh." She grinned. "You *do* know how to show your teeth."

He let the smile linger for a moment before putting it back to rest. "I'm not made of stone, Miss Smyth."

She rolled the apricot around between her palms. "Would you please stop calling me that?"

He took a bite of his fruit. "I can't call you by your real last name. At least not right now. Not after whatever just happened tonight." He chuckled. "What just happened?"

"I don't know." She pulled her knees to her chest. "It felt like fate. Like we were all dumped here on purpose."

"Purpose." He scoffed. "The root of my existence."

She leaned her cheek on her knees and turned her head

toward him. "You're an old Magnificent who hasn't aged. Vira said it's because you haven't completed your purpose yet."

"That's how it works." He focused on the apricot, avoiding her stare.

"But you must have done *something* all these years," she pried. "You mentioned your life getting ruined by a golden witch." She paused, giving him the opportunity to stop her. "What happened?"

He finally glanced at her. His face warbled in the lantern light. A dark piece of hair hung between his eyebrows. "Estell was a golden witch."

"Estell, who is dead, Estell?"

"Estell who is dead," he said in an airy tone. "Yet her memory taunts me."

She wanted to reach out and offer him comfort, but she was still afraid he would react. "How did she die?"

"Old age."

"So you knew her a long time ago?"

"I was your age when I met her."

She snorted a little. "You *are* my age."

"Kind of." He flicked a grin. "But I was *actually* your age."

"So what did she do?" She dug her fingernail into the apricot. Uneasy. Nervous.

He rubbed his eyes. "You know, I don't think Estell's story matters right now."

Her heart crashed. "So I'll have to guess for the rest of my life what the mysterious Magnificent meant when he said his immortal life was ruined?"

"I'm not immortal." He leaned back, resting his head on the cot. "I'm semi-mortal."

She scrunched her nose. "Is that the technical term?"

"It's the best way to describe it."

She studied him as he closed his eyes. "So that's it? That's all you're going to tell me about yourself?"

He laughed. "Relax. You'll have enough time to pry me open."

"What do you mean?"

He lifted his head, opening his glistening eyes once more. "I'm not leaving."

"You're not?" She had to swallow a joyous cry.

"You think I'd leave you now? After what happened?"

"But you could. You could leave now and no one would stop you."

He shook his head. "I know. But maybe Vira had a point."

"Oh, the golden witch had something worthwhile to say?" She gave a sly smile.

He narrowed his eyes even further. "Don't."

"Is it what she said about your purpose?"

"I'm still young," he said. "There is only one other Magnificent I know of who is older than me, but he looks old. It must be because my purpose hasn't found me." He sighed, dropping his head. "I need to carry out my purpose. One-hundred-eighty-seven years is enough. I need to age. I *want* to age."

She gazed at him. "Will you age rapidly? Once you fulfill your purpose, I mean."

He shrugged. "Some Magnificents do. Some don't. Nothing is certain."

"That's true." She gave a soft laugh. "Nothing is certain. I like the reality of that phrase."

"If you live as long as I have, you learn that uncertainty is the norm. It's better to embrace it than to cower from it."

"Is that why you've decided to stay?" She squeezed the fruit even harder now. "To embrace the uncertainty?"

He lifted his gaze, staring at her through the fading lantern glow. A far-off laugh erupted from outside, reminding the two that they weren't alone, though it felt like they were. "You were uncertain," he breathed, appearing to contemplate his every word. "I didn't wake up one morning in search of a Le'Garian refugee. Yet I found you. And you were so...so..."

"Lost," she snorted.

He dared to smile. "Lost, yes, but you were also searching. For help at first, but then searching for yourself."

"Well," she fidgeted with the fruit, "I've lived as someone else since arriving in Le'Gar. Of course I'm searching for my true self."

"But your bloodline isn't uncertain to me," he said, hushed.

She subconsciously leaned into him. "What are you saying?"

"I've known a Massoud." His expression turned cold, then sorrowful. "It was over one hundred years ago, but I still remember every inch of his existence."

His existence. She couldn't fathom why someone from her bloodline would be on this side of the Desarian Sea. Massouds lived in Beezus and further inland in the desert regions. Why was a Massoud in the mountainous regions over one hundred years ago? And who was he? "Why do you remember him?" she asked.

"Because I was supposed to help him," his voice slipped. "Just like Vira feels called to help you. I once felt that calling." He pressed his palms into his eyes. "But I failed, and I never wanted to meet a Massoud again."

She sat frozen. His hard shell was melting before her. He was admitting his past mistakes, opening the door just a crack for her to see why he wanted to flee from here. Fear plagued him. Hiding felt safer than facing the uncertainty of failing again. But he had remained hidden for so long that his purpose couldn't find him. He was trapped by his fear.

"So that's why I'm not leaving you." His words struck her in a tender spot between her ribs. "I may be able to do something right. You might be my chance at redemption."

No longer feeling hesitant, she placed a light hand on his arm. "I want your help. If you'll let me rely on you, I will."

To her surprise, he placed a weathered palm over her fingers. "You can put your security in me. I don't mean to fail you, Naomi Massoud."

Her stomach tightened. "Thank you."

He smiled.

"For saying my name," she said gently.

"You can't be Miss Smyth forever, I suppose." He pulled his hand away. "Not if we're going to be partners." He looked down at her apricot and frowned. "Are you going to eat that or are you just going to gouge at it with your fingernails?"

She hung her head and chuckled. "I'm going to eat it. Why? Do you want it?"

He stood, stretching his back. "No, I'm just making sure you get nutrients. It's important. Especially when we don't know where our next meal will come from."

She took a bite of the nail-punctured apricot. "Embrace the uncertainty."

He looked down at her. "I already have."

CHAPTER TWENTY-FIVE

awn was still two hours away, but Ferrin crept to his feet from his spot on the tent's dirt floor. His cloak prevented the soil from tarnishing his face while he slept but his left arm had sprawled out clumsily during his slumber. He brushed at a long, brown smudge on his tan sleeve, nicking away loose particles of dirt. Heaviness sat in his eyes, longing for more sleep, but his mind wallowed with fog and throbbing memories. He often thought of Estell, and every time he did, he would end up harboring hatred and rage in his heart. He carried his hatred like a boiling kettle and it burned him. Maybe he should have revealed his history with Estell to Naomi. Perhaps that would have ensured him extra hours of sleep. But he hadn't, so he was stuck tossing and turning.

He moved toward his quiver and bow leaning against the side of the tent. Naomi's breathing continued in a steady rise and fall behind him. He slung his bow onto his shoulder and strung his quiver and arrows across his chest. Turning, he studied her. Her hair was a matted mess scattered about her shoulders and over her face. She twitched once, breathing quickly, dreaming. He found himself smiling at her passive state then yanked his lips back down. Estell may be preventing his sleep, but Naomi wasn't entirely off the hook for his insomnia either.

Shaking his head, he ducked out through the door of the tent into the chilling air. The sky was still dark but fading gradually from black to royal blue. The smell of burning logs trailed to his nose from somewhere deep in Zul's community. He made his way down the quiet row of tents, their occupants still asleep. He would be back in time to guide Naomi to the Rooted Lady landmark. It was a well-known spot for golden witches and Magnificents. To humanity, the Rooted Lady was just an oak tree with roots that crawled out above the ground and creeped away from the trunk like millions of tentacles, surrounding the tree like a nest. Humans passed the tree with awe. Witches and Magnificents stopped with relief. The roots offered relaxation and calm to anyone who could channel into the life that coursed through the oak. He had visited the Rooted Lady twice, and both times he had felt mental relief when he pressed his hands against her legs. But he was aware not to visit her too often or she would withdraw her services to him. She gave peace to the needy, not the greedy.

The east mountains sat directly in front of him now. What little foothills remained before him were absent of tents, allowing the tall grass and wildflowers to grow. But the spring weather had only just begun to call up the wildflowers from the ground, making their presence sparse. As he waded through the soft blades of grass that reached his fingertips, he fell clumsily into a memory. For a moment he saw Estell sliding a red flower into her white, shimmering hair, smiling at him as she did so. Her bright eyes and high cheek bones pierced his heart. *"What do you think?"* she had said. *"Should I try the yellow flower?"* He remembered the way he had moved toward her, wrapping his arms around her waist, pulling her in. He had mumbled something in her ear about how she didn't need flowers to add to her beauty. His exact words were lost on him. Decades can do that to the mind. But he never forgot the way she laughed and fell into his arms. *"I love you,"* she whispered. *"I really do."*

He snapped his mind back to where he was: hiking up the east mountainside, sidestepping shallow streams and weaving around skinny pines. "Curse you, Estell!" he shouted into the air, digging his fingernails into his palms. "I'd wipe my memory of you if I could."

He tarried on in silence, his glare ceasing as he watched the multitude of streams trickling down the steep, rocky, moss-covered crevices. The east mountains were known for their waterways. Sparkling streams covered the ground and water-falls cascaded from cliffs embedded into the heart of the mountains' lush foliage. It was a beautiful land. Some parts enchanted. Like the Rooted Lady.

Estell's face lingered behind his eyes again. *"I know how to cast lots of enchantments,"* she had once said. *"Enough to rule this world."*

"Oh, shut up," he grumbled at invisible Estell.

He stopped near a cluster of birch trees with their roots embedded in the dirt between smooth stones outlining a stream. His bow now rested perfectly against his shoulder, secured with a steady palm. Getting into position took hardly any effort, and cocking the arrow was swift as a breeze. He aimed at a birch. Estell's golden face flashed before him and he let the arrow fly.

The arrowhead speared the birch, thwacking with power. A perfect shot.

Ferrin swept his aim right. He heard Estell's laugh. Another arrow struck the next birch. He reloaded, unthinking. Drawing back the bow, he breathed once. *Estell again.* The arrow soared.

The fourth arrow was between the bow's string already when his mind changed course. *Naomi.*

He paused, adrenaline shaking through his fingers. The thought of her had surfaced amid his vicious contemplations of Estell. All night Naomi's face had warbled above Estell's, drawing his attention. He kept shoving it down, but suddenly he couldn't. He squeezed his bow, his grip weakening. The tension in his shoulder dropped. Naomi didn't cause him to fall into fits of rage. In fact, just knowing her calmed him. He had tried so hard to keep her at a distance. To be short with her. To prevent an alliance. Yet, he failed.

He uncocked the arrow and dropped his hand, the arrow hanging at his side, letting his bow down on his other. He stood staring at the first three arrows sticking out of the birches. Estell influenced him to strike nature. Naomi coaxed him down. She was gentle. Something about the way she knew next to nothing about life outside of Le'Gar. Her innocence. Her blind trust in him. Her kindness even when he was cruel. It drew him in.

A grove of elm trees sat behind him. He dragged his bow and arrow to the grove and tossed his weapon to the ground, sinking to his knees. Rubbing his eyes, he gazed up. The sky was brightening. No more stars were visible. Only a hazy, morning fog. He swallowed and attempted to steady his breath. Worry grappled at his throat. What if he had suppressed his power for so long that his next words would come back void? Or worse, what if Old Man Magnificent *chose* to turn his ear away from his voice?

"Eli?" He could hardly breathe. "Old Mag." His voice lodged in his desperate throat as he spoke into the air. "I hope you recognize my voice."

The awakening woods surrounding him seemed to grow quiet again, listening.

He grabbed at the soil surrounding his knees, digging deep for support from nature. "Eli, I need you to know about her. In case I lead her into danger." He shut his eyes, feeling for Eli's mind. "If what she told me is true about an old man helping her at the docks upon her arrival in Le'Gar, then I believe you already know who she is." He paused. "I know I'm a disgrace, but I'm going to help her. I just need you to know." He dropped his head. "Just to be safe."

There was no way to know if Old Man Magnificent had received the words, but Ferrin relaxed, having done all he could. He leaned against the tree nearest his bow. The back of his head pressed into the bark and he closed his eyes. Dawn had an hour, meaning he had ten more minutes to rest before he had to head back down to the tents. And he would take those ten minutes.

But his breathing became shallow. His arms went limp. The heaviness in his eyelids surrendered to sleep. And soon he was deep in a dream.

———

Naomi lay still in the safety of her cot but her mind was miles away in a dream. She stood in the middle of King Tal's cathedral. Alone. No Riders stormed in to usher her out and King Tal wasn't roaming the floors. Even the seven foot lanterns hanging along the interior walls weren't lit. It was eerily silent. Gray like a storm.

Behind her sat the king's throne. Emerald velvet and gold. Behind the throne hung the curtain. The thick, dark purple curtain that was never pulled aside.

Her feet made no sound as she crossed the floor, and even though she was moving at a steady pace, she wasn't getting any closer to the curtain. Two steps forward, three steps back, over and over again. It was like the curtain had no intention of being touched.

A scuffling sound made her glance over her shoulder to the cathedral doors. It sounded like wind with claws. Then both doors crashed open, nearly flying off the hinges. Her heart lodged in her throat as the Dark Hand's five fingers expanded into the cathedral. King Tal tumbled in behind it, his throat sliced open. She shrieked, staggering backwards. The shadowed Dark Hand rose above her head, filling the cathedral ceiling. She didn't dare look straight at it. Instead, she forced herself to focus on Tal's lifeless body lying slumped near the doors. But her eyes looked through the doors and out into Center Square. Ferrin. He was there, standing flexed and shocked. Shocked to see *her*.

A presence made itself known to her left. She spun her head to the cathedral wall where Le'Gar's flag and statues of kings and queens lined the entire length of the hall. There was a human face.

She jolted awake.

The cot tipped with her sudden movement and she clattered to the dirt floor. She clambered up to her feet just as spastically. Ferrin was gone. And the sun was up. He had abandoned her.

Her heart boomed with adrenaline. She spun in a circle, making a full sweep of the tent. Yes, he was truly gone. He had left her. But her body didn't shake from fear of being alone, it was from the image of Tal's open throat. Of The Dark Hand's expansive fingers. Of being in a place that felt so real it couldn't have been a dream.

She staggered to the tent's exit and stumbled out into the walkway. A man passed by as she emerged, sidestepping her frantic movement.

"Watch where you're going, lass," he growled.

She gasped, unable to form words to apologize. Her ankles wobbled as she tried to run. To find Vira. Or Hux. They wouldn't abandon her like Ferrin had. But where was their tent? Which way? Her mind raced and she lost all sense of direction. The ravine was...east? West? No matter which way she chose, it was just another row of tattered tents and scuffed dirt roads. She broke into a jog, glancing behind her when she feared someone might jump at her back. But she was alone.

She looked ahead and slammed into someone.

Ferrin.

"Naomi." He gripped her biceps, holding her close to his face. "Are you all right?"

She grasped the front of his shirt, breathing heavy. "You *left* me." She shook her head. No, no that wasn't the problem. "I saw King Tal *die*."

He was panting too, sweat dripping down his forehead. "I know, I—"

"I saw you in my dream." She leaned in even closer, eyes bugging.

"No, that was *my* dream." He was just as distraught.

"What are you talking about?" She shoved away from him. "I don't need to be teased right now, you were there. You were standing right there as—"

"As Tal's throat slit open, Naomi, I know." He dug his palms into his eyes. "I saw it happen. It was my dream. But for some reason my vision dispersed to you."

She moved back a step. "You invaded my mind?"

"I shared a dream against my will," he corrected. "That only happens when Protection sees it fit. And it's only happened to me one other time. With Eli."

"You mean," she let her arms fall to her sides, "The Hand of Protection acts on the people of Thãen?"

He stood frozen. "Do you think The Hand of Calamity can influence Thãen but The Hand of Protection can not?"

She turned away from him. "This is too much." She whipped back around. "This is crazy, you know that?" Wild heat from hysteria claimed her face and lungs, but she couldn't stop it. "The Hand of Protection gives you a vision and somehow your vision just wanders its way into my head?"

He stepped closer to her. "Keep your voice down, Naomi, this is beyond serious."

She didn't obey. "If The Hand of Protection has a say in what happens to Thãen, why is The Dark Hand still allowed to roam our land? Some protection that is."

He watched her. "You think you have the mystical void all figured out, huh Ms. Smyth?"

She fumed. "I dare you to call me that one more time."

"Then live up to your true name," he challenged.

"*Excuse* you?"

He stepped up to her nose. "I said live up to your name. Be *strong*, Naomi. Come down from this panic. This anger. You're losing your sense of self."

She breathed in his face, hot, flustered breaths. Her eyes searched his, looking for an ounce of agitation, but she found none. He was being serious.

He spoke softer now, but steady. "Come back." Placing a hand on her shoulder, he offered her a sense of support. "Don't tread in the realm of confusion and anger. You're better than that."

She froze beneath the weight of his hand. What was she supposed to do with those words? Accept them? Obey them? Trust them? She swallowed a few times, grounding herself in the facts that he had shared, searching for a logical place to take the conversation. "Who is Eli?"

He almost raised an eyebrow at her deescalating tone. "He's

known as Old Man Magnificent. He's the oldest Magnificent alive to this day. He lives in Le'Gar but only a select few people know of him because he lives in the secret tunnels and spaces behind Le'Gar's stone walls."

"I know some of those spaces." She nodded. "I've been in some."

Now he did raise an eyebrow. "How were you able to find the entrances?"

"I work when the sun starts to make shadows. Shadows distort things enough to reveal what is otherwise hidden. And I'm quick. And irrelevant. No one pays me any mind, so I can go places without being noticed."

"Do you believe you ever met Old Man Magnificent?"

She thought back to the day she was crowded on the docks of Le'Gar with all the other children from Beezus and how the strange old man had crumpled and smudged her name papers. She stared at Ferrin with sure eyes. "Yes. Yes, I do. I think he knew who I was the moment he laid eyes on me."

"I think so, too," he affirmed. "That's why he's still in Le'Gar. He stayed to protect you."

A warmth touched her core. "Why would he do that?"

He dropped his eyes. "Because his life purpose is to enable a Massoud to complete the task that will bring destruction to The Dark Hand in a way that won't destroy our world completely." He glanced up. "I know because I used to work alongside him."

Her spirits rose. "So does Eli know the task that I must complete?"

Shaking his head, he let out an exhausted breath. "No. He has bits and pieces, but not the full picture. When we..." He cleared his throat, forcing himself to look directly at her. "When Eli and I worked together, we were protecting a young Massoud from being discovered by King Jomal, Tal's great grandfather."

"How young was the Massoud?"

Ferrin squeezed his eyes shut. "Much younger than you, Naomi. He was barely a teenager."

She tucked her hair behind her ear, noticing the visible pain he expressed. "But if I'm here today and still considered valuable, that Massoud must be..."

"Dead." He snapped his eyes open. "He's dead, Naomi. And it's my fault."

A bird squelched, drawing her eyes up to the sky. Dawn was over. The morning light expanded from the mountains into Zul. Surely Vira and Hux were already at the Rooted Lady landmark. "We should go," she suggested. Even though she itched to ask how the royal blood of Le'Gar was intertwined with The Dark Hand and *why*. She saw how Ferrin's past ate away at his conscience. She would creep into his past little by little and only push when absolutely necessary. "We can talk about the dream later?"

He considered her, taking in her calm demeanor and a set of eyes that didn't condemn him. "We'll tell Vira and Hux about it," he decided. "They need to know, too."

She pointed to the mountains. "Well then let's go. I'm itching to do something. Otherwise I'm just going to keep seeing Tal's bloody throat."

He stepped into stride with her, moving briskly. "Yeah. Not a pleasant thing to witness."

"Why do you think you would dream something like that?" She shuddered.

He pulled her elbow to the right, weaving down a narrow trail leading away from camp and through the tall grass. "Some dreams are prophecies."

"What?" She side-eyed him. "Magnificents can see the future too?"

"Not all of it." He was calm, level. "Just hints of it through dreams. And it only happens to some Magnificents. I just happen to be one of the lucky few." He shoved a prickly weed out of his way. "It's a wretched curse, Naomi. Going to sleep wondering if you'll be given vital information that could alter the future." He chuckled then. "If you haven't realized it yet, I almost despise my life."

She trod quietly next to him, her stomach sinking with his words. "I understand why you feel that way."

He motioned for her to move ahead of him as they started their ascent up the mountainside. "I know it seems selfish to hate being blessed with life and power, but it's caused more harm than good."

She looked down, careful not to trip on the loose rock. "I don't think you're selfish. I think you're just experienced. Experienced in life, I mean. You've seen all the bad stuff and some of it has affected you personally. So no, I don't think you're selfish, just hardened."

He followed behind in silence.

Birch trees began to pop up along the way, streams weaving between them. Moss crept over the loose rock, getting thicker and thicker as they climbed.

He finally spoke. "Aren't you hardened?"

She glanced over her shoulder at him. "I don't have one-hundred-eighty-seven years of strife on my back."

He bounded up next to her, dodging a pale trunk. "But you've witnessed The Dark Hand in your own home. You lost your family to it and have lived in solitude since you fled. Doesn't that bother you? Didn't that callous your heart?"

His words dug like a graveyard shovel into the darkest corners of her soul. "It did harden me." She leapt over a stream only a foot wide. "But ultimately that experience just made me stronger and placed me exactly where I needed to be." She watched as he stepped over the stream too. "I escaped Beezus because my parents prepared me for that exact moment. And by luck my tall ship traveled to Le'Gar. If I had been on the ship to Ode, I still would have met death. It just would have been eleven years later."

Ferrin tilted his head to the right, directing her to follow. "So you took your hardships and found the good in them," he said, amused.

"Not necessarily the good, but the reason." She trailed just behind him now, the chill of the low hanging fog pressing against her skin. "There's a reason I didn't die by The Dark Hand in Beezus." She quieted. "There's a reason I'm alive. I've always known that. Even before I knew about my bloodline."

A breeze fluttered through the dark green foliage, moving Ferrin's hair in a gentle wave. "You're right."

She darted questioning eyes his way.

He smiled with only his lips. "You do have purpose." His smile fell. "Even if you lived in Le'Gar as a lantern snuffer for the rest of your life, you would still have purpose."

"Well, I'm part of a sacred bloodline," she said in a pretend proud tone. "That's my purpose, isn't it?"

"That's *a* purpose." He took her hand and pulled her up onto the first boulder of seven that climbed to a cliff edge hidden amid the towering trees draped with vines. "But you yourself have purpose before your actions give you purpose."

She steadied herself with his arm before climbing onto the second boulder. "What do you mean?"

"Your personality," he stated, continuing upward, avoiding eye contact. "You have an easy way about you." Waiting for her on the next rock, he stared up at the cliff, hands on his hips. "You're my first partner in one-hundred-seventy-seven years. That should go to show you how much I loathe company. Yet here we are. Here you are." He reached down and took the underside of her arm, lugging her onto his rock. "What do you think that means?"

She tried not to focus so much on his touch and more on his words, which were equally as jarring. "I'm good at convincing?"

He shook his head, scolding her teasing tone with a smirk. "You're all right to be around. You listen." He looked away. "You have a willing spirit."

His words caused an anxious uproar in her nervous system. "Thank you, Ferrin. That's really kind of you to say."

"See?" He shook his head with a half-moon smile. "You have a gentle way with words."

She used her own strength to climb onto the last boulder. "Are you warming up to me, ranger?"

"Only a little." He stood shoulder to shoulder with her. "But don't test your luck."

She caught one last smirk on his lips as he stared up at the cliff edge just above their foreheads. The ledge was covered in moss—just like everything else on the mountain—and a stream trickled over the edge, free falling in a miniature waterfall. When Ferrin looked at her next, his expression was serious. Maybe a little inquisitive.

"Did you really think I left you this morning?" he asked softly. "Even after I promised I was with you?"

Only the sweet sound of the falling stream preceded her response. "Most people say things but don't mean them. I'm sorry for doubting you."

"I'm not leaving." He glanced up at the cliff again. "You have my word."

A voice came from the topside of the cliff. "Ferrin?"

Naomi recognized Vira's steady voice before her face peered over the ledge.

Ferrin waved half-heartedly. "Yes, it's us. We got distracted. You can blame me."

Hux's toned body showed up next to Vira's, his blonde hair

tied back in a stubby ponytail. "Here, Naomi." He lowered his arm. "Grab on, I'll hoist you up."

She reached up and clung to his forearm as he gripped hers. His hand was stronger than steel. Even as he elevated her body to the lip of the cliff, he never wavered. He helped her to her feet and gave a humble smile.

She smiled back. "Thank you."

Whereas Ferrin was getting easier to talk to, Hux was still practically a stranger, and it caused her to retreat back to her casual, quieted self.

Ferrin appeared behind her, actually accepting Vira's hand when she offered it as he pulled himself up onto the cliff.

"I'm glad it was just a distraction and not a betrayal." Vira looked at Ferrin when she said it.

He, for once, didn't look away. "I told Naomi and now I'm telling you: I'm not going anywhere."

Vira nodded. "Let's move further into the trees. The Rooted Lady waits."

Hux took to Vira's side and the two led Ferrin and Naomi further into the vine laden terrain brimming with wide Kapok trunks.

Naomi leaned into Ferrin's side, talking out of the corner of her mouth. "Does Vira scare you?"

He scoffed. "Not even remotely."

"She does me." She stared at the back of Vira's glossy black hair. "She's intimidating. Or wise."

"She is wise." He didn't even act like it hurt to say it. "Her kind may put a bad taste in my mouth, but I'd be ignorant to think her not wise."

Vira tilted her chin over her shoulder. "Say something?"

"No," Naomi said too quickly. "I mean yes, but we were talking about how we didn't have breakfast."

Ferrin nodded, exposing nothing.

Vira looked ahead again.

She and Ferrin shared wide eyes and a mischievous grin.

The Rooted Lady appeared in the middle of grounded vines and winding streams. Her roots were five hands thick around and mimicked the shape of tentacles. They sat above the ground and dove beneath the dirt only at the tips. Her trunk was wide enough to hide all four travelers from whatever was on her other side. Her leaves were oblong and glossy dark green on the top, waxy yellow on the underside.

"Wow." Naomi tilted her head up, breathing slow.

Vira stepped to her side. "First time seeing it?"

"It's my first time outside of Le'Gar in years." Her cheeks blushed. "Everything is new to me."

Hux climbed over the twisting roots, examining just how thick and powerful they were. As his hands grazed them, Vira and Ferrin watched him with anticipation. Hux must have felt their stare, because he turned around, half swallowed up by the Rooted Lady's legs. "What?" he said. "I've only ridden past her. I've never stopped to marvel."

Vira and Ferrin exchanged a look of common knowledge. Like they knew something Hux didn't. That Naomi didn't. It made Naomi feel slightly left out, but then she realized that maybe Vira and Ferrin should connect. If they were to be working together, some sort of trust had to ensue.

Vira stepped closer to the roots, but avoided touching them. "The Rooted Lady gives rest to those who can tap into the life within her veins. I was curious if you would be able to feel it, but I didn't expect you would. Humans can't."

Hux was at the tree's trunk now, his massive frame looking miniscule next to her majesty. "Yet another thing humanity misses out on." He called behind him. "What about you, Naomi? Have you ever wondered what it'd be like to wield powers like Vira and Ferrin?"

The mountain grew quiet as all eyes turned to her. Hux meant it as a casual conversation starter, but the fact that she was a Massoud hung in the air like a topic that was not to be discussed. Like a fact that was known, but mysterious. Possibly dangerous.

She cleared her throat, attempting to sound as casual as possible. "Sure I've thought about it, but I can run. That's enough for me."

He raised an eyebrow. "An athlete. I like it." The tone in his voice held a fatherly stature. It softened Naomi's heart and she felt a tick of trust toward him.

Ferrin moved into the sea of roots, climbing carefully, not using his hands. "Come on, Naomi, you can touch the roots. It won't stir you." He continued on to where Hux had situated himself comfortably in a rooted nook.

Vira placed a hand on Naomi's back and glanced down at her. "Do you still have the necklace?"

"In my pocket, yes." She shook her right trouser leg with her hand.

"Is it still glowing?"

She nodded. "It's never gone out."

"Same as the quill." Vira looked up to the men who were talking quietly at the tree's trunk. "Do you trust him?"

Naomi lowered her voice. "Which one?"

"The ranger."

"Ferrin." She felt a shocking wave of defensiveness.

Vira softened. "Yes, Ferrin."

She watched him for a moment as he moved his hands, explaining something to Hux. "I do." She couldn't explain it, but she truly felt he was trustworthy. If it came back to bite her, she would accept the consequences, but it wasn't fair for Ferrin to be treated with suspicion when he had no obligation to remain with her yet chose to do so. "We're partners now."

"Is that what he said?" Vira sounded skeptical, yet hopeful.

She nodded. "And I'll take his word for it."

Vira smiled, then motioned for Naomi to enter into the tentacles. "Go ahead."

Even though Ferrin assured her that the roots couldn't infiltrate her spirit, Naomi stepped onto the first one with caution, moving across the bumpy arms like she would stones across a river. "Why don't you and Ferrin touch the tree?" she called over her shoulder. "Wouldn't rest from The Rooted Lady be a gift?"

"Of course." Vira moved swiftly, catching up to her. "But we need to build trust with her first. You can't show up and take something as valuable as rest without appreciating her first."

"Oh." Naomi looked down at her feet. The root holding her up felt normal. Gigantic, but normal. She longed to feel its life like the golden witches and Magnificents did. But she moved on, stepping faster now, attempting to not slow down where she could lose her balance.

Vira stayed right with her, never letting her drag behind.

They were almost to the tree's trunk when the tip of Naomi's shoe caught on a root as she leapt from one to the next. She fell like a loose marionette puppet. Her knees slammed at different times and she flung her arms out to stop her face from colliding with another root. As her palms smacked against the tree's root, red light exploded behind her eyes, filling her vision like fire. She gasped, attempting to stand. She stumbled again, grabbing onto another root. The red light happened again, this time so bright it seemed to block her hearing, if that was even possible. She collapsed to a fetal position, pressing the heel of her palms into her eyes. But the red stayed. It moved like molten lava. Thick and slow. Then a voice hummed in her head, like a woman singing a single note. *"Let it flow,"* it said. *"Let it flow."*

Naomi sucked in a desperate breath then snapped her head up. She opened her eyes.

Vira's face was directly in front of hers. "Naomi!" she shouted, shaking her shoulders. "Naomi, talk to me."

Through blurry eyes, Naomi saw Ferrin bounding down the roots toward them. "What in grave's sake happened?" he hollered. "What happened to her, Vira?"

Naomi touched Vira's hand on her shoulder. "I'm okay. I think I just—I felt The Rooted Lady."

Vira sat back on her heels, gazing into her eyes. "But you didn't get rest from her. You were screaming."

Ferrin dropped down next to Vira. His eyes were round with concern. "Naomi, what happened? Are you alright?"

Hux hovered over Vira and Ferrin's shoulders, worry flooding his face as well.

She felt like a child. "I'm okay. I was just taken over by The Rooted Lady's voice, that's all. It startled me and I wasn't expecting to see her light."

Vira looked at Ferrin, sharing yet another knowing glance, only this time they both seemed distressed.

Ferrin's eyebrows arched in confusion as he placed his focus back on Naomi. "The Rooted Lady doesn't talk. And she doesn't give visions. She only gives the body a feeling of temporary rest."

"How did she feel anything from the Rooted Lady at all?" Hux pointed out. "She's human."

Vira helped her to her feet. "You're a Massoud. We don't know what you can do."

Naomi glanced down at her own hands, wondering what they were capable of. "I'll try to be more careful. I'm sorry."

Ferrin rested a hand on her shoulder. "You didn't put anyone in danger. You don't have to be sorry."

Tears brimmed her eyes when she looked up at him. "I saw

red flowing light and a voice that said *let it flow*." She let out a shaky breath. "It made me think of Tal's blood. What if I have something to do with his death?"

Hux straightened with a snap. "King Tal *died*? When? Last night?"

Vira's mouth hung open, stunned.

Ferrin held his palm up to Hux. "No. No, King Tal isn't dead. It was a dream." He pressed his lips together. "We shared a dream. Naomi and I."

"Why would your dreams connect?" Vira crossed her arms, her black hair cascading down her arms.

"The Hand of Protection saw it fit to share it with her." He turned his head to Vira. "You believe in Protection's divine intervention, yes?"

She nodded. "Of course. But it's rarely so evident."

"Divine intervention how?" Hux piped up. "I know Protection holds Thãen, but isn't Protection's only job to never let us fall? Not drop us?"

Naomi nodded at Hux, agreeing with him. "Yeah. That's what I always thought, too."

Ferrin shook his head. "Why would Calamity have more power than Protection?"

Hux crossed his massive arm over his other. "Calamity is the only one that shows itself. Why *wouldn't* we think Protection is lesser?"

"Hux." Vira held her arms out, surprised at him. "Why do you speak this way? We were raised to put our faith in Protection."

"No, Vira." He let his shoulders drop. "*You* were raised to put your faith in Protection. You have a connection to spiritual entities and power runs through your veins. I'm a man. A crippled man. I was raised to fight for myself. And it's worked. What has Protection ever done for me?"

Naomi's pulse rapped at her neck. Hux's words struck her, and she could feel the tension building within the conversation. She'd had those same thoughts about Protection but never dared voice them. Not because she worried what others would think, but because she feared what would happen to her if Protection found out she doubted.

"What has Protection done for you?" Vira said, her breaths short. "You were the lone survivor of a mission to Ode. And you left the rubble with an enchanted quill. Wouldn't you call that favor?"

Hux had naturally easy eyes, but now they were sharp. "*You* got me out of Ode, Vira. Don't give the credit to Protection."

"Protection kept me safe," she argued. "Don't you see? Sometimes the ways of the entities outside of Thãen aren't clear. But that's just the intricacies of the Outer Void."

He remained fixated on her. "I'd stand by you through death and destruction, you know that."

"I do."

"But for grave's sake, Vira, don't let blind faith guide you."

She didn't reply. She only stood taller and turned away from him.

Ferrin cleared his throat, attempting to regain control of the group. "Listen, if we're going to bicker over beliefs, it will drive a wedge between us. Protection or not, The Dark Hand is at work and we all have a role to play."

"Yes," Vira said stiffly. "You're right, Ferrin. Tell us about the dream you had with Naomi."

CHAPTER TWENTY-SIX

The four waded out of The Rooted Lady's legs to sit under the dancing shade of a Kapok tree instead. Naomi's hands would be safer near nature that wasn't enchanted. Even so, she sat slowly, wincing when her fingertips touched the grass, afraid that she would summon nature to speak to her again.

Ferrin described the dream to Vira and Hux from his view. How he saw The Dark Hand sweep through Le'Gar and topple building after building. Then how its five fingers reached the king's cathedral where King Tal stood outside the doors, as if he expected Calamity's arrival. But Calamity swiped one finger right across Tal's throat, killing him on the spot. When The Dark Hand rushed into the cathedral, Ferrin saw Naomi in the throne hall. Then the dream was over.

Naomi described her part in detail all the way up to seeing Ferrin, but she paused, remembering something that was there but also wasn't. "A face," she said. "I looked to my left and there was a face. But I can't remember anything about it. I don't think I even saw a body attached to it. I just knew it was a face. Then I woke up."

Vira leaned forward, legs crossed. "And you believe this was a prophetic dream?"

"It was." Ferrin rested back on his palms. "I don't have to question it. The only debate is which parts of the dream were prophetic."

Naomi felt an ounce of hope. "So Tal's death isn't certain?"

"Not exactly." He rubbed the back of his neck. "But from what I know about Tal's family lineage, it doesn't surprise me that he's connected to The Dark Hand. It was the same with his father, grandfather, and great-grandfather."

Vira frowned. "What kind of involvement does his ancestry have with Calamity?"

Ferrin rolled his shoulders back and inhaled to reply, but the sound of crashing leaves in the treetops and a frightening caw sounded above their heads.

Naomi had no time to react. Something dark gray dropped from the trees. She ducked as Hux threw his arm around her neck, pulling her down beneath him. His body hovered over hers, his heart slamming against her shoulder blade.

Ferrin leapt to his feet and drew an arrow. Vira pressed her back into Ferrin's, hands hovering out in front like she was ready to throw something invisible.

"Watch it, Ferrin!" Hux shouted, his chest shoving Naomi further into the ground.

Naomi stared up in panic as the gray thing, which she identified as a bird, swooped toward Ferrin. Its wings made a grinding noise, not soft and fluttery. And something was rolled between its talons. "Wait!" She threw an arm out from beneath Hux. "Ferrin, don't shoot!"

But he had already lowered his bow.

"What are you doing?" Vira held an arm across his chest. "It's enchanted."

The bird was a gnarled crow, and it landed right at his feet. It was made of stone. A gargoyle.

He lowered Vira's arm. "I'm aware it's enchanted, but it's not harmful." He dropped to a knee. "It's from Le'Gar."

Hux rose, pulling Naomi up with him. She brushed dirt from her stomach, arms and face.

"Sorry." Hux brushed the last smear from her shoulder.

"Don't be. Now I know you'll keep me safe."

He gave her one last pat before they both joined the others near the gargoyle. She watched Ferrin turn his palm upward, letting the crow place the rolled-up parchment into it. As soon as the crow released the paper, it stepped back, turned its head to Naomi, and gave a slight nod. Her stomach tightened. There was a split second of quiet before the crow crumbled to ash. A pile of dusty rock. The result of disobeying the enchantment rules. She shut her eyes, not wanting to feel the sorrow of watching something disappear because of her.

Hux watched with an open mouth, not entirely familiar with Le'Gar's gargoyles and their enchantment. Vira didn't seem so taken back as much as in awe.

Ferrin rose, parchment in hand. He turned to Naomi first, offering her the first look with him. She wondered why, but inched closer to him instead, peering down at the paper as he unrolled it.

The paper had a short, written message, but when she read it, she knew how important the simple words were.

"*Tal questions you, young Mag,*" Ferrin read aloud, his voice cracking when he reached what she guessed was a nickname for him. "*Riders are seeking you. Keep your possessions safe.*"

And that was it.

She looked up from the paper at him. His glassed-over eyes were still glued to the words. He chewed the inside of his lip, either trying to compose himself or thinking. She let her shoulder touch his, a silent way to remind him she was with him. Partners. A word that stuck in her mind since he said it. Partners meant that if Tal sent Riders to find him, she was a target too.

He seemed to agree, but for a different reason. "You're my possession."

She shook her head. "What do you mean?"

"Eli didn't want to write it plainly. In case the crow got intercepted before it reached me." He touched the word possession, letting his finger linger. "The Riders must be after me because they've linked me to you."

"How?" she strained, annoyed. "When they searched your cave they didn't find me."

He clenched the paper, crumpling it in an enraged fist. "Le'Gar doesn't like me. I have Tal's great grandfather to blame for that. If Le'Gar is looking for someone to accuse, it would be honey to their souls if it were me."

"Why is that?" Hux gruffed.

Vira lifted her chin. "I won't read you, Ferrin. Your history isn't mine to know. But remember that her safety depends on our honesty."

"You think I don't know that?" His voice shook. "She's my responsibility, not yours, not Hux's."

Naomi swallowed words, feeling a sensation that rarely came to her. It wasn't a pleasant sensation either. One that usually preceded a breaking point.

Vira rose her voice above his. "We are entering this debacle together. She is under *all* of our care."

Oh no, thought Naomi. *I'm going to snap.*

"Yet if something happens to her," Ferrin thrust a hand toward her chest, "I'll be the one to carry the blame."

Vira took one long stride to be close to him. "Because you'll choose to. You are destroying yourself over something from your past and you're letting it consume you."

He spoke through clenched teeth. "Don't. *Read*. Me."

"I don't have to." Her focus trailed from his forehead to his chin. "It's written all over you."

Naomi clenched her fists, watching Vira and Ferrin stand nose to nose, neither of them breathing. Did they clash so intensely they were blind to the fact that she was able to speak for herself? She was inexperienced, yes, but not helpless.

"I can go at it alone," she said, sounding more bitter than she meant to. "If you two can't keep your heads on straight, I'll leave Zul tonight. Without you. And I'll figure out my bloodline myself."

Hux shifted. "She has a valid point."

Vira stepped away from Ferrin. "I'm sorry, Naomi. I know this is a lot, and we aren't helping any."

"No, you're not." She crossed her arms. "I need help figuring out what a Massoud can do, but I need to be treated like a human in the process. I'm not a possession. I'm a person."

Ferrin dropped his chin to his chest momentarily, then looked up. "Okay. We hear you, Naomi." He glanced at Vira. "Right?"

"Of course." She sighed. "We know you're a person. You're just a very important one."

"But so are you both." Naomi waved a hand toward Hux. "And him. My life isn't the only one that matters."

Ferrin looked down.

Vira shrugged her hair behind her shoulder, her face twisting a little.

"So let's focus on what to do next," Naomi went on, feeling a surge of confidence. "Where do we go from here?"

Hux came to stand next to her. "We can't stay in Zul. Not if the Riders of Raina know I'm here."

"And we can't go back to Le'Gar," she added. "So what does that leave us? Ferrin? You know the territory well."

He glanced up the mountainside. "That leaves us with the east mountains which run into territories I haven't spent much time in."

"I know a place." Vira stood taller. "A perfect place."

Ferrin studied her, frowning. "In the east mountains?"

"Yes. You know of it, too."

He let out a long breath. "Are you sure we should?"

Vira's lips rested gently into a small smile. "What better time than now?"

Naomi's focus bounced back and forth between Ferrin and Vira. "Take us there," she decided for them. "Wherever it is you're talking about. Don't worry about the danger."

Hux dropped his hand onto her shoulder. "The Massoud has spoken. Listen to her."

"As we should." Vira agreed. "You are wise, Naomi."

She wanted to hide, but she wasn't finished yet. "And one more thing. Can I hold onto the quill?"

Ferrin arched an eyebrow, but turned to look at Vira.

Without hesitation, Vira pulled the quill out of her satchel. Its glow still matched Naomi's necklace. "I have no grounds to deny you the quill."

"I only want to see if it will react to me differently than you," Naomi hurried to add. "I don't know the connection between me, my necklace, and the quill, but maybe I can find one."

"It's a good thought." Ferrin nodded at Vira. "Naomi and I can both keep an eye on it. I promise."

Vira passed the quill to her. It was lighter than she thought it would be. Almost the weight of a real feather quill. She winced, afraid it would react at just the touch of her palm, but it didn't.

"We can leave tomorrow," Vira directed. "At dawn. Today we will prepare for our departure. Ferrin, you and Naomi came by horse, correct?"

"Correct."

"Good." She strolled down the mountainside back toward Zul. "That gives Hux and me my horse. We'll combine our food supply. That's all we'll need."

"How long will the journey be?" Naomi jogged behind her, closing the distance between them.

"That depends on if the east mountains cooperate." She stopped, letting Naomi catch up to her.

Naomi matched Vira's stride, feeling insignificant next to her towering figure and poised facial features. "The mountains are alive?"

Vira only grinned.

"There's so much I don't know." She shook her head, exasperated.

"But you'll learn," Vira reassured. "You aren't lesser because you don't have the knowledge that we do. What matters is that you're eager."

CHAPTER TWENTY-SEVEN

Ferrin's back was to Naomi. Her back was to him. Neither of them spoke. Night had fallen and Zul had awakened, full of the sounds of distant, joyful shouting and laughing. Inside their tent, the lantern lights danced in amber waves against the material walls. Naomi latched the last buckle on her backpack, finishing her preparations for tomorrow's journey. Her trousers were uncomfortable against her waist, but she couldn't let the button loose until she climbed into the cot to sleep. It'd be strange to walk around loosely like that with Ferrin so close. But her tattered blouse had come off hours ago as Zul experienced one of the first hot days of the turning season. Her undershirt was less modest, but still covered everything, save for her shoulders.

Ferrin turned away from his own backpack. "Where is the canteen I gave you?"

She pointed to her cot. "There. Would you like me to fill them?"

He strode over to retrieve hers. "No, I can." His arm brushed hers as he reached down and grabbed it.

"I don't mind doing it." She crossed her arms, feeling

synched with awkwardness. "I don't want you to have to do everything."

He paused with both canteens slung across his chest. "I don't think you're incapable, if that's what you're getting at. But some of the people in Zul can be rough."

She flopped her hands to her sides. "I want to help."

"You'll have plenty of time to help," he reassured. "I'm not going to keep you on the outer circle when it comes to decisions." He smiled then. "You're the reason we're doing any of this."

"So where are we going then?" she tested. "Vira wouldn't say."

He cleared his throat, looked around the tent, then shrugged off the canteens. He went to his backpack and drew out a rolled-up piece of paper. "Here." When he flattened it on the cot, she saw it was a map.

He pointed to a place that had a title banner saying Zul. "We're here," he said. He lifted his finger and moved it to a terrain that had multiple peaks. "These are the east mountains."

She leaned in, almost touching heads. "Wow. The east mountains stretch farther than I thought."

"Right. They're beastly. See the marks all over the mountain range? The curved lines?"

She nodded.

"Those are waterfalls."

"All of them?"

He cut his gaze to her, watching her amazement. "Yes. And this one," he moved his finger to one that seemed to be in the dead center of the mountain range, "is where we're going. If a golden witch or Magnificent slices through the center of this waterfall with a sword, a doorway is revealed; it leads to a land that lies within Thãen. Like a parallel territory. It's called Mira Isla."

"Those kinds of places exist?"

"This is the only portal land we know of, so this kind of place exists," he corrected. "Remember when I asked you where you think all the Magnificents went after the slaughter?"

"This is where they all went?"

He nodded. "A sanctuary. Only a golden witch or a Magnificent has access. Humans can only reside there if they are brought in with a witch or a Mag." He paused, staring down at the map. "It's beautiful there, Naomi. Unlike anything you've ever seen."

Her heart swelled. "I look forward to seeing it. To see something different than the stone city of Le'Gar. Even Zul is a sight. I can't imagine what a land possessed by witch and Magnificent will look like."

He turned to smile at her. "I'm happy you get to see it."

She was close to his face, staring at his genuine look of excitement for her. She thought back to how reserved he had been toward her only a few days ago. It had been like he didn't want to build a relationship with her. As if friendship were a burden. Or dangerous. Surely something had happened to him that made him believe friendship was cursed. "What was it?" she found herself saying.

His dark eyes that had been gleaming, hardened. "What was what?"

"What was it in your past that makes you so fearful of friendship?"

He shoved the map aside and sat next to it on the cot. She remained standing in front of him. She shook a little, the result of adrenaline from asking such a personal question, and he must have noticed.

"You don't have to be afraid to talk to me," he said in an easy tone. "I know I can be brash, but I don't mean to be frightening."

She felt her face grow warm. "I'm not afraid. I'm just... hesitant."

"Well, you don't have to be that either." He placed his palms on his knees. "I'm no stranger to loneliness. And I'm learning that neither are you. So why don't we just," he shifted, rubbing his hands against his trousers like he was trying to get rid of sweat, "just trust each other?"

For a moment, she waited for him to start laughing. This had to be a joke. Trust? *He* was speaking about trust? He who was full of secrets and shadows. How could she trust him?

"Sometimes I feel that I can," she admitted. "But you keep a lot from me. Why do you hide things?"

He did laugh. Only once. "I may be a Magnificent, but I'm not made of stone. My past hurts." He glanced down at the dirt floor. "I'll admit."

"So does mine. But I'm not afraid of what's to come because of it."

"Your past hurts because terrible things were done to you." He readjusted again, sitting even closer to the edge of the cot. His knee bumped hers. "My past hurts because I did terrible things to others."

She felt his presence like she would expect to feel a spirit's. Haunting, powerful and all consuming. "What did you do?"

He shook his head. "If I told you, you'd want me dead."

"I don't think that's true." For one impulsive second, she almost reached out and touched the side of his face. His rough cheek looked like it needed to feel something other than his own calloused hands. "Please tell me."

He wouldn't look at her. "My job was to keep the young Massoud of Le'Gar safe. His name was Oliver Massoud." When he said the name, his voice struggled to remain steady. "He was in his adolescent years and living under an alias, just like you."

She wanted to drop to her knees and beg to hear all the details. Oliver Massoud. A relative. A boy who went through the same thing she was now. But she tread carefully, knowing Ferrin's fragile state. "How did Oliver get to Le'Gar?"

He finally stared up at her. "He was left at the doorstep of Eli Thrane, now known as Old Man Magnificent. Then, Eli was in his forties and didn't have to keep hidden because hardly anyone knew he was a Magnificent."

"Did Eli raise Oliver?"

"He did." Ferrin nodded, picking at his nails. "Eli gave Oliver his own last name. Oliver Thrane. Everyone in Le'Gar thought Oliver was Eli's grandson because that's what Eli claimed."

"Did you know Oliver when he was an infant?" She imagined Ferrin codling a baby, believing he would be gentle even with his intensity.

But he shook his head. "I didn't. He was seven when I met Eli. I was eighteen and hiding my powers. My parents had to flee during the slaughter, as I told you, and I was terrified I'd be murdered if anyone ever found out about me." He looked off, lost in the memories of his true young adulthood. "One evening, Eli came to the blacksmith shop where I was apprenticing. The owner of the shop was away on a brief trading trip, so I was alone and in charge. Eli knew it. He came in not for service, but to talk to me. He told me he knew I was a Magnificent and that he was too. He offered to help me."

"What kind of help?"

"Mentorship." He focused on her, seeming to anchor himself in her steady eyes. "He gave me tips on how to use my powers without drawing attention to myself, but he also urged me not to be afraid to let others see. He left it up to me to decide who, but he believed Magnificents had a unique opportunity to prove our powers weren't evil, but blessed."

She watched his shoulders fall, the tell-tale sign of regret. She stepped to his side and slowly sat next to him. "Did you choose to show your powers?" she asked gently.

He breathed long and slow. "Not at first. But eventually I did, and I wish I hadn't."

"Was it your powers that killed Oliver?" she whispered.

He curled his fingers into his palms. "The answer to that is twisted, but if my powers weren't known, maybe I wouldn't have been used as a pawn."

"Eli used you?" She dropped her chin to catch his falling eyes.

He jerked his head back up. "No. Not Eli. He would never."

"Who then?"

He stood, hands shaking with violence. "This is why I didn't want to tell you." He paced in front of her, the side of his neck visibly pulsing. "Because I get like *this*." He slammed his arms down at his sides.

Naomi could see all the ways his body physically took the toll of his emotions. His trembling, his misty eyes, his tight fists.

She rose to meet him. "It's okay, Ferrin."

He stepped away from her. "No, it's not. I'm a Magnificent for grave's sake. I shouldn't be affected by something as ridiculous as emotional turmoil." His voice rose. "I'm above that. I'm above this." He held his arms out, revealing just how much they were shaking.

"Ferrin." She reached for his arm.

He withdrew. "Please don't."

She pulled her hand back into her abdomen.

He ran shaky fingers through his hair. "You asked me what it was that made me despise friendship."

She kept her lips pressed closed, afraid that if she responded, he wouldn't continue.

"But it's not friendship that I detest," he said. "Eli never did me wrong. Nor did Oliver." It suddenly sounded like a hand was clamped around his throat. "What I hate is love. I loved a woman with all my heart and she used that love to kill Oliver."

"That's not your fault." She exhaled with relief.

"Of *course* it's my fault. I let love blind me when I was supposed to keep Oliver's secret." His shoulders sagged in overwhelming defeat. "Love is poison, Naomi. I hope to never love again."

She froze in disbelief. He had lived 187 years, most of it without love. She marveled at how the loneliness hadn't killed him yet. And to think that he wanted to live that way. She understood the feeling behind it. Aloneness meant no harm from someone else's hand, but it was a promise of self-inflicted damage. Which was worse? When she thought about it, she didn't know. Losing her parents was like ripping an artery from her heart, but living in solitude had numbed her. Both hurt. But there was a moment that made her feel valuable for the first time since her arrival in Le'Gar, and it was when Ferrin offered to help her. She was a stranger to him, yet he had offered his hand. That moment she knew. Loneliness wasn't made for humanity, witch or Magnificent. It was made *by* them. And it wasn't healthy.

"No." She said it firmly, but refused to raise her voice to match his. "Love is *not* poison."

His bottom lip dropped the slightest centimeter, shocked that she verbally disagreed with him.

With caution, she stepped closer. With every inch that disappeared between them, he tensed. She stopped before him, close enough to feel his presence, far enough not to feel his breath on her forehead. They stood face to face, the lantern light swimming around them. Where he was rigid, she was relaxed.

She shrugged her shoulders back, straightening. "You help me uncover what a Massoud does, I'll help you learn what real love is."

His eyes became soft, the rigidity leaving the lines in his forehead. "I don't love you, Naomi. I'm afraid you've got that all wrong."

"And I don't love you." She didn't flinch, just leaned forward even more. "But love isn't only romantic. That's where you've got it all wrong." As she said it, her chest tightened. To openly challenge a Magnificent like this was unlike her. Yet she was willing to defy her natural instincts to get through to him. Something about him sunk into her. She needed him in this time of chaos, but she saw he needed her, too. "You said let's trust each other," she reminded him. "So let's. Trust that I won't hurt you." She smiled.

He watched her for a whole minute before speaking. "You are not what I thought you were when I picked you up outside of Le'Gar."

Worry leapt to the surface of her skin. "Oh no, I've made it worse?"

"No." He touched her arm.

She stiffened.

He didn't let go. "Just different. And I think it's a good thing."

His hand fell away, leaving her reeling at the strange sensation left behind by his touch.

"Naomi?" Vira's voice came from outside the tent.

She cleared her throat. "Yes. Come in."

Vira swept into the tent. For the first time since Naomi met her, she was dressed down. She wore linen slacks, similar to her own. But she had on a buttoned, long-sleeved blouse that matched the material of her trousers. Even dressed down, she was beautiful.

Vira paused for a moment, perhaps feeling the leftover tension in the room. "I've come to check on your progress."

Ferrin picked up the canteens again and held them up by the straps. "Filling these, then we'll be set."

Vira moved past Ferrin to Naomi. "Mind if I stay a moment?"

Ferrin shrugged a shoulder out of the tent flap. "Keep Naomi company while I fill these."

Naomi wanted to huff out loud. She didn't need a babysitter. But she had no intention of insulting Vira, so she nodded instead, welcoming her to stay.

With Ferrin gone, Vira seemed to relax some. "Has the quill done anything?" She sounded hopeful.

Naomi had kept the quill while Ferrin held onto the necklace. They both felt that keeping the items separate was best. When she took the quill out of her deep trouser pocket, it looked exactly the same.

"Nothing has changed," she said, exasperated. "It still just glows. And glows and glows and glows."

"Well," Vira laughed quietly, "I suppose we should count it a blessing that the quill isn't doing something monstrous."

Naomi flipped the quill over in her hands. "I suppose you're right." She noticed Vira's hair. It didn't flow freely anymore. It was braided from the top of her head all the way down her back. The shaved sides of her head made her appear warrior-like, as if ready for battle. "Do you think you could teach me how to braid?"

"I sure can try. We'd need to find a mirror." She pointed to the single table and chair. "I can braid yours for now if you like. I always set my hair in this style before I travel. Loose hair on a long horseback ride can be a menace."

"I've experienced that on Ferrin's horse," Naomi said as she moved to the chair and sat. "I'd love if you braided it for me. Thank you."

Vira stood behind her and gathered her thick, brown hair into her hands. "You have almost as much hair as I do," she marveled.

Naomi smiled. "So did my mom."

Vira grew quiet, running her fingers into the top of Naomi's head, beginning the braid. "So does my daughter."

"You have a daughter?" For a fleeting moment, Naomi felt a wave of pain at the thought of her own mother.

Vira's fingers moved steadily, gathering more and more bits of hair. "I do. Her name's Millicent, but she goes by Millie. We'll see her when we reach our destination in a few days."

"She lives in Mira Isla?"

"So Ferrin told you," she chuckled. "He really does view you as an equal."

"He just agreed that I should know the plans."

"And he's right," Vira said. "But where we're going is a sanctuary for golden witches and Magnificents. Revealing the site to humans can be dangerous. I thought perhaps he would feel more cautious."

She frowned beneath Vira's hands. "I'm not dangerous. And most of humanity isn't either." She thought of Le'Gar, remembering the golden witch who owned the apothecary. Her name was Sadie Hepstein and she was revered, cherished, loved. Sadie healed people with enchanted medicine. Sometimes her concoctions even saved lives. "I think we need more witches and Magnificents roaming about us."

Vira reached the base of her skull with the braiding. "With time, that will come. Thãen has shown signs of healing since the Magnificent slaughter. Especially now that the Dark Hand has been revealed as the culprit of destruction."

"Did you send your daughter to Mira Isla to keep her safe?"

Her hands slowed. "Yes. Although it wasn't because I thought humanity would harm her. It's because of the way I live. I'm nomadic."

Naomi slouched, relaxing under her touch. "You think Millie would have minded the way you live?"

"Not exactly." She wove the hair faster now, trailing the braid down her back. "But I mind it. Millie needs stability and a community that is safe. I don't offer either of those things."

"What about her father?" A pang of nerves hit Naomi's core. Vira obviously wasn't married. If she was, it was a secret.

"Millie doesn't know her father." Finished with the braid, she rested both palms on Naomi's shoulders. "And I'm not positive I do either."

Naomi's stomach wrenched. It wasn't exactly the answer she expected. "I'm sorry. I was almost violated a few weeks back in one of Le'Gar's side streets. It's a terrifying moment. I'm sorry you suffered from it."

"Oh, Naomi," she breathed, giving her shoulders a slight squeeze. "I wasn't violated. I made unwise decisions."

A stale beat passed between the two. Vira began to lift her hands as if she thought Naomi wouldn't want to be touched by her anymore. But Naomi reached up and stopped her, allowing her hands to stay settled. "Thank you for braiding my hair," she said. "Your hands remind me of my own mother. I'm grateful."

Vira didn't say anything. Not for a long time. Naomi thought perhaps she overstepped or dug into wounds that Vira didn't wish to address.

Then Vira spoke. "You're a breath of fresh air, Naomi."

Naomi smiled, her back still to her.

"For me *and* for Ferrin," Vira finished.

Gingerly, Naomi stood, feeling her hair to examine what

Vira had accomplished. "He's lost in the dark, isn't he." There was no question in her remark. Only certainty.

Vira faced her. "No one lives without darkness." She paused, pressing her lips together. "But Ferrin, I'm afraid, has a darkness that consumes him. It will either strengthen him, or kill him."

Naomi felt her height difference standing in front of Vira. She knew she was shorter, but this close, she felt shrunken. "I don't think Ferrin will let it kill him." She tried not to sound so quiet, but her courage was low. Vira thought his darkness could eat him alive. She could be right. But Vira hadn't heard the things he had said. The little drops of confessions about his actions. The admittance of pain. "He wants to defeat his darkness."

"Keep him believing that," Vira urged. "He's a powerful being if he'll allow it to be so. Unlike golden witches, Magnificents can summon power into existence. As much as I dislike to admit it, I'm limited where he is not." Vira gave her a final half smile before turning for the tent's door. She walked a few steps then stopped and turned. "Hux and I will come to retrieve you and Ferrin in two hours. Be ready."

"We'll be ready."

Then she was gone.

CHAPTER TWENTY-EIGHT

Ferrin still hadn't returned when far-off shouting drew Naomi from her tent. She slunk into the night, keeping quiet in the shadows. The voices came from the heart of Zul—near the main tent—along with a collective clobbering sound of hooves. Her row of tents remained quiet. Everyone bunking in Zul most likely knew better than to investigate mysterious commotion, but Naomi knew her situation was different. Strange noises could be related to her.

She sucked in the courage to move down the dirt row toward the main tent. It towered over Zul, illuminated with hanging lanterns and manned by permanent residents of Zul. Residents who kept the order. The man whom Ferrin had paid to rent a tent frightened her. He was burly like Hux, but unkempt like a merciless warrior. She had no business approaching the main tent alone.

Stopping in her tracks, she recoiled. Her curiosity was making her a fool. Not just because she was alone at night in Zul, but because she caught a glimpse of three Riders galloping past the entrance of her row with Raina's flag hanging off each horse's flank.

She threw a hand to her mouth and backpedaled. Riders of Raina. They were here for Hux.

Turning and running, she headed for the ravine, knowing that was the last place Ferrin had gone. But she took an unexpected left toward Vira's tent instead. She didn't need Ferrin. She needed to get to Hux. Before the Riders did.

Her newly braided hair swished against her back as she flew. The night air infiltrated her lungs and chilled her arms. It was invigorating. And it distracted her. Because the next moment someone slammed her to the ground.

The body came from her right. She landed on her left shoulder. Her face ground into the dirt. A stabbing pain pulsed between her ribs as she scrambled to crawl away from whoever was on top of her.

A hand grabbed her ankle. "Not so fast, beauty of Le'Gar."

She kicked at the hand. "Release me or I'll scream!"

The face above her had teeth that glowed in the inky night, but her shimmering hair shone even brighter. Like Vira's, but vibrant white. "Scream away, darling." The woman didn't let up on her icy grip. "No one will come. Zul doesn't poke its nose into other people's business."

Naomi kicked with her free leg again, slamming her heel into the woman's knuckles. "Then don't poke your nose in mine!"

The woman pulled her closer, sliding her on her back.

Naomi swung her fingernails out like claws, swiping at the woman's face. "I'll try to kill you, I swear I will. Let me go!"

And the woman did let go, but she just as quickly grabbed the front of Naomi's blouse and began feeling around as if searching for a weapon.

Panic suffocated Naomi. She lay on her back in the most defenseless position and the woman's hands were treading closer to the pocket that held the golden quill. With a fighter's adrenaline, she slammed her hands into her attacker's chest. The woman jerked backward at the force. Naomi flipped onto her hands and knees, crawling a few feet before the woman yanked her back by the hair.

The woman pulled Naomi's ear close to her lips. "What are you hiding, Le'Garian miss? I sense it all over your naive face."

Naomi drove her elbow into the woman's abdomen. The woman gasped and let go. When Naomi jumped up, the quill spilled from her pocket.

The woman was still on her knees, and she watched the quill fall right in front of her. Solid and glowing.

Naomi dove back to the ground, swiping for the quill.

The woman reached, too.

Naomi won.

In ferocious haste, the woman tackled her again. The back of Naomi's head collided with the ground. She clenched the quill in her right hand, and the woman grabbed her wrist, prying her fingers up. Naomi felt helpless. The quill was loosening under her grasp and the woman's forearm pressed into her neck. Without thought, Naomi opened her mouth and screamed.

"Ferrin!"

The woman's eyes flickered with shock. For a moment, she lessened the pressure against Naomi's neck.

Naomi felt the sudden change and shouted again. "Ferrin, help!"

Down at the ravine, Ferrin sat on his knees, slowly rinsing days of dirt from his forearms. Crickets and peeper frogs chimed around, calming him. But the beautiful songs of the night were silenced when a voice screamed inside his head.

Ferrin!

He jerked his arms from the water and stood.

Ferrin, help!

His heart clogged in his throat. His muscles burned with urgency.

He spun and sprinted up the ravine.

———

Naomi gripped the quill harder, resisting the woman's sharp fingernails.

The woman leaned into her face, sneering through exuberant distaste. "You wouldn't fight me if you knew who I was." Her breath sat stale against Naomi's cheeks.

"I'll fight whoever dares to touch me." She squirmed beneath the woman's chest. "Especially a thief like you."

"I am no thief." She shoved her forearm deeper into her neck. "I am a willing servant."

Then Ferrin's voice roared through the night. "Release her!"

The woman flew backwards as if tossed by a wave. Her body landed in the dirt a few feet away from Naomi, mangled and flailing.

Naomi scrambled to her feet, clutching the quill against her chest. When she saw Ferrin behind her, both of his palms were facing outward, as if he had thrown the woman without touching her. When the woman jumped up and lunged for Naomi once more, he thrust his hands forward and the woman froze in place. Naomi backpedaled to him.

He kept one hand up and used his other to pull Naomi into his side. "Are you hurt?"

But she didn't get to answer, because the woman—still paused against an invisible force—grinned. "Ferrin," the woman seemed to seep his name. "You're practicing your power again."

Naomi felt a vibration streaming through Ferrin's body. She didn't know if it was his magic or anxiety, because his face was the color of white sand.

"You're deceiving me, witch," he wheezed. "You aren't who you want me to believe you are."

"Oh, but I am, love." She reached forward, testing if he would allow her to approach. But her feet remained rooted to the ground. "Let me come to you."

Naomi gripped the back of his shirt. "She wants the quill, Ferrin, don't trust her."

"I *don't* trust her," he snapped, tightening his arm around her side. "Did she hurt you?"

She didn't know how to reply. She was alive. She was safe. Her left shoulder throbbed, but—

"Did she hurt you!" he shouted.

"No," she choked. "She only tried."

"Curse you, witch!" Spit flew from his mouth. "Let go of my mind and show me who you really are."

"But you see clearly." The woman touched her chest. "It *is* me. Estell, my love."

He had told her Estell was dead. Estell knew Ferrin in his real twenties. This couldn't be her.

"You were mortal," he whispered. He lowered his palm, sighing when his power stopped flowing from his hands.

Estell dramatically shook out both feet, as if the hold had caused her discomfort. "You aren't the only one who is granted longevity," she said, pulling her hair to her front and draping it over her chest in gorgeous white waves. Gorgeous even after the fight. "I live because the one who holds the power gives me life."

He took a step forward.

Naomi kept a grip on his back.

"Who holds the power, Estell?" He drove the words with a menacing chill.

Estell crossed her arms, swaying side to side. "Darling, you know who hovers over Thãen."

"Protection," he said with hot haste.

She tsked. "And yet Calamity still succeeds in crushing cities to their bones."

He rolled his shoulders back. "Calamity doesn't hold Thãen."

"Not yet." She held a long finger up. "But soon."

Naomi tugged Ferrin back. He was moving too close to Estell. "She's Calamity's servant, Ferrin."

He glanced back, his eyes catching hers. "I know."

"Of course you know." Estell smiled, tilting her chin down. "You've known me more than most." Somehow her eyes shimmered. "Don't tell me you've forgotten so easily?"

Ferrin's muscles turned to rock beneath Naomi's grip.

"I gladly blotted out our time together," he said through gritted teeth. "I celebrated when I thought you were dead."

Estell ran her fingers down the sides of her arms. "And yet I've missed you every second of the passing years."

He stood in silence.

"I have to do what my Master says," she whispered. "Even if I don't want to."

Naomi saw the game Estell was playing. "But you want to," she accused.

Ferrin put an arm across to block her. "Naomi, don't."

She shoved his arm away and stepped to his side, facing Estell. "You must be a fantastic servant if Calamity has kept you around for so many years. Calamity doesn't do that for anyone."

Estell sneered.

Ferrin spoke through clenched lips. "Naomi, *stop*."

"Why?" She faced him, anger brimming her eyes. "Because she's powerful? Because you loved her?"

His eyes matched hers. "Because she'll kill you if you provoke her. For grave's sake, Naomi. I'm trying to *protect* you."

Estell's words ripped through the air with malice. "Like you protected Oliver."

"Don't speak his name," Naomi sobbed. A reaction she didn't expect from herself. She never knew Oliver. But he was a blood relative. One who shared a similar life as her. And if she wasn't careful, perhaps they would share a similar fate.

Estell raised an eyebrow. "You speak as if you knew him."

Ferrin shoved her behind himself. "She knows his story."

Estell looked beyond him to Naomi's tear-stained cheeks. "Only the story. And yet she cries."

Naomi trembled behind Ferrin, resisting the urge to claim Oliver as her blood. It would be the ultimate revenge. A moment to tell Estell, *you succeeded before but now I'm here in his place. Try me.*

"Perhaps she's a Massoud," Estell tested.

In one beautifully timed moment, Ferrin and Naomi said at the same time. "A Smyth."

Estell's shoulders lowered slightly. "But the quill glows in her presence."

Naomi glanced down to her chest. She had forgotten about the gold feather pressed against her heart.

"It glowed in someone else's possession first," said Ferrin. "So your hunch is mistaken. Naomi Smyth is simply a Smyth."

Estell took a step forward. "Ah, so there are more of you involved. I assumed as much. My darling Vira seemed put off by me the other night."

He kept a composed face. "Any man or woman in their right mind should be put off by you."

"Were you not in your right mind when we held each other?" She tilted her head, sorrowful eyes searching his.

Naomi's body thrummed with nerves, sensing a fire rising inside Ferrin.

"You weren't always cold." His voice was oddly calm. "Why you chose Calamity over yourself, I'll never understand."

His words seemed to pierce her, because for once her sinister grin subsided. "Would you believe I had no choice?"

"Everyone has a choice," he said with darts flying from his tongue. "You choose to die if it comes down to it, but you always have a choice."

Her lip curled. "Is death so easy to welcome? To lie motionless beneath the ground for eternity?"

He moved back a step, pressing into Naomi. "I'd choose death over service to Calamity any day of my life. You're alive, but you're a slave, Estell. Calamity will give you life until you prove to be useless."

Useless. Naomi watched the word ignite Estell. The woman's eyes blazed with the overwhelming want to rip Ferrin to shreds.

"I will still be here," Estell threatened. "Even if you escape today, I will be trodding at your heels, ready to swipe your ankles and drag you down. Calamity offers me life now, yes, but power later."

He titled his head slightly. "An empty promise."

"A promise stronger than yours." She stood tall, readjusting her voluminous white hair. "Calamity stands by me, even in my darkness."

"You purposefully created your darkness." He took another step backward, taking Naomi with him.

"Love does not judge." Estell hung her head. "But you cast me aside."

He wrapped a hand around Naomi's wrist. She assumed it was to keep her behind him, to make sure she was still protected, but she felt his hand trembling. The gesture was a plea for support. A subconscious action that screamed, *I need your help.* She moved his hand down to her fingers and intertwined them, hoping he could sense her response: *I'm right here.*

He squeezed her fingers. "It wasn't love, Estell. It was manipulation. You manipulated me."

Estell's figure sagged in the middle of the row of tents. Her shoulders hunched forward. The way her lips drew down made Naomi believe she was truly hurt by his words. For a flickering moment, Naomi felt twisted sympathy.

Then Estell readjusted, regaining her stance of strength. "I toyed with you to get what I needed, yes. But you can't believe my love was nonexistent."

"I don't believe," he bellowed. "I know."

Behind Estell, a figure morphed out of the darkness.

Vira.

Before Estell could turn around, Vira placed her hand on the woman's white-haired head. Estell dropped to her knees, then collapsed to her side. Asleep.

Vira stepped over her, unapologetic. "You knew her." She said it to Ferrin.

He dropped Naomi's hand. "Too many years ago. She should be dead."

Shouts rose from the north side of Zul. Heads popped out of the rows of tents, peeking around for the commotion.

Vira stepped closer to Ferrin and Naomi, hiding together in a dark shadow, away from Estell's body. "What did she want?" she whispered.

Naomi lowered the quill from her chest. "She tried to get this."

Ferrin eyed her wrist, noticing deep red skin from Estell's vicious fingers. He held his hand out, asking for the quill. When she transferred it to him, his fingers grazed her wrist and hand.

His motion was sly, but intentional, searching for any further injury. She lifted her eyes to his and smiled with soft lips, allowing him to see that she was okay.

"Does Estell know who you are?" Vira questioned Naomi.

"No." She was still shaking. "But she's Calamity's disciple. She may know things she shouldn't."

Vira glanced back at Estell's body lying in the path. "I must admit, Estell has been atrocious to be around, but I never assumed she was a disciple. We spent quite a bit of time together."

"If she befriended you here in Zul, she deceived you," Ferrin assured, half grumbling.

Vira swallowed, eyes flickering with remorse. "She claimed to be a golden witch, like me."

Naomi glared at the woman sleeping on the ground. "Is she a witch, Ferrin?"

"Yes," he said, sharp. "But a dangerous one."

"Can Calamity really give mortals longevity like Estell said?" She bounced her eyes from Ferrin to Vira.

Vira shared a glance with him. "I don't know. There is new knowledge arising and we must learn as we go."

Naomi sniffed in the ever-chilling air. "Perhaps she was the one to tell Saul of Hux's survival and the quill being found."

Vira nodded slow, thoughtful. "You make a valid observation."

Ferrin peeked at Estell. "How long does your sleep touch last?"

"Not long enough." She put a hand on Naomi's shoulder and gave a gentle nudge north. "Let's leave while we can."

"Where's Hux?" Naomi followed her with purpose, letting the breeze invigorate her and the specks of lanterns comfort her.

Vira moved only a step ahead, swiftly guiding the way. "In our tent."

Ferrin grabbed the two women's arms and pulled them back, dipping back into the shadows. "No. No he's not."

The three crouched together in the dark space between two neighboring tents. Horse's hooves and boot buckles rattled by, passing the place where they hid. There were eight Riders of Raina.

Following on foot, bound at the wrists and attached to the last horse with rope, was Hux.

CHAPTER TWENTY-NINE

The Riders of Raina plowed through Zul, drawing stares. Lanterns ignited in surrounding tents, concerned residents awakening. Raina's men ditched their horses outside of Zul's main tent and dragged Hux inside.

Naomi, Ferrin and Vira trailed the Riders, but hung back near the residential tents when they reached the clearing surrounding the main tent. They pressed themselves against the side of the last tent in the row. There was too much light surrounding the hub to hide. Massive lanterns staked around the tent cast a wide, golden ring of light. It was bright enough to get one last glimpse of Hux as he was pulled into the tent by the elbows, a Rider of Raina on each of his sides.

"How did they find him?" Naomi's breaths were quick.

"Zul is an obvious place to search." Vira leaned her head out ever so slightly, then pulled it back in. "As to how they knew what tent Hux would be in, my intuition tells me Estell had something to do with it."

Ferrin's eyes darted around the main tent, examining who was where. Eight Riders of Raina had gone inside the tent with Hux. Eight more stood around the perimeter of the structure to guard. The man who had rented him a room was nowhere in sight. In fact, none of Zul's self-proclaimed authority was present. Perhaps they were inside with the other half of the Riders of Raina. "Does Zul protect its residents?" he asked grimly. "Or do they surrender them to whoever comes to make a claim?"

Vira looked back at him. "Zul is a loose territory. No one interferes with the lives of others. But they won't prevent arrests. There is no motive to."

"But why are they arresting Hux?" Naomi asked, her chest tense.

Vira stared ahead again, eyes sharp and poignant. "He committed treason against King Leeland. The Riders of Raina are doing what they're supposed to do." She swallowed, glancing around, inspecting the layout. "But King Leeland sent a crew to Ode to find the quill, an object that most don't know about. So King Leeland is not innocent either."

"We need to get him back," Naomi blurted. "Right? Hux didn't mean to get wrapped up in all this. He's as lost as I am. What is he supposed to do? Accept arrest? He can't fight using powers like you both have."

"He did accept arrest." Ferrin nodded toward the tent. "That's why he's in there. It doesn't look like he tried to resist."

"Because he knows he committed treason," Vira's voice was steel. "He's a man of honor. But I will not give him up to Raina. He wouldn't allow it if it were me in his place. And we need him. He's a skilled fighter."

Ferrin fidgeted, antsy. "So are we going in? Or are we going to sit out here and chit chat about it?"

"Do you *want* your head on a stake?" Naomi whispered. "If we waltz in there blazing on a trail of anger, we will end up bound right next to him."

He waved a hand toward the guarded tent. "He's one of our men and he's being held captive. It's our duty to get him back."

Vira looked him up and down, almost admiringly. "You're absolutely right. What can we do?"

Naomi watched as Ferrin and Vira examined one another. No words passed between them, but they appeared to be communicating. Not in a literal sense, but in a discovering type of way. Since the witch and the Magnificent met, they had gone head-to-head. But now, for the first time, they seemed to meld. Accepting each other, knowing they could be a force together. It made her shrink back, having nothing to offer.

Ferrin squinted. "How well can you deceive the mind?"

"Well." Vira nodded. "But for a whole slew of men? I'm unaware of how long I can keep a hold on them."

"Then we'll move quickly." He turned to Naomi.

Her eyes widened. "Do you want me to fetch the horses?"

"No. We need you."

"I don't think you do." She sagged back even more, wishing to melt into the tent's material.

"Naomi." He sounded stern, but there was reassurance, too. "There is something you can do that we can't."

She frowned. "What is it?"

"You can move within the visuals we create," he smiled, looking as if he were growing excited at the thought.

"The what?" she asked.

Vira lowered her voice when a Rider casually glanced their way as he continued his stroll around the hub tent. "I can make the Riders both inside and outside the tent believe they are seeing something that they really aren't. In this case, I will make them think they can see Hux, even when he's gone."

"But someone has to go in and get him," Ferrin took over. "And that will be you."

"Me?" Naomi gasped. "Why not you?"

He touched her shoulder, calming her. "Magnificents can't use their powers on themselves. It's our largest downfall. So I will have to use my powers on you."

"What are you going to do to me?"

"I'm going to make you invisible."

"I'll be like a ghost?"

"You won't feel any different physically," he promised. "But you'll be able to walk into the tent unnoticed. When you find Hux, touch him, and he will become invisible, too. But Vira will make sure that it looks like he's still there." He hesitated, reading her petrified look. "Then you and Hux will walk right out into the open and we'll all make a break for the horses."

She examined every inch of his sure expression. His forehead down to his chin was relaxed, no worrisome lines or tautness. He truly believed this plan was going to work. He had faith that she would accept.

"Okay." She nodded, trying to match his courage. "Send me in."

CHAPTER THIRTY

Word of the appearance of the Riders of Raina spread through Zul. By now, brave groups of people trickled into the pathways and crept toward the main tent. Whispers bounced around the night wind: *The Riders of Raina have a man captive. A dangerous man is inside the hub. Zul is being taken over by Raina.*

Naomi heard fragments of the whispers as she bounced on the balls of her feet, waiting for Vira to give the go-ahead.

Ferrin wrapped his fingers around her elbow, stopping her. "Hey. Relax."

She scowled. "I'm allowed to be anxious. I'm not the one with powers to protect myself."

"I've got you. They won't be able to see you. I promise."

Vira cut her eyes at Ferrin. "All right. Ready?"

Ferin nodded. "Let's hide between these two tents." He looked behind him, watching more and more residents of Zul meandering their way to see what all the gossip was about.

The three slipped into a foot-wide space between the tents. Vira and Ferrin stood shoulder to shoulder. Naomi hung on the end, pressing as close to Ferrin as possible.

"You ready?" he whispered down to her.

When she looked up to nod, her heart seized. She wasn't ready, but he promised that he would keep her safe, so she forced herself to believe it.

"It'll be fine." He touched her wrist and smiled softly.

She frowned, but finally nodded. She was as ready as she could be.

Vira linked elbows with Ferrin. He glanced down at her touch briefly, but accepted it. She shut her eyes and seemed lost to a different world. Her breaths were steady and he matched the pattern.

"Now, Ferrin," Vira said, fast.

He didn't even move. He merely stared at Naomi for a few seconds then said, "Go."

She didn't budge.

"Go, Naomi," he whispered. He pointed to his temple. "You're safe right in here."

She backed out of the shadowed space and into the main path now streaming with people. She had to sidestep one, two, three bodies who nearly plowed into her as they sauntered toward the main tent. They couldn't see her. Her body, once vibrating with nerves, pulsed with excitement. Whatever Ferrin and Vira were doing was working. She was invisible.

She set her shoulders back, lifted her chin, and stared ahead at the towering tent. Eight Riders of Raina wandered around the perimeter, swords in hand. She would simply walk past them. Moving slowly at first, she weaved her way through the people filling the path. She made sure not to touch a single one. She didn't want to spook them or make them invisible, like what Ferrin had said would happen once she touched Hux.

Too soon, she was on the outer edge of the center clearing. She hesitated for a moment, but remembered what Vira had said: *I'm unaware of how long I can keep a hold on them.* It urged

Naomi to move into the clearing. She took a tentative step, then another, and another.

The Riders outside the tent didn't even glance her way as she glided into the surrounding lantern light. They only kept walking in their patterned steps, monitoring and alert.

Her heart pumped in petrified thuds, but she felt something else, too. Pride. Excitement. *Enjoyment.* She shook as she neared the front of the tent, but it was an addicting feeling of jumpiness. She was walking, unseen to any eye, right into a heavily guarded tent to retrieve one of her men. It was invigorating. She felt the weight and intensity of the situation. And she loved it.

She stopped just outside the tent's entrance. A Rider stood broad and firm, staring out at the residents of Zul who were lingering like stray dogs across the clearing. He was making sure no one entered or exited the tent. Naomi knew he couldn't see her, but surely he would see the flaps move when she snuck inside. Wouldn't that give her away?

She closed her eyes and took a deep, hopeful breath. *Vira,* she thought. *Make the tent remain still to his eyes.*

She waited. For what, she wasn't sure. Vira was the golden witch, not her. It wasn't like she could pass messages as Vira could. But Vira could read thoughts. Or intervene with them, at least. Maybe she would catch her thoughts in the wind.

When she felt she had waited long enough, she gave the Rider one last hard stare and slipped past him. She slid her body into the tent, moving the flap as little as possible, but the Rider didn't budge. Even when she was fully inside the tent, the Rider remained frozen. It worked. Vira had heard her.

It took a moment for Naomi's eyes to adjust to the warm glow of the lanterns' firelight inside. It would have been inviting had the situation looked different. Her back was to the entrance. In front of her, seven Riders of Raina stood in a cluster behind one Rider. The lead Rider. The lead's hair hung under her helmet in dreads that reached to her waist. At her feet, Hux sat on his knees, hands tied behind his back. In front of the lead Rider was a man Naomi didn't know, but she pieced together that this man must be the authority of Zul: Simeon. Unlike the man who rented Ferrin the tent, this man had no tattoos and was clean shaven.

"He's wanted for treason against King Leeland," the lead Rider stated, crossing her arms. "Your opinion on the matter holds no weight."

Simeon crossed his arms, too. He stared down at Hux, then back up to the lead. "Zul is a place of refuge."

"This man is an unloyal Rider." The woman's voice was smoky. Thick with power.

"You hold authority in Raina, not in Zul," Simeon challenged, holding his ground.

Naomi remained still at the front of the tent. Why was this man attempting to keep Hux out of the hands of Raina's Riders? Vira said Zul didn't interfere with such things.

The woman tilted her head. "Zul has no authority. Not even you."

"We have honorary authority." He stepped closer to the lead. He kept his arms crossed and tense, matching her stance. "And I've been chosen to keep smooth operations in Zul. Letting outside powers infiltrate our camp and snatch away our residents is far from smooth."

The lead Rider grabbed Hux's hair, pulling his chin upward to face Simeon. "This man once stood in my position," she spat. "And he stole from my king. I will be leaving with him as a whole, or with his head in the crook of my elbow. Your resistance to his arrest will be the determining factor."

Simeon gazed at Hux. "Do you wish to go with her?"

Hux swallowed.

Naomi felt desperation in the air.

"I wish to go with her," Hux barely vocalized.

The lead let go of his hair. "A wise decision."

Fearing this conversation was nearing its end, Naomi dared to move across the ground toward Hux. Ferrin and Vira still had a hold on the situation, but time was ticking, and she had stalled enough.

The lead stood over Hux, staring down at him like a dog. "Where is the item you stole from our king?"

He looked up. "It's no longer in my possession, Maya."

She kneed him in the ribs.

Simeon flinched, visibly wanting to drag Hux away from her.

Naomi quickened her pace. No one turned to look at her.

"Then whose possession is it in?" Maya's voice rose, no longer smoky, but flaming.

Hux shook his head. "It lies at the bottom of the ravine, taken downstream to the wide mouth river to be washed away into the wilderness."

Maya dropped in front of him, leaning her face close to his. She wrapped her hand around his throat. She didn't squeeze, but her eyes vowed that she would. "Who are you protecting?"

He didn't even blink. "No one. I speak the truth."

Naomi was only a foot behind Hux now. She could see the menacing chill in the lead Rider's pupils. Hux's back rose and fell with heavy breaths.

"If you have help," Maya continued, "they're only assisting you because they know what power the quill holds."

"Do you know of its power?" he asked, unwavering.

Maya hesitated, examining his face. She seemed to search with genuine curiosity, contemplating whether she would give in to his question or not.

"I know King Leeland means to free us from The Dark Hand and I share in his desires," she said.

"As do I," Hux stated honestly. "But Leeland seeks power of his own."

Maya sneered. "Don't we all? Didn't you, as lead Rider, seek power?"

"I sought to protect."

"Spoken like a man with no drive," she scoffed. She lowered her hand from his throat and balanced on the balls of her feet, grinning. "You believe you're high and mighty. A man with one working arm who rose to the top. But look at you now."

Naomi clenched her fists. She wanted to scream. *Don't speak to him like that!*

The woman continued to smile. "If it's not just you, I'll find the others. And they won't be spared like you."

He dared to lean toward her. "I'll die with secrets if I have to. To the grave with anyone who believes power is the remedy that will heal the fear of death."

Maya's eyes dropped, losing their viciousness. She looked over his face for an uncomfortable amount of time. "You were a good Rider, Hux."

He stared right back, unwavering and calm.

"Why would you throw that all away?" she whispered.

But Hux gave no answer.

Maya stood and faced Simeon. "I'll be taking him now. Raina wants no ill relations with Zul. We will leave in peace."

Naomi blinked. It was almost too late. She had idiotically sat behind Hux and listened to the conversation when she should have snagged him minutes ago. She thrust her hand forward and rested it on his back. He snapped his head backwards and his eyes widened. She held a finger to her lips. He just gazed at her, frowning, confused. He could see her. She could see him. But Maya acted like he was still the only one at her feet. Vira and Ferrin's scheme was working.

Naomi waved a hand toward herself, beckoning him to

follow. He shook his bound wrists once. Balancing on his knees next to Maya, he couldn't use his hands to push himself up. He needed help.

She tucked her arms under his bound ones and tugged upward. He rose.

Maya still spoke to Simeon. The seven Riders behind remained standing in a cluster. No one under the main tent's tarp moved.

No one except Naomi and Hux.

They strode right through the seven Riders, moving brisker now. Hux nudged his broad shoulders sideways so as not to knock into a Rider. When Naomi exited the tent with him on her heels, shouts of confusion erupted from inside.

"Time to go," she gasped. She grabbed his arm and dug her fingernails into the knotted rope at his wrists.

The Riders inside the tent grew louder.

She yanked at the rope, burning away some of his skin as she broke the bonds loose. Her own strength startled her, but panic and adrenaline surged through her, taking control.

He threw the rope to the side and shoved her forward. "I'm right behind you."

She took off. The surge she always felt with running engulfed her. She was on a high. She sprinted with the speed of a stallion. Hux kept up with her, but still trailed a few feet behind.

Zul passed by her peripherals. Tents, people, firelight, smoke. The world grew darker as she skidded down the embankment to the ravine. Ferrin and Vira sat atop their horses, having retreated when they could no longer manipulate the scene surrounding Naomi and Hux.

Ferrin tugged his horse toward the sprinting pair.

"They know I'm gone," Hux panted.

Ferrin reached down and launched Naomi up onto his

horse. She tottered behind him, unapologetically wrapping her arms around his midsection to steady herself.

Hux more gracefully joined Vira.

Vira smiled, even in the midst of the chaos. "But they won't know where you've gone." She kneed the horse into an instant sprint.

Naomi tightened her grip around Ferrin as his horse followed Vira's. They sailed up and over the embankment toward the east mountains that sat black as night. She dared to look back. Zul shrunk to specks of campfires and rising smoke behind them. The smaller Zul became, the blacker the mountain grew in front of them. Naomi's heart rapped. The marrow in her bones pulsed with pride.

Maybe this was what a Massoud did. A Massoud saves those in need.

CHAPTER THIRTY-ONE

The east mountains were quiet, but Naomi could sense their life. Six foot ferns blanketed the ground. Trees with branches that curled into swirls sat like silhouettes above her head. Alcoves were filled with pools of water clear as glass, even in night's light. The beauty of her surroundings struck her into serene surrender.

The four traveled in silence, wanting to be able to hear anything or anyone approaching. It wasn't until the sky started to turn a dusty, pale pink that Vira spoke the first words. "The sun's rising," she said. "We'll make a brief stop here."

They guided the horses to a rocky outlook. From there, the ridges of the mountains in the distance could be seen sitting masked against the low clouds and faint morning sky. The pink light filtered the air, washing over the four as they dismounted the horses and sat in a circle, passing around sunflower seeds and berries.

Naomi placed a berry into her mouth and watched Hux hold his handful of sunflower seeds in his lap. He stared out at the vast expanse of mountains in the distance. His eyes had dark smears under them, like he hadn't slept since he arrived in Zul.

"You should have let Raina have me," Hux said.

No one said a word.

He moved the seeds around in his palm with his thumb. "The Riders of Raina will be coming for me, which means they'll be after you, too. If I go with them, you won't have them at your back."

"Yes, we will," Naomi was quick to correct. "We have the quill. Sure they want you for treason, but King Leeland wants the quill. Whether you stay or go, Raina will hunt us down."

He nodded, considering this. "I can never go back to Raina. And I can't safely live in Zul." He offered a forlorn smile to the others. "My home is with you now. That's how I see it, anyway."

Naomi smiled back. *He* may not know it yet, but she didn't feel he was made to be a lead Rider. His heart was too warm. He deserved to be with people who felt like home. It was a feeling she herself longed for. Le'Gar used to be home, but it was a cold home. Even though she now was on the run with strangers, she felt a sense of belonging with them that had been absent from her for quite some time now. She understood what Hux felt, and she was thankful he voiced it. If he felt it, too, maybe there was some truth to what she was feeling. Maybe she was closer to finding home than ever before.

"What about Estell?" Vira breathed, keeping her voice low. "I never knew she was a disciple of Calamity. Estell and I were friends, I suppose." She cleared her throat. "Maybe not entirely. We both had to find ways to make a living so we were, in a way, business partners."

Ferrin cracked a sunflower seed with his teeth. "I know Estell. If she was in business with you, it wasn't to benefit you. It was for personal gain."

Vira's gaze fell. "She gained from me, I gained from her. It was as fair as it could be. But it harmed me, and if it ever harmed her, she never showed it."

Hux pressed his lips together, his scruff twitching. "Well, she won't harm you again."

Vira nodded, accepting his promise.

Naomi looked sideways at Ferrin. In her heart, Hux's promise was meant for him, too. Estell had clearly toyed with Ferrin in a way that permanently altered his life. Naomi would do anything to prevent that from happening again. If this was home now, she was going to protect it.

Vira leaned forward, taking note of the way Ferrin kept staring at the rising sun, avoiding eye contact with anyone. "Ferrin," she said.

He finally looked at her.

Her lips remained in a straight line, but her voice swelled with power. "Whatever Estell has on you, it won't translate to how we interact with you."

His face softened. "She has murder on me, Vira."

Naomi sat cross-legged next to him and didn't budge with his words. She knew he thought Oliver Massoud's death was his fault, but he hadn't revealed the full story. Sooner or later he would have to tell. And with Estell being a common enemy now, perhaps, knowing Estell's backstory would be beneficial in outsmarting her.

"It might help us to know," she offered, slow in her approach, but the way he looked at her told her that he was planning on revealing it all anyway.

His face screamed defeat. No secret could hide behind his stone walled eyes anymore. The walls he once held up had crumbled. Seeing Estell again—alive—tore those walls down. "Estell isn't just after the quill like King Leeland is." His voice trailed. "She's after a Massoud. Once she finds out who Naomi is, she'll take any opportunity to kill her." He paused, perhaps making sure his words sunk in deep enough. "That's the only reason I'll tell you what happened."

Hux gave a single nod, urging him onward. If Ferrin were to trust anyone, it should be Hux. A treasonist. A man of crime himself.

Ferrin must have felt Hux's approval as encouragement, because he began. "When I lived in Le'Gar, I met a man named Eli. He was a Magnificent, and openly so. When I met him, I had no family left. I lived where I worked in the blacksmith shop and I was hiding my powers." He focused on Vira and Hux since Naomi already knew this part. "I was born a few years after the slaughter, so openly practicing as a Magnificent was terrifying." He paused to breathe in, then out. "But when I met Eli, he took me under his wing and encouraged me to use my powers for good.

"Eli had a grandson named Oliver. Oliver was always around when Eli would work with me. In the evenings, when Eli would train me on how to use my powers properly, Oliver would hang back and watch. I never questioned his presence. I always assumed Oliver might be a Magnificent, too, and Eli wanted him to learn from our sessions as well. But sometimes Oliver was afraid. Especially during our sessions. He'd look at his hands with terror and say to Eli, *'I can't control what my hands do like you two can'*. Oliver was truly afraid of who he was."

Naomi's soul lurched with pain. She had been swallowing that same feeling. The feeling of not knowing what she was capable of. The fear that she might harm someone because she didn't know enough about herself.

Ferrin continued. "I grew incredibly close with Eli. He was like my father. Eventually, I spent more time with him than I did at the blacksmith shop. I ended up losing my apprenticeship." He gave an airy laugh, perhaps remembering the goodness of those times. "But I didn't care. I loved learning from Eli. And I enjoyed Oliver's company, which was like having a younger brother." His lips fell straight again. "Around that time

I met Estell. She worked as a cobbler. I went in one day to get new shoes and I saw her. She was sitting, hunched over, shining a shoe. Her white hair fell over her shoulders. I remember thinking she was beautiful. I was taken aback. And then she looked at me." He bit the inside of his bottom lip. "She smiled at me and said that she'd seen me around and that she'd been hoping I'd come for her services someday." He rubbed his eyes. "I started seeing her after that. Every day."

Vira shifted from leaning on her left arm to her right. "Did you know she was a golden witch at the time?"

He nodded. "She told me right away. And because I fell so hard for her, I told her I was a Magnificent. I was with Estell for a year. Spring to Spring. And that winter, Eli trusted me with Oliver's secret. Oliver was a Massoud. Dropped at Eli's doorstep. I didn't know about the Massoud bloodline then. But Eli did. He knew of an ancient story where a Massoud had powers that were unheard of. Powers that not only worked here, in Thãen, but in the Outer Void, too. The realm where Calamity and Protection reside."

Cold sweat sprung over Naomi's skin. Powers that reached the outer realm? All Massouds had this? She had this?

Hux lifted his chin when he noticed her twitching and read-justing. He aimed his palm at her and slowly lowered it toward the ground. *Calm down,* he was saying. *Don't be afraid.*

His gesture was enough to bring her pulse back down. Not all the way, but low enough to avoid a full-blown panic.

Ferrin's shoulders slouched forward. "Of course, I kept Oliver's real identity a secret. I understood the weight of his existence. It was similar to mine. Being a Magnificent was dangerous enough, but to have powers that were nearly unheard of? I knew it was crucial to keep his secret safe.

"Around the same time, King Jomal Demar—Tal's great-great-grandfather—hired Estell to work for him." He flicked a sunflower seed onto the ground. "It was strange. She had been a cobbler all her life, barely making a living, and King Jomal decided to pluck her off the streets. Like a charity case."

"He hired her to do what?" Naomi probed.

"Jomal told Estell he hired her to be a castle hand." Ferrin chuckled, an angry sound. "And that's what she told everyone, too. But he had hired her to be a spy."

Hux scoffed. "A spy amongst his own residents?"

"Unfortunately, yes." He closed his eyes. "Not knowing the truth, I was so excited for Estell. So happy that she had a turn of good fortune in her life. But she started to grow cold toward me. She spoke less. When she did have words to say, they were often bitter or distant." He sighed. "Most of our relationship was just physical after that." He cleared his throat. "And that's what our love was based on."

Naomi didn't know whether or not it was appropriate to look at him or to avoid eye-contact all together. She felt the confusing swirl of emotions that seemed to spin around him like a swarm of flies: confusion, love, disconnection, anger, regret.

Ferrin thrusted his voice forward as if he were trying to avoid losing composure. "I eventually told Estell I couldn't go on like that. I told her it was time we ended our relationship. But she placed all the blame back on me. She said she felt distant from me because she knew I was keeping a secret from her. In her heart, she couldn't love me fully because she couldn't fully trust me." His face fell flat. "I believed her. Because I *was* keeping a secret from her. I was keeping Oliver's secret."

"But for good reason," Naomi justified.

"Of course it was for good reason," his voice swam with agony, "but I loved Estell, and the thought of losing her hurt. I thought that if I told my secret—Oliver's secret—that she could love me wholly again. So I told her." He dropped to a whisper. "I told her who he was. And she told me her trust in me was restored. I was so thankful. Because she was a part of me, and my naive heart relied on her."

Naomi's own heart burned. How dare Estell twist his spirit the way she did? To manipulate a man into love—the most sacred, active emotion—only with plans to destroy him. How *dare* she?

The sun broke over the purple ridges in the foggy distance and shone gold across Ferrin's eyes. He breathed in, feeling Thãen's awakening. "And a week later I discovered her true motives." His stare was blank, zoning out across the expanse of mountain and sky. "The king's cathedral has many hidden passageways. Some underground, some within the walls, some crossing the roof. One morning, while it was still dark, I used the rooftop to make my way to the room Estell occupied inside the cathedral. I was going to surprise her with a visit. But I didn't make it to her window because I saw her standing at the rooftop edge, facing the alley behind the cathedral. She had Oliver in some sort of trance. He was limp in her arms. And as I reached out to shout her name, she tossed him over the edge."

Acid burned in Naomi's stomach. Nausea followed quickly after. She held her hand over her mouth.

Vira squeezed her eyes shut.

Hux remained stoic.

"I screamed at her." Ferrin's words shook. "She was surprised to see me standing behind her on the rooftop, but as I was shouting, she flung herself on top of me and thrust me down on my back. She dug her nails into my throat and took hold of my mind. I knew she was a golden witch, but I didn't know she was that powerful. She wasn't just reading me, she was controlling me. She displayed, right then and there, that she could make me do whatever she wanted."

He stood. The sunflower seeds left in his hands scattered to the ground. He ran his fingers through his hair, leaving behind seeds that had been stuck to his sweaty palms. He walked to the mountain ledge, his back to the others.

Naomi started to rise, but Vira signaled her down.

For a few agonizing moments, no one spoke. Ferrin didn't turn around. No one approached him, either. They just waited for him to collect himself enough to finish his retelling.

Finally, he did. "Estell told me that I could either leave Le'Gar and never speak of what happened, or that she would control me to make me love her for the rest of my life." His back rose and fell with heavy breathing. "I chose to flee. I couldn't fathom the thought of being in Estell's presence ever again, and I knew my relationship with Eli was over. So I left that night, after a civilian found Oliver's body and King Jomal deemed it a suicide." He turned, facing the three. "King Jomal Demar had hired Estell to find the Massoud living in Le'Gar and to murder him. The throne is tainted. Calamity works amongst the Demar royalty to achieve its plans. Even to this day. King Tal is just as corrupt as his kin."

"Is Estell still working for the line of Demar?" Naomi rose to her feet. "Is that why she came after me in Zul?"

He wandered back over to the others. "It's deeper than that. Estell works for Calamity itself, as we've established. She doesn't need to report to royalty at all, only The Dark Hand, which is a hundred times worse."

"So she is a willing pawn," Vira said, letting out a minor groan.

Hux ran his thumb and finger down his short beard. "We have the Riders of Raina, Estell, and the Riders of Le'Gar on our heels." He exhaled. "We need to get to Mira Isla now."

CHAPTER THIRTY-TWO

Maya removed her chest plate, letting her fingers graze Raina's lead Rider emblem designed into the bronze: an elephant head with raging tusks. Since being in Raina's cavalry, she'd always dreamt of holding the position of lead. And now she had it. But a bitter force surrounded her heart. She felt it because Hux had given it up. *Why?* Why would he do that? How could treason have been more appealing than being lead Rider? She fought to hold those questions down, but they kept resurfacing.

Estell lowered to sit next to her at the small fire the Riders had built at the base of the east mountains, just outside of Zul's territory. The night around them made Estell's skin and hair glow even brighter in the flame's light. Maya had been shocked when Estell offered to help recapture Hux and even more surprised when she said she had her own motives to find him and those who helped him escape Zul.

Maya glanced back at her Riders, who were settling down for the night. Hux had escaped right under all of their noses. One moment he was in their presence, the next he blinked away. It was a trick that Maya knew could only be a golden witch's doing.

She faced Estell. "You said a woman named Vira helped Hux escape?"

Estell stretched her feet toward the fire, leaning back on her palms. "Vira and two others, I'm certain."

She drilled her stare deeper into Estell's shimmering face. "I knew a woman named Vira once. We were the same age. But she was cast out of Raina for stealing from our king."

"Of course," Estell scoffed. "That sounds like something Vira would do." With a wicked grin, she leaned toward Maya. "And were you aware back then that Vira is a golden witch?"

Maya's stomach dropped. "I was not."

"Now you know." Estell sat back, satisfied. "That's how Hux was able to escape."

Maya groaned and leaned into the fire, the right side of her face warmer than her left. "With a golden witch helping him, we have only a small chance of retrieving him."

"But you have a golden witch helping you."

Maya sat straight. "*You?*"

"Yes, darling." Estell waved her fingers over the ground and made the grass ripple with invisible energy. "You have an advantage now, too. I can feel the ones we seek. Their energy. Their presence. In my mind, I can feel that they aren't far. You see how I will help you, don't you?"

"But why?" Maya shook her head. "Why would you want to help me and my Riders? What will you gain?"

Estell's teeth appeared behind her soft lips. "The one I'm after. The other girl. The Massoud."

Maya's heart fluttered once. She had never heard that word before, but the sound of it caused a stirring within. "What is a Massoud?"

"A sacred bloodline. A dangerous one."

"Dangerous how?" She leaned closer.

Estell bit her lip, looking perplexed. "She could bring the end upon Thãen. She can do things golden witches and Magnificents can't." She lowered her voice. "And not only in this realm. The Outer Void, too. Her powers can affect the Outer Void. She could provoke Calamity into unleashing its full wrath on us."

Maya sucked in a sharp breath. "She has influence in Protection's realm?"

"And Calamity's," she rasped. "It's both of their realm, and don't you forget it."

"But Protection holds us," Maya countered. "It has the stronghold."

"For now," she spat. "Don't underestimate The Dark Hand's capabilities."

Maya hesitated, watching the fire's reflection line Estell's pupils. "So you want to get hold of this Massoud and prevent her from provoking Calamity into demolishing us?"

Estell's smile broadened, a light laugh seeping from her throat. "Eye for an eye."

"What?"

"The girl could demolish Thãen, so I will demolish her."

Maya stiffened. "You mean to murder her?"

"What else is there to do, darling?" She threw a rock into the fire.

"You take her captive and hand her over to authority."

"What authority?"

"Zul," Maya said, almost pleading. "That's where you're from. Those people are who you answer to."

Estell shot her a viscous glance. "I answer to no one."

She stood. "When you're riding with my company, you answer to me."

Estell stood, too. "So what are you saying? Are you implying that what I do with the girl is your concern as well?"

"That's exactly what I'm saying." She bit the insides of her cheeks to keep from lashing out. "This mission is one of retrieval, not murder."

"You're retrieving a treasonist and I'm seeking a threat to Thãen. What cause is there to keep them alive?"

"Decency," Maya bellowed. "My company and I are *Riders*. We aren't executioners."

The forest around them swished in the night breeze. The other Riders glanced their way as the women's voices rose, but kept to their circle, hunched and chatting.

Estell breathed fiery huffs. "So what does your king want with the golden quill?"

"To eliminate the threat of Calamity."

"By doing what?" she hissed.

Maya leaned forward into her face. "By using the quill, that's all I know. But I commend him for seeking such a dangerous task. If only someone would have done it years ago. Thãen has long been under the fear of The Dark Hand's clutch."

"Your king will start a war between Thãen and the Outer Void," Estell said, voice raising. "Don't you see? You go after Calamity, it will come after us. You will all be murderers in the end. War means death. And it will be your fault."

"We are already in a war," Maya retorted. "Just because Calamity doesn't hold onto us doesn't mean we are free from its schemes. People can still turn to Calamity and become its disciple. Cities are still crushed. If we don't smite Calamity, it will be crowned the winner in the end."

"We will face death," Estell snapped. "Better to live with oppression than not live at all. We must not push Calamity to its limits."

Without thought, Maya grabbed Estell's arm and yanked her near. "Are you on Thãen's side or Calamity's?"

Estell tried to tug from her grasp, but didn't get free. "I'm on *my* side. I'll do whatever I have to do to live."

"In the end we all die," Maya spoke through clenched teeth. "Choose your path wisely."

"And if I choose a path you disagree with? What then?"

"I'll leave you behind."

"You need me to locate your treasonist."

Maya breathed through flared nostrils. "I can find him without you if I have to."

Estell gave a vicious yank and freed herself from Maya's hold. "I can sense fragments of Vira's thoughts. She's still near enough. Leave me and you won't have a clue if she's close or far."

The women quieted, staring each other down, challenging.

"Agree to retrieve the Massoud and hand her over to authority," Maya demanded. "Or you'll be searching for her alone."

Estell sneered. "You're acting foolish. I'm able to find them on my own."

"Then leave now," she dared. "Head into the mountains without my Riders. But when you come face to face with the ones we seek, you will be overpowered."

Estell grabbed Maya's wrist, clenching with malice. "Fine." She took a large breath, calming herself. "I'll retrieve the Massoud and bring her to Le'Gar. Not Zul."

Maya frowned. "Le'Gar?"

"Yes." She grew a triumphant look. "Le'Gar knows what to do with Massouds."

CHAPTER THIRTY-THREE

Ferrin woke drenched in sweat. The night air chilled his moist skin, causing him to shake. He sat up and looked around. Vira and Naomi were still sleeping on the forest floor while Hux sat next to a miniscule fire, warming his hands.

Rubbing his eyes, Ferrin focused on his breathing. The image of Oliver falling over the side of the cathedral of the king had infiltrated his dreams. He hadn't had a nightmare about it in months.

"I get them, too, you know," Hux said, keeping his voice down.

Ferrin lifted his eyes to Hux's face, which glowed with the fire's light. "Get what?"

"Dreams." He threw a stick into the fire. "Nightmares."

Half reluctant, half tempted, he rose to join Hux by the fading fire. He sat across from him. Sleep deprivation hung over Hux's eyes like a mask.

"I haven't had dreams about Oliver for quite some time now." He tilted his palms toward the fire. "Must have resurfaced after speaking about him openly again."

Hux let his right arm drape into his lap and he pulled his

cloak tighter around his neck. "It's not weak to have nightmares."

Ferrin noted how Hux's massive body slumped forward like he was at ease with his thoughts. They had barely spoken since coming together. Honestly, Ferrin didn't think they were relatable to each other. Riders were never on his side. He was a ranger, and Riders were often put-off by the fact that he did odd jobs for multiple kingdoms, even if it was in the name of peace.

"What are your nightmares about?" Ferrin wondered.

Hux kept calm. "Lately, my second in command. My friend. Geoff."

Ferrin hung his head, nodding. "Was he harmed?"

"Consumed." Hux stared into the fire, appearing lost. "Calamity claimed him by a swarm of flies in Ode on our quest to retrieve the quill. All of my Riders were taken. Except for me." He focused back on Ferrin. "When I sleep, I hear Geoff shouting my name before I see him swallowed by a black swarm."

"Good *graves*," Ferrin said.

"You can bet I always wake up in a cold sweat." He grunted and gave a sorry smile. "Maybe the more I see it, the less it will affect me. Eventually."

"There's some truth to that," Ferrin affirmed. "Although I've found, after over a hundred years, there are some nightmares that still have their claws embedded into my mind."

"I fear you're probably right."

Ferrin lowered his voice and leaned forward an inch. "Why didn't you bring the quill back to your king?"

Hux opened his bleary eyes. "King Leeland thinks if he rids Thãen of Calamity, then everyone will bow to him in reverence and he will gain control of any land he wishes. They're motives built on greed. Besides," he gestured his head toward Vira, "she confirmed there is something supernatural at work here. She's been living a nomadic life for years, all because she believed that one day she would find a Massoud, whom she had *felt* arrive on this side of the Desarian Sea eleven years ago. If I can give Vira the chance to figure out what this all means, I will. I think there is a right way to defeat The Dark Hand. Naomi might be the lockbox, and the quill may be the key."

Resting his eyes on Naomi's sleeping body, Ferrin saw a woman who had no idea what she was capable of. It was perfect, really. If anyone were to possess power, what better person than one who thinks so little of themselves? So powerless.

"There is extreme power in Massoud blood." Ferrin drew his stare away from her frizzy, braided hair and back to Hux. "I fear for her."

"You fear what she's capable of?"

His voice fell gruff. "I fear what may happen to her."

Hux's eyes softened. "What happened to Oliver wasn't your fault."

"I gave his secret away," he snapped in a whisper. "I'm the reason Estell was able to achieve what she did."

Hux rested his hand on his knee. "Did you really love her?"

"Yes."

"Then you should have been able to trust her."

CHAPTER THIRTY-FOUR

The hike the next day was slower. Rain had come in the middle of the night, soaking Naomi to her bones. She shivered for an hour before the warmth from Ferrin's body finally eased her chill. Clouds covered the entire eastern ridge, keeping the moisture clinging to the terrain. The forest floor had leveled out again, but the air was thinner now. The trees were sparse, mostly skinny pines. All the Kapok trees had disappeared an hour ago. Soil gave way to rock, and when the four neared a ledge, a basin holding a turquoise lake sunk far below.

Ferrin and Vira let the horses peer over the edge.

Naomi peeked around Ferrin to see the immaculate body of water glistening hundreds of feet down. "Can I dismount to get a better look?" She attempted to adjust her tone to not sound like a child begging for sweets.

Ferrin smiled. Her effort must not have worked. "Sure."

She slid from the horse's rump and landed on wobbly legs. Her stomach growled for a proper meal, but she could ignore it for now, with the ledge at her toes and a sparkling body of water flooding before her eyes.

Vira joined her. "See the other side of the basin?" She pointed.

Naomi nodded. "It looks green on that side."

"It is," she confirmed. "That's where the waterfall to Mira Isla is. We're almost there."

Ferrin and Hux joined the women, stretching their stiff legs and cricked necks.

Naomi subconsciously picked at her nails, removing dirt that had built up over the last few days. Most of the dirt was from her scuffle with Estell. She cradled her wrist, remembering the way Estell showed her ferociousness in her grip. She was frightened until Ferrin showed up. Seeing him calmed the storm.

Now, she sought to examine the bruises Estell had left. But there were none. Her pulse sped. There used to be faded purple skin in the shape of fingertips. Bruises get worse over time, not better. Where had they gone?

Ferrin let out a long breath. "Shall we ride? If we keep on, we could get there by midnight."

Naomi tilted her chin up at him. He turned to head back to the horses and caught her stare. Her hand was still around her wrist. He noticed her stance and flicked his eyes to her wrist, her face, then smiled. She watched as he meandered away. He had touched her wrist right after Estell had attacked her. The missing bruises were his doing. He had healed them.

She followed him, still processing, when a tingling sensation pulsed up her legs. The feeling crawled up her vertebrae and struck the base of her skull. Words screamed with urgency inside her head. *They're coming.*

She spoke before she could stop it. "They're coming."

Hux drew his sword. "Who's coming?"

Ferrin stopped and glanced around.

For a moment, Naomi stood stuck, wondering what her own words meant. "I don't know."

"Did you hear something?" Vira scanned the pines behind them.

"Not out here," she stammered. "Only in my head."

Ferrin stepped closer to her. "A voice?"

Hux held his sword up, silencing the crew. "Listen."

Hooves clicked against rock in the distance, coming from where the four had just traveled.

"Riders." Ferrin placed himself in front of Naomi. "Vira, get back here."

Vira didn't budge. "Ferrin, they're too close. If it's Raina, there will be too many."

"Vira, I said *get back here*," he demanded. "I can't make us all transparent if you're standing so far away."

Realizing his plan, she dove for Hux's side.

Naomi stayed close to Ferrin's back, feeling both his cloak and the edge of Hux's.

Ferrin held his arms up and shut his eyes as the Riders of Raina came into view between the pine trees.

Maya, the lead, held a fist up to halt the rest.

Naomi held her breath. All sixteen Riders were right in front of them, but thanks to Ferrin, the Riders couldn't see them. They were invisible.

Maya leaned back to speak to the person sitting behind her on the same horse. "Is there a clear path around the top of the basin?"

"When the weather is favorable, yes," Estell answered.

Maya craned her neck to the left, seeking a natural trail. "Is it possible they fled the other direction? Back toward Le'Gar?"

"Unlikely," Estell said, monotone. "Le'Gar is their enemy, too."

Naomi pressed closer to the backside of Ferrin and Hux, trembling.

Vira stood firm next to Hux, but cast a glance at Ferrin. She watched him for a moment, and her eyes became taught. Naomi noticed the look and focused on Ferrin again. His arms were shaking. Sweat dripped down the back of his neck. His powers were fatiguing him. It looked like he could fail at any moment.

No. Naomi squeezed her eyes shut, praying in desperation. *I wish a mountain could rise up between us and the Riders.*

The ground vibrated. She clutched at Ferrin as a deep, horizontal crack split through the rock between the Riders of Raina and them. The jolt teetered Ferrin to the side. His arms dropped and he lost the flow of his power.

Maya's eyes bulged when the four became visible to her and her Riders in a blink.

Hux raised his sword.

But the crack between the two groups groaned and widened. Like a geyser, a jagged stone mountain erupted from the ground. It rocketed to the sky, towering upward and cutting off the sun. Naomi braced herself as Ferrin fell into her. She caught him by the elbow. He clung to her shoulder, avoiding a spill down the basin.

"What in *grave's forsaken name,*" Vira whispered, hand to her mouth. She backed up and ducked behind Hux as shards of loose rock rained down.

Hux blocked his head with his shield. "Thãen is altering!"

Naomi gasped for air, but none would come. She wished for a mountain, and a mountain arose. Now their backs were to the basin, cutting off all escape routes. Even if the Riders and Estell couldn't get to them at the moment, she was sure Estell could find a way soon enough.

Vira and Ferrin's horses skittered to the side, wanting to flee from the erupting mountain.

Naomi looked down into the basin. "Can the horses swim?"

"What?" Ferrin followed where she was looking. "Down there?"

She pierced her eyes through his. "Will the horses be alright?"

He squinted. "Yes."

She turned and focused on the lake again. *Rise to meet us, and take us to Mira Isla.*

The lake, still as glass, started to ripple. Like a bucket filling with water, the lake began to rise. It filled the whole basin, floating upward toward the top lip.

Ferrin touched her arm. "Naomi, wha—"

There was no time to explain. The lake was at their feet now.

"Jump in," she instructed.

Vira grabbed her horse by the neck and obeyed. She pulled her stead to the edge and coaxed it in before following.

Hux gave Ferrin a quick look, wondering if this was his doing, then jumped in, too.

Ferrin grabbed his horse's mane with one hand and Naomi's hand with his other. "Ready?"

Her nerves surged. "Yes."

They jumped in together.

The water flooded over her head. Crisp, clean, and quiet. She opened her eyes underwater as her body tumbled like she was falling down a hill. Panic overtook her. She couldn't feel Ferrin's hand in hers anymore. Light shone from both directions, up and down. There was no obvious way to the surface.

Vira's black hair floated past her like wispy seaweed. Then Vira's face appeared right in front of hers. Naomi jolted, letting bubbles escape her mouth. Vira grabbed her shoulders and pointed downward.

She looked. Below her feet was black water. Deep and never-ending. The light underneath her was gone. Only pale light shone above.

The women rose together, kicking heavily as their air dwindled. When they broke the surface, Naomi let out an explosive gasp. Ferrin's head bobbed up next, gulping for air all the same.

"Where's Hux?" Naomi spit water.

He exploded from the water like a boulder splashing out instead of in.

Ferrin treaded to his side in case there was need for assistance. Hux wiped his eyes then waved, signaling he was fine.

Naomi swam in place and turned her head. The lake was at ground level, but the basin was gone. In fact, the surrounding forestry looked nothing like where the four had just been. Overgrown vines climbed ancient oak trees and the sound of waterfalls called from deep within the spring greenery.

"I'm not ungrateful." Hux swam toward shore, following the horses. "But what in the name of Thãen's roots just happened?"

Naomi swam after him, keeping her mouth shut. What *had* just happened? Somehow, she had controlled nature. And it cost her no energy. She merely wished, and it happened.

They found their footing near the shore and waded, slow and soggy, to the pebbled beach. Ferrin stayed oddly close to Naomi as Vira led them and the steads into the cover of the trees.

Ferrin tossed his bow to the ground and dropped to his knees.

Naomi bent to his level. "Are you alright?"

His breathing was laborious. "Using my powers took a lot

out of me. That's all." He searched her concerned eyes. "You're not exhausted though."

Vira wrung her hair out over her shoulder slowly, listening. "Naomi. Was the mountain you? And the lake shifted not only upward, but turned into a portal. That was you, too?"

She straightened, leaving Ferrin at her feet. "I only prayed. I prayed for the mountain."

"And it listened to you," Hux said, in awe.

The oaks swished above their heads, gentle and inviting.

"I guess it did," she whispered.

Ferrin stood, using her as a crutch. "Don't be afraid, Naomi." He turned his face toward her, hair dripping at the tips. "It's a triumphant self-discovery. You just found your first true power."

CHAPTER THIRTY-FIVE

Dusk fell in golden blankets as Vira guided the group through waves of ivy bushes. A rapidly moving stream cut its way through thick underbrush. It headed away from an alcove that was created by a stone wall towering twenty feet up. The wall was covered in moss and vines. Falling down the center was a waterfall.

Vira slid off her horse and waded shin-deep into the stream. She approached the waterfall, facing it with a stance of respect.

Naomi leaned around Ferrin from her place on his horse to watch her, anxious for her to *do* something already.

The sword Vira pulled from the sheath at her side shocked Naomi. Through everything that occurred in Zul and even during the Rider incident at the basin, she had never drawn her sword. Its pristine blade proved that it didn't suffer from overuse. But then again, why would she need to resort to a weapon when she could put someone to sleep with the touch of her hand?

Vira gripped the sword and raised it above her head. It glinted in the falling sun before she sliced it down the middle of the waterfall. A crack of light burst forth in the path left behind by her blade. The falls parted in two, the blinding light creating a thin, narrow doorway into whatever lay behind the water. Or, inside the water. Inside Thãen. How that worked, Naomi wasn't sure, but she would find out soon enough.

Hux nudged his horse forward and the stallion obediently slipped through the bright crack. Both he and the horse disappeared from sight.

Ferrin hesitated. He didn't move his horse forward like Hux had. In fact, it seemed that he would rather turn around than plunge into the waterfall.

Vira waved him forward, searching the trees behind him. "Quickly, Ferrin."

He snapped to it, squeezing his thighs into the sides of his horse. The horse pranced into the strip of light.

Naomi buried her face into the back of his cloak. The light was blinding, and she feared they would burn up as they crossed between worlds. But all she felt was a warm wave of air and then the smell of oranges and cinnamon. When she opened her eyes, Hux was still mounted on his horse ahead of her, but he was no longer standing in the middle of the east mountains' jungle. Instead, a mix of cinnamon and orange trees towered above shin-high grass that was dotted with white wildflowers. They were on a cliff overlooking something she couldn't quite see from behind Ferrin.

Vira joined them through the waterfall. When Naomi spun to face her, she saw that the waterfall on this side of the world was crystal blue and falling from the tip of an orange tree branch. Like the branch itself was the source of the water. Vira drew her sword and sliced it through the waterfall, closing the strip of light. Blocking out the real side of Thãen. The side that Naomi knew, at least. Mira Isla wasn't separated from Thãen, only hidden within it. A concept that fogged her mind and rendered her speechless.

Vira swished past and strode to Hux's side. He had dismounted and was staring out over the cliff. "What do you think?" she asked him.

He put a hand on her shoulder. "I've never seen anything like it."

His comment made Naomi squirm. She and Ferrin were still too far back to see below the cliff. "Let's go look, Ferrin." She tapped his shoulder. "Come on."

He looked over his shoulder and smiled at her. "You go ahead. I'm just," he shrugged, "readjusting to being here."

She didn't dismount, but looked at him. "You've been here before?"

His smile actually deepened. "I grew up here."

"What?" She smacked his arm. "Why didn't you say?"

He shrugged again. "It wasn't important information."

She almost asked if his parents were still here, but remembered he was 187 and both his parents were dead. But his mother had to have been here with him when he was young. Perhaps the memories were saddening to him. Or too far away now.

She hadn't been to her own childhood home in eleven years and the thought of returning to her rickety bed in her damp room set an ache in her throat. Something about her past felt haunting. Like if she ever returned, there would be no comfort. Only melancholy nostalgia. The quilt that used to drape over her seven-year-old body wouldn't say, *"Welcome home, come and get cozy."* Instead, it would whisper, *"Remember the good days? They're gone now. You can't ever get them back."*

"Naomi?" Ferrin lowered his gaze to meet her far-off look.

She blinked up at him. "Sorry. I was just thinking. I get it. I get why it's strange to be back."

He swung his leg over to the side and dropped to the grass.

"When does home not become your home?" He reached up to help her down.

She took his hand and joined him at his side. "When you leave it?"

He shook his head. "When all the people who made it home are gone."

She tilted her head. "So now you're a visitor in your own land."

He turned his back to Hux and Vira, blocking Naomi from seeing whatever lay beyond the outlook. "That depends."

"On what?" She crossed her arms.

He looked at the stray hair falling loose from her two-day-old braid. "Who my home is now."

They matched each other's quizzical stares for a long beat. Their eyes reflected one another, searching. What were they searching for? Naomi couldn't pinpoint it. But it made her heart beat back and forth. Did he feel like he was gaining a home within her presence? Or was he simply saying that he truly wasn't sure where, or who, he considered his home now?

"Want to go look?" he broke the strange air. "It's beautiful."

She nodded, finding it difficult to look away from his facial features that had somehow softened since she met him. She didn't realize until she started to follow him to the edge of the overlook that her palms were sweating. Wiping them on her pants, she nudged up next to Hux. Her breath caught in a sharp gasp when she stared out.

The ledge they stood on was higher up than she originally assumed. Way down below, a city of white rock, pale brown turrets of stone, and golden domes was built into the soft brown rock that towered up on either side of a wide, turbulent river. The river split the city in two. It stretched from the horizon line, through the city, and disappeared into the dense treetops below. The sun sat like a weeping, orange splotch where the river met the sky. It cried over the city in gold, showering every dome, arch, and statue in its glow. The sky itself was a soft, evening violet, preparing for night.

Now that Naomi was right at the edge, she saw that the cliff wasn't just a drop-off. It slanted downward gradually and a dirt trail weaved through thin wisps of sage grass.

Hux glanced down at her over his massive shoulder. "A lot prettier than Le'Gar, huh?"

She tilted her chin up. "Much. Although I do miss the gargoyles sometimes."

"You don't find them spooky?"

"No." She laughed. "They're protection for the city. What's spooky about that?"

"The fact that they're alive," he chuckled back. "Didn't you ever fear that you'd wake up to see a griffin or a demon staring through your window?"

She put her fists on her hips. "I was friends with the griffin outside my window."

His brows rose.

"And there are no demons," she finished.

He squeezed her shoulder. "Friends with the griffin. Of course you were."

"What's that supposed to mean?" She felt small beneath his touch.

His eyes glimmered. "Only that you're brave."

Vira smiled quietly behind them. "All right, let's ride the horses down the trail. Two golden witches stand guard at the entrance to the city, but they know who I am."

Ferrin swung onto his horse. "And me."

Vira stared up at him, hands on her hips. "You?"

He winked. He actually winked. "I grew up here."

Naomi suppressed a grin and joined him. "But you're very old now. Everyone you knew is probably, uh, you know."

"Dead." He leaned his head back, letting his hair touch her face. "Oh, I know they are. But I'm the second oldest living Magnificent. Wouldn't you think people know about me?"

She swatted his hair out of her face, unsure of how to handle his sudden playfulness. "I guess I never thought it through." And she truly hadn't. To her, Ferrin was a quiet mystery. A fog lingering in the mountains. She never thought that maybe he wanted it to be that way, that maybe he hid away in the mountains because he desired to go unnoticed. But he was right, he was the second oldest living Magnificent, of course people knew of him. He was probably folklore at this point. The thought gave her a swell of pride as they rode together down the cliffside. She was friends with a legend.

The cliff's trail snaked back and forth and downward until it connected with a wide dirt road that led to two stone turrets covered in ivy and violet and peach flowers. The turrets stood side by side like pillars, the dirt road passing between them. Two women in black trousers and chest plates over tight, black, long-sleeved tops blocked the passage through.

One of the women stepped forward, her wheat-colored hair woven into a ball on top of her head. "Vira?"

Vira dismounted her horse and approached the woman. "Dina." She opened her arms for an embrace.

Dina practically dove into her. "Why are you here?"

Vira's body draped over Dina's in a secure hold. "We have business to accomplish." She withdrew from the hug and held Dina's shoulders, locking eyes. "And we need a safe place to seek refuge."

Dina looked at her, then shifted her eyes to the others behind Vira's towering shape. "Who are they?"

Vira stepped to the side and pointed. "Hux. My oldest and truest friend."

Naomi saw Hux's back go rigid as he sat up straighter. He offered a nod to Dina.

"And Ferrin," Vira continued.

Dina went stiff. "Ferrin the Magnificent?"

Ferrin gave a two fingered wave.

Dina was still gaping wildly at Ferrin while Vira moved on. "And Naomi. The Le'Garian refugee."

Dina snapped her eyes back to Vira. "*The* Le'Garian refugee?"

Naomi scowled in confusion. How should Dina know of her?

"Is she," Dina whispered, stealing a glance at her, "dangerous?"

"Dina," Vira scolded through a chuckle, pulling the curious woman's eyes away from Naomi. "Mind yourself. This is why they put you on entrance duty. You ask too many questions. Which is good for entrance duty, but inappropriate in conversation."

"But you've been gone for so long," Dina strained, "and it's *because* of this task. This belief that you needed to find someone from Le'Gar."

Naomi's cheeks burned. Dina seemed to really miss Vira. How much had Vira given up just because she felt the urge to help *the* Le'Garian refugee?

"Listen, Dina." Vira dropped her hands and sighed. "We are in slight trouble and we need a place to stay. This is the only place I could think of that would protect us."

Dina glanced back at the other woman standing guard who hadn't budged. Her pale skin and red hair hung to her waist in two braids and her eyes were cold.

"Mira Isla is a place of peace," the redhead grumbled, glaring at Vira. "You haven't visited for years. Why should we welcome your danger now?"

"*Amani*," Dina hissed at the other woman. "We don't turn away our own."

Amani shifted forward. "Vira, you know all of Mira Isla trusts you, but an unknown friend, a refugee and..." Her eyes trailed to Ferrin. "A legend?" She paused. "It's strange."

"I know." Vira shut her eyes. "But we need Mira Isla. At least until we figure out our next move."

Amani stole one more glance at Ferrin before sinking her stare into Vira again. "What danger should we be looking out for?"

Naomi's shoulders relaxed. Amani would let them through. Strange situation or not, Vira held a lot of impact here, clearly.

"We have a group of Riders from Raina, who obviously can't enter through the waterfall themselves," Vira stated quickly, "but they're now accompanied by a golden witch who will help them get in if she can find Mira Isla." Her eyes flicked to Ferrin then back at Dina. "I'm not sure if this golden witch has been here before."

Ferrin cleared his throat. "I'm unaware as well."

Vira paused, then nodded once. "So she could find us, or she could not."

"And what if she does?" Dina's face was stone. "Do you suggest military pushback?"

Amani shook her head. "Only Captain Bromulin can order battle or not."

"I'll speak to Bromulin," Vira settled. "Then he'll relay to you what to do."

Dina and Amani nodded at the same time.

"But," Dina tilted her head, "why would a golden witch work against her own kind?"

Vira breathed in. "She serves The Dark Hand."

Dina and Amani shared a nervous glance.

"So you know what kind of danger she possesses." Vira

brushed her hair from her shoulders and walked back to her horse. When she mounted in front of Hux, he put a hand on her back. Naomi caught a slight tremor beneath his palm. Like Vira was vibrating. Or shivering.

Ferrin nudged his horse up next to Vira's. "If she gets in, she won't be able to touch us," he said quietly.

She drew her face back into complete seriousness. "You knew her when she was truly young. I knew her as of late. She's off the hinges, Ferrin. A wild spirit searching for chaos."

"She *won't touch us*," he said, harder. "I'll use up all my energy to keep her away from us. She won't succeed." Anger flashed across his eyes. "Why do you assume she will prevail?"

Vira pursed her lips. "You're growing tired."

He gave her a warning look. A sign that subtly whispered, *don't remind me*, or, *don't let the others know.*

The image of Ferrin dropping his arms in fatigue in front of Maya and Estell came back to Naomi. He did look tired then. But didn't he just need rest? They all did. A full night's sleep would rejuvenate him. It had to. He was a legendary Magnificent. He couldn't grow so weary. Could he?

Dina stepped forward. "Speak to Captain Bromulin for us and we'll do whatever is necessary to keep this golden witch out."

Vira turned away from Ferrin and smiled at her. "Thank you." She collected herself. "Where do you suggest we stay? Is Millie staying with Heatheren still?"

Amani looked down, avoiding eye contact with Dina, leaving her to do the dirty work.

"Heatheren drowned in the river during a summer storm last year," Dina said with a tremor in her voice. "She was out in a fishing boat and the storm came too fast."

Vira's words slung out like venom. "And no one sought me out? Who has Millie?"

"Millie is attending school and doing well," Dina rushed to say. "She stays with Professor Som and his wife now. They treat her well."

"Why wasn't I told of this?" she accused again. "That my own daughter lost her caretaker?"

Hux's cheeks went rigid. Naomi noticed his wide-eyed shock, revealing he didn't know about Millie. Until now, at least.

Dina tugged on her chest plate. "You were gone on important business. You sent your daughter here to be cared for, so that's what we're doing. We're making sure she's cared for."

Vira bit her bottom lip and directed her horse forward. "What lodges have availability?"

"Take the librarian's turret," Dina said, sounding ashamed. "He's off on a six-week trade journey. He would want you to use it."

Naomi remained quiet as Ferrin allowed his horse to follow Vira's between the two ivy covered entrance turrets. Vira left her own daughter to one day find Naomi. It was unfair. To Millie, to Vira, to the people of Mira Isla.

"Vira," Dina called after them.

Vira turned, but only slightly.

Dina hesitated. "She goes by Millicent now. Not Millie."

Apparently that was the drop of water that broke the dam. Vira leaned forward and urged her horse into a gallop. Hux held on for dear life at the sudden jolt.

Naomi clutched Ferrin's cloak, prepared for him to follow just as fast, but he let his horse mosey forward. They traveled away from Dina and Amani and rounded a bend and out of sight. Vira and Hux were far ahead.

"I know what you're thinking," he said.

She dug her teeth into the inside of her cheek, holding back tears.

"You didn't make Vira do anything." He let his horse walk slowly. They strolled through the grass, staying close to the tree line, still able to see Mira Isla glistening below in the dying sun.

"How could Vira know about my bloodline before I even did?" she groaned, defeated. "She shouldn't have left her own daughter for me."

"Vira is a golden witch." He looked at her. "Important things are revealed to golden witches and Magnificents that must be taken seriously. Your existence was one of those important messages."

She gazed down at Mira Isla. "But who revealed my existence to her?"

He ran a hand through his horse's mane. "Protection."

"Do you fully believe in Protection's involvement with Thãen?"

"It's hard to determine exactly what I believe. I'd believe in Protection wholeheartedly if it would just wrap its fingers around Thãen and keep Calamity out. That would make more sense to me."

"Of course it would make more sense to us," she agreed. "But would that make more sense in their realm?"

He tilted his head, looking back at her again. "What do you mean?"

She waved her hands above her head. "The realm up there. Out there. Whatever. The Outer Void. What if we don't understand it because it's totally different than down here? The rules could be different. Our reality isn't the same as, well, the sovereign powers."

He wore a half smile. "You have a decent point, Miss Massoud."

A butterfly took flight in her stomach. "I thought you couldn't call me by that name."

"Mira Isla is a safe place," he countered. "And we're alone right now. So we're safe. You're safe."

His last words rolled into her heart with gentle reassurance. *You're safe*. She believed it. With him she was protected. It was a beautiful revelation for her soul. To be guarded by someone else other than herself. "Do you feel safe with me?" She almost choked as the question spilled out. She regretted asking it, but he didn't even flinch.

"Because you move mountains?" He chuckled. "Literally."

Naomi swallowed, but nodded, wanting to hear the truth.

He halted the horse. "I'm not afraid of you. What you did back there was impressive and gave me hope."

"Gave you hope?" She drew her chin back. "I turned Thãen's terrain around. That should be...alarming."

"Alarming to who?" He dismounted.

Hesitantly, she joined him on the ground. "I don't know. Just, alarming."

He flashed a fake grin. "Then consider me alarmed."

She scowled. "You're teasing me."

"Of course, I'm teasing you." He stepped in front of her, blocking her from walking away. He rested both of his hands on her shoulders. "You might be able to beat The Dark Hand. Do you understand that? Do you realize what that means? It means no more cities destroyed. No more shadows snatching kids from their beds."

"I might be too late." She felt her breath catch.

He softened his touch on her shoulders. "Late?"

"My Papa," she said, blinking away memories. "He told me that one day Calamity might hold too many of Thãen's people in its hand. When that happens, the scales will tip. Thãen will roll from Protection's hand into Calamity's."

Ferrin must not have heard it explained that way before because his eyes lit up with understanding, like a student finally comprehending a mathematical equation. "So you're not too late."

She stepped back from his hands. "Not today, but what about tomorrow? If Calamity takes one more person, the scale could falter."

"But that hasn't happened yet." He turned and began to walk, his horse obediently following.

She jogged after them. "You think there really is a chance to defeat Calamity?"

He let her catch up. "Like I said, Naomi, seeing what you did back there gave me hope. I've seen golden witches and Magnificents do incredible things, but none of them could move mountains."

CHAPTER THIRTY-SIX

The librarian's turret sat alone on a piece of elevated rock that jutted out from a tree line of weeping willows. The turret had a pointed roof and was the same light brown as the pillars Dina and Amani guarded. One arched window sat at the top facing west to overlook Mira Isla and its grand river. The bottom portion of the turret didn't have a window, only a thick wooden door.

Ferrin let his horse rest outside and opened the door for Naomi. She stepped into the dim space. The single room was circular, fitting the shape of the building. A ceiling of wood cut the turret in half and a set of stone steps edged along the wall upward to the second floor. A ropey, woven rug covered most of the floor and an oak kitchen table took up the rest of the main space. A sink with a water pump and cupboards sat against the wall, shaped to fit the rounded stone.

Vira and Hux stood next to a hearth, leaning into the fire they must have just lit. They both stopped talking when she and Ferrin entered. Naomi's eyes darted to the stairs where a child was running down.

"It's cool in here, Mum," the little girl said. Her hair was jet black, exactly like Vira's, and it was pulled back into a messy ponytail. She stopped at the bottom of the steps when she saw Naomi and Ferrin. Her mouth dropped open. "Mum, is that her?"

Naomi itched to run away. *Mum, is that her? The girl you left me for?*

Vira moved toward Millie, who looked to be no more than eight-years-old. "Yes, this is Naomi."

Millicent grinned. "You're very pretty, Miss."

Naomi pointed to herself.

"Yes," the girl blushed, "you."

"Oh," she found her voice. "Thank you." She felt Ferrin staring, but didn't look his way.

Millicent cocked her head. "She looks normal, Mum."

"Millicent!" Vira playfully covered the girl's mouth.

Her daughter laughed and pulled away from her touch. "Mum, can I show you my drawings from school?"

Vira got down on her knees, facing her. "Yes, of course you can. I just need to get settled here, then I'll meet you at Professor Som's house. Does that sound okay?"

Millicent looked like she was about to argue, but she hung her head and nodded. "Yes. But don't be too long. You've been away a long time and I sort of miss you."

"Sort of?" Vira smiled with angst.

"A little more than sort of," she admitted.

Vira kissed her forehead then stood. "I'll see you soon. Are you okay walking back alone?"

"I always walk alone, Mum."

Vira's cheeks wavered. "Alright. See you soon, love."

With Millicent gone, the room was quiet. Stale even.

Hux busied himself with buffing his shield in the fire's light.

Vira touched Naomi's sleeve. "Are you well?"

"I'm tired," she caved. "Really tired."

"You look it. Go upstairs and rest. After what you did today, your body probably needs it." She cast a hard, meaningful stare at Ferrin. "You, too."

He matched her intensity. "I'm fine, Vira."

She ignored him, turning back to Hux, who looked up cautiously.

Ferrin gently nudged Naomi forward. "Come on. We'll go upstairs and rest."

Sweat gathered on Naomi's palms again, but she headed for the stone stairs. Vira and Hux seemed out of touch, like they needed to square something away with one another. She would rather be hidden upstairs with Ferrin than in the middle of an argument between those two.

The upstairs was the same size as the main floor but a bed with tall, cherry-wood posts filled most of the space. A flat clothes trunk sat under the stone window sill. There was no glass to block the outside air from getting in. The window was carved out, agape. The view drew Naomi in. She crossed the wood-planked floor to stare out. By now night had fallen, and the wind seemed to announce a storm coming. Flames of light flickered like specks in the distance within Mira Isla, but the silhouette of mountains behind the city brought her focus upward. Stars appeared occasionally when there was a break in the blowing storm clouds. A low rumble sounded in the distance, and she leaned against the sill. The thunder was calming. The wind was gentle. Even though a storm was brewing, Mira Isla was like a warm cup of tea and a feathery blanket.

The breeze blew in through the window and flicked the edge of Ferrin's cloak. He shed the layer, tossed it onto the bed and undid the top three buttons of his shirt.

Naomi glanced back at him. "You can sleep on the bed first. I'm too awake to rest."

He stepped up behind her. "You told Vira you were exhausted."

She turned, facing him. "I am, but my mind is not."

"You should rest anyway." He rolled up his shirt sleeves.

Watching him reveal his wrists brought her thoughts back to her own skin. "Did you heal the bruises? On my wrists?"

He looked up from his sleeve and smiled.

She smirked. "Why'd you have to be so sneaky about it?"

He took a step closer to her. His closeness sent an unfamiliar shock through her limbs. "I didn't want to frighten you," he said plainly. "Just like how you thought what you did with nature could make me think you're dangerous."

She watched his forehead. "Oh."

He took yet another step toward her, the space between them shrinking, almost disappearing.

She looked up at him, heart wailing with anxiety. She wanted to ask what he was doing, why he was so near to her. But she couldn't come up with the words. Though his body didn't touch hers, she could feel it. His presence. His warmth.

"I feel safe with you," he finally said through a hurried breath.

She stayed looking up at him, fighting the urge to pull back. "Why is that?"

"You're similar to me. Sometimes I see myself in you." He glanced out the window. "Only you still have the chance to do things right the first time." He set a gentle gaze on her again. "I want to help you do that. I want to help you control whatever powers you find within yourself. But more importantly, I want to protect you from making poor choices with them."

"Ferrin." She straightened, attempting to look as stern as she could. "I appreciate you wanting to help, and I know I need it, but I can read it all over your face. You think helping me will fix you."

He blinked. "Isn't that how you attain redemption? You do the right thing to blot out the wrong."

"Why do you have to *do* something to feel restored? Can't you simply forgive yourself?"

"You fix past mistakes with better present decisions." He pressed his palms together and shoved them her way, trying to drill home the thought.

"No." She held a finger up to his desperate gesture. "You can't fix the past. You learn from it and you do things differently the second time around, but you can't fix what was done. You've tied yourself to your past. The reason you still despise who you are is because you're trying to fix yourself by correcting something that can't be undone. You've trapped yourself in misery."

The side of his neck visibly pulsed. "So what am I supposed to do? Say, *oh well, Oliver died because of me, but I'm still worthy of life?*"

"*Yes.*" She grabbed his arms. "You're still here, aren't you?"

He stayed silent.

"You still have a purpose. You've said so yourself. If you keep swinging back and forth on a pendulum of restoration and condemnation, you're going to get confused and incredibly tired, Ferrin."

He pulled his arms away from her grasp. "I *am* tired, Naomi." His voice slipped away. "I'm going to lay down."

She watched him meander to the bed. With his back to her, she allowed her expression to reveal the pain she felt for him.

With a sigh, he crawled onto the bed and collapsed face down on top of the covers. His shoulders rose and fell with steady breaths, eventually slowing to a sleeper's pace.

"I wouldn't be here without you," she whispered, though she knew he couldn't hear her. "You have purpose."

Downstairs, a fire leapt in the hearth. Vira and Hux sat in two wooden chairs on either side of it. Though there were no windows in the circular room, Hux could tell it had started raining by the soft tink of water hitting the turret's stone.

He leaned into the flames, his elbows resting on his knees. "Why didn't you tell me about Millicent?"

Vira closed her eyes and pressed two fingers to her forehead. "I didn't find it necessary."

"Necessary?" He resisted sounding strained. "We're friends, Vira. Lifelong friends. I could have helped."

She snapped her eyes open. "Helped? You, the lead Rider of Raina, helping the exiled golden witch." She leaned forward, too, rubbing her face. "I appreciate how willing you are to be there for me, but I am simply not who I was when we knew each other in Raina."

He gazed down at his hands. One stronger than the other, but both willing to work. To help. "Yet you came to my rescue in Ode," he pointed out.

"Yes, Hux, because though I am different, I still care for you."

"So why is that so hard for you to understand when it comes to me?" He clutched his chest. "You're different now, I'm different now, but we still have the same level of care for one another. Why can't you accept my help? Or even my trust?" His hard stare lingered on her. "Vira."

She barely looked at him.

"Vira," he said again. "Trust me with who you are. If you've changed, I want to know the new you."

"And that," her voice shook, "is what I've been petrified of since we've reconnected."

"What?" He sat back in his chair. "Why? Please, tell me. You made poor decisions? Well so have I. So has Ferrin. Probably Naomi, too. We all do it."

"It's worse than poor decisions, Huxton." She stood in rage, her chair falling backward behind her.

He stayed seated, staring up at her. "*Vira*. Explain it to me. Please."

She crossed her arms and faced the fire. "How do you think I got Millicent?"

"Well." He squirmed. "I don't think that's very hard to figure out."

She almost dared to laugh, but swallowed it, feeling an upcoming sob instead. "Millicent wasn't made with someone I love. In fact, I don't know who her father is."

"Okay," he said slowly. "I see the picture you're painting here."

"It's a beautiful picture, isn't it?" she spit with sarcasm. "It's detestable, really. Horrendous. It was how I made money in Zul. Estell introduced me to the idea of it. I didn't dare use my magic to make money and corrupt my powers. So I decided to corrupt my physical body instead."

He rose, approaching her side. She flinched back, creating more distance.

"Please." He held his hands up. "Trust me when I say I don't detest you."

"And why shouldn't you?" She faced him, the fire burning to her right, Hux's eyes reflecting its flames.

"Because I know you," he tried to convince her. "You did what you felt you needed to do."

"But I had every opportunity to turn away."

"And didn't you?"

She flashed a haggard look. "Yes, but only after Millicent."

"But you did it. It's done. Over."

"It's over." She laughed, a wild, sickening sound. "But it will never truly be over. Because I remember what I did. I regret it. And I'm full of distaste at myself for it."

"Don't say that about yourself." He reached for her arm.

"Please don't touch me." She withdrew, her voice slipping into a controlled sob. "I can't bear to taint your hands."

His eyes clouded with sorrow. "Do you believe this? Do you believe you're covered in filth because of what you did?"

"I know I am." A tear slid to her nose. "I've accepted it. Now you know. You can leave if you'd like."

"Leave?" He held a fist at his side. "I'm not going anywhere. The only going I should have done was eleven years ago. I should have ditched Raina and followed you."

The tears dotting her cheeks stopped on her taut skin. "There was no reason for you to follow me."

He groaned, wildly exasperated. "Of course there was. I was madly devoted to you."

She paused, perplexed. "Madly devoted." Her tone was stale, as if in disbelief.

"Wasn't it obvious?" He sighed. "I was starting to love you. Then you were cast out of Raina. My heart felt like a sinkhole." He held an arm across his chest. "It was too early to love you, but too late to forget."

She stood still, rubbing her arms slowly, swallowing every word he dared confess.

"Please don't put a wall between us." He held his hand out to her once more. "I've waited years to be next to you again."

She held a hand over her face, covering her tears. "Hux."

He waited for her to say more, but all he heard were sobs. When he touched her free hand, he expected her to pull away. But she didn't. Instead, she clung to his fingers like she would be swallowed up by the ground if she let go.

CHAPTER THIRTY-SEVEN

Naomi threw herself forward, wincing in pain as her neck creaked with stiffness. She had fallen asleep sitting on the floor and leaning against the stone wall. The turret's upstairs room was still dark, but a hazy, pink morning light seeped through the window.

Rising to wobbly feet, she scanned the room. Her heart pounded. A sound had snapped her awake. Ferrin was still lying face down on the bed. She hadn't had the heart to wake him and ask for a turn on the mattress. And she didn't have a clear conscience to lie down beside him.

Movement near the window snagged her attention.

A man.

He stood tall with hunched shoulders, his face shielded by shadows. Shadows that bounced off him.

She froze, limbs going numb. "You," she called out. "Who are you?"

The figure turned his head, slow like a thick, heavy gear. His face met hers, red irises and expanded pupils gazing through a shadow-laden face. When he opened his mouth to snarl, three flies flew out.

The sudden appearance of the bugs sent her staggering into the wall farthest from the figure. "Ferrin!" she screamed.

Ferrin stirred.

The man moved forward, sending dust swirling behind him in miniature tornados. He was either dressed in flowing silk or he was completely made up of the same material.

Shadows, Naomi realized with terror. This man was made up of shadows.

"Ferrin, wake up!" she tried again.

The figure crossed the room toward her. She bolted to the stairs and not so much ran down as fell down, screaming at the top of her lungs. "Hux! Vira!"

Hux leapt up from the floor, out of sleep in half a second. The blanket that was draped over his body fell to the floor. His sword was in his hand before she reached the bottom stair.

"Behind me," she gasped. "He's right behind me." She landed on the floor, cracking her foot, and sprinted to Hux.

He pulled her to him, shoving her behind his wide stance. "Where, Naomi? Who?"

"Calamity!" She shook behind his protective body. "The Dark Hand has come for me."

"Naomi." He lowered his sword. "I don't see—"

She searched the bottom room, eyes frantic. "Where's Vira? Calamity took Vira!"

He eyed the stairs one more time then turned to face her. "Calm down, it's okay. Vira stayed with Millicent last night."

Naomi could hear her own breaths. Hux's face was inches from hers, scrunched and concerned, but behind him there was nothing. No shadow man with red eyes and a mouth full of flies following her down the stairs.

"He's after Ferrin." She shoved past him. "Ferrin!"

"What? What?" Ferrin came bounding down the steps. His shirt was wrinkled and the side of his face was covered with lines from uninterrupted sleep. He staggered down the last step, tearing toward her.

"Naomi, he's okay." Hux said it gently, but the words held a hint of concern.

She stood between the two. Hux at her back, Ferrin at her front, his eyes still slogged with sleep.

"Did you see him?" She grabbed the front of Ferrin's shirt. "The man? It was Calamity, Ferrin, I know it!"

He held her shoulders, frowning. He flicked his eyes up to Hux.

Hux shook his head. "I didn't see anything. I'm sorry."

"*No,*" she cried. "He was in the room with me!" She shook Ferrin. "You have to believe me. Please. Flies flew out of his mouth. He was evil!"

Hux touched her back. "Flies?" He looked up and around. "Okay. Let's say this did happen. What—"

"It *did* happen." She yanked her hands away from Ferrin and waved them spastically toward Hux. "We're in danger."

Again, Hux focused on Ferrin. "I believe her. I never told her about how a swarm of flies took one of my men. She couldn't think that up."

"Of course I didn't think anything up!" She wanted to shove him. "I'm not *crazy.*"

"No." Hux steadied her by the tops of her shoulders. "But dreams can feel real when you're truly frightened. Although a dream would be a logical explanation for this situation, I believe you. I don't put anything past The Dark Hand."

Ferrin paced the length of the room. "A man." He mumbled something to himself. "Calamity in the form of a man?"

"He was hardly a man," she justified. "He was made of shadows. And had red eyes."

"I've never experienced Calamity presenting itself as a whole, physical figure," Ferrin doubted. "The Dark Hand destroys and steals in utterly disgusting ways, but I've never seen or heard of Calamity walking around Thãen amongst its people."

"It'd do something different for me." Naomi drooped, feeling Hux's hands fall away. "I bet it would break every rule to get rid of me." Her insides lurched. "I need to leave. I need to get away from all of you."

Ferrin spun on his heels, nearly tripping as he strode toward her. "Are you joking? With as much respect as I can muster, no. Absolutely not. You will not carry the task alone."

She swallowed a protest, but knew he was right. She simply couldn't survive alone. "Then we need to make it as hard as possible for Calamity to gain any sort of advantage." She dug into her pockets. "Here. Here's the necklace."

He caught it as she threw it at him with haste.

"Who has the quill?" she demanded. "Vira?"

"Yes," Hux confirmed.

"Good. Let's keep the two items separated." She spoke like a military leader, but shook. "I have no idea how they're connected to me, but Calamity might. If Calamity does get to me, then at least it can destroy me and not those."

Ferrin stared at the piece of jewelry in his palm. "I have an idea." He curled his fingers around it, shaking his fist with thought. "Is the sun up yet? Where's Vira?"

"She's in the city with Millicent," Hux said for the second time that morning. "I don't know what time it is, but something tells me Naomi doesn't care if the sun's up. Am I right?" He raised a brow at her.

"Time is not on our side," she stammered. "So sunrise or not, let's do whatever Ferrin has planned."

Ferrin's lip curled into a smile at her urgency. For a moment he saw a flash of himself in her. His past, willing self. And in this moment, he wanted that part of himself back. "Alright. Get ready to head out. It'll take us half an hour to get to the heart of Mira Isla from here."

"Shouldn't we tell Vira?" Naomi was already heading for the stairs.

He followed. "She'll know. I've already sent the message into the air. She'll get it, I'm sure."

She looked over her shoulder at him as they climbed the stairs. "Must be nice to speak without actually having to open your mouth."

He put on a wry smile. "Must be nice to command the mountains to move."

She froze at the top of the stairs, towering over him. "Did you just make a joke?"

"Are you laughing?"

"No."

"Why not?"

He moved up the stairs to be one step away from her.

She stood above him only slightly now, able to see the swirls of greens and browns in his eyes. "Because it's not all that funny that I have powers that scare me."

His grin disappeared. "Why are you afraid?"

She breathed a few times before speaking. "What if I wish for the ground to do something out of anger or revenge, and then I regret it?"

"Most powers rely on extreme emotional control." He joined her at the top of the stairs, put an arm around her shoulders and walked her into the room. "That's what I'll help you learn."

She tried to sift through what she was feeling at his friendly arm, but she could only focus on the overpowering sense of comfort. "What if you don't teach me in time? What if tonight I mess up and send Mira Isla skyrocketing to the clouds?"

"Why do you bother yourself with what-ifs?" He dropped his arm and faced her.

She looked up at him. "I've personally heard you live by what-ifs as well, ranger. Don't point fingers at me."

He held his palms up. "I'm not pointing fingers, *Miss Smyth*. I'm learning the game of life right alongside you. Can't my words be for both you and me?"

She puckered her lips. "I'm not Miss Smyth."

"You resorted to calling me ranger first." He was smiling again. "I'll play the game, Naomi."

"What game?" Though when she said it, her heart leapt with the knowledge of what he was talking about. The game of enemies. They coped through a strange, shared vibe of sternness and spit-fire. It kept them grounded but also pushed each other forward. But was it truly a game? If it was, what was the reality? What is the opposite of enemies?

"Stay sharp, Massoud," he whispered, and brisked past her to gather his cloak.

CHAPTER THIRTY-EIGHT

Naomi walked sandwiched between Ferrin and Hux as they entered Mira Isla's city. They crossed the river over a high arching stone bridge with twisted gold rails. Waterfalls fell from pockets within the cliff where the city was built. The streets wound through white buildings capped with gold domes or terraces. Trees with amber and yellow leaves sat wedged in crevices between buildings or clung to the edge of the cliff, leaning out to hang over the city. With the sun rising, the city appeared pink as the light reflected off of the mist from the waterfalls.

A few residents of Mira Isla were awake, opening the shutters over the windows of their businesses or sweeping leaves away from their front doors.

"It seems like it's early fall here," Naomi noted as she glanced around.

Ferrin strode up the cobblestone street, seeming to take his time now that they were in the heart of his home. "It is. The seasons here are opposite of Thãen. When it's spring there, it's fall here. And when it's summer here, it's winter there."

Hux's eyes remained upward the whole time. The city

towered above, planted in the ledges of the cliff. Stacked. "To think this place has existed and I didn't know about it. Raina has never seemed so irrelevant in my life."

Naomi looked back at Hux. "What is Raina like?" She realized she had never asked him.

He finally looked down. "Raina." He stepped up to be shoulder to shoulder with her as they continued wherever Ferrin was leading them. "Every city has a reason for its name. Take Ode for example. Ode was a city filled with color and art. They were an ode to themselves. A song within the barren, rocky side of the west mountains. And Le'Gar? It means, *the dear*. The gargoyles watch the city as if the stone architecture is precious to them. Near and dear to their stiff hearts."

"Wow," she whispered. "I never knew that."

Even Ferrin tipped an ear to listen now.

"But Raina," Hux's voice dropped. "The reason for its name isn't so beautiful. The city is stone, like Le'Gar, but lacks in height and detail. And no gargoyles." He gave a slight smile. "Which I'm thankful for, though I know you don't mind them." He went on. "But Raina has rivers. A lot of them. They flow through the city. The city was actually built around them. They're needed because Raina sees a lot of rain. Hence the name."

Dry leaves crossed the cobblestone in front of Naomi's shoes. "That's not a bad story. Rain isn't always terrible."

"I agree. But our rivers are deep red. Even after it rains and the waters flow faster, the red remains."

Her eyebrows drew together. "Your rivers are red?"

He nodded. "From ground clay. That's the consensus anyway. But there are other suspicions."

Ferrin perked up. "Suspicions like what? I've seen your rivers. It always struck me as odd that clay could alter the water that significantly."

Hux looked to Ferrin. "Years ago, a doctor in our city had his students take samples of the water to see if it was safe to drink. If clay was the only culprit of the red color, then filtering the water would leave it fairly clean. But the doctor's findings showed something very strange."

"What did he find?" Naomi pried.

"Hints of ink."

"Ink?" Naomi asked.

Ferrin matched her skewed look. "In the water?"

"It makes no sense." Hux held his palm up in confusion. "But that's what the doctor claimed. It's unknown where the traces of ink come from. Some believe it comes from the rain itself. Perhaps a curse over Raina. Nowhere else that we know of has red rivers. So though Raina is blessed with storms, it's cursed with toxins."

"I see why the name carries both good and bad connotations," Naomi pondered. "Though it's interesting enough."

The street curled around a tree with roots protruding through the cobblestone cracks. Another walkway snaked between two buildings to the left, wet with runoff water. The way was dim, unlit.

Ferrin stopped and glanced around, straightening when he saw Vira striding toward them from the direction they had just come.

She waved. "Sorry for the delay. I saw Millicent off to school." She reached them. "What's the urgent matter, Ferrin? Your message in the air startled me."

He quieted his voice. "We may not be in Mira Isla alone. It's possible The Dark Hand has found us here."

"In Mira Isla?" Her lips were taught, and she spoke just as softly as he. "Calamity has never put a finger on this city."

"But I saw it," Naomi spoke up. "This morning. Upstairs in the turret."

"You *saw* it?" She snapped her head to Hux. "All of you?"

Hux and Ferrin shared a glance.

"No," Hux admitted. "It disappeared before I had a chance to look and Ferrin was still sleeping."

Naomi's muscles tightened with irritation at Vira's skeptical eyes. "I saw it." She made sure to keep her stare leveled and unwavering. "I don't care if you think I'm lying, I know what came after me and I know I'm not crazy."

"You aren't crazy," Vira said hastily. "And I never thought you were lying. I'm just trying to make sense of it."

She nodded, sensing the truth in her words.

"We need answers," Ferrin took control. "You have the quill?"

Vira stuck her hand beneath her cloak. "I do."

"Keep it hidden," he commanded. "The man we're going to visit won't need to see it. He'll only need to inspect the necklace." He stepped into the dark walkway. "Follow me and keep quiet. His workshop is hidden for a reason."

Naomi stuck close to his elbow as her feet splashed in cold puddles. "Who is he?"

"A jeweler." He put an arm around her shoulders and leaned into her ear. "He makes enchanted pieces."

His breath against her ear sent prickles down her arms. "Why is his work hidden if Mira Isla is full of magic anyway?"

He didn't remove his arm from her. "Just because those who live in Mira Isla have abilities doesn't mean they're all good. Thieves still prowl. Alliances and questionable tasks still occur. Better to keep enchanted items a secret than to reveal them with blind trust."

"Won't the jeweler be skeptical of four strangers plowing into his workshop?" she asked, a hint of fear riding on her words.

Ferrin pulled away and faced the alley wall. He waved his

hand sideways in a wiping motion and an unnoticeable rock door slid open. "He knows me."

Naomi followed after him through the door. Stone steps led down. She tried not to step on his heels as the darkness intensified with their descent, but Hux wasn't so graceful. His toes grazed the back of her heels three times before he grunted, apologizing. But once they reached the bottom, a tunnel came into view that was brighter than the stairway. Flames behind metal lanterns sat like cages in the walls, illuminating the way. The walls were wet with threads of water that trickled through the stone's cracks like broken spiderwebs.

"Did the jeweler put these lanterns in?" Naomi asked Ferrin's back.

"No." He cut right. "I did."

"So you knew him well?"

He chuckled. "I had to install them as punishment when I was fifteen. I tried to steal one of his watches from the market. I was caught, so my punishment was physical labor."

Vira scoffed from behind them. "And you think he'll be glad to see you?"

Ferrin stopped at a wooden door at the end of the tunnel. "He grew to like me enough."

"You better hope so," Naomi said.

He held his knuckles over the door and took a deep breath before knocking. When he did, the door opened right away.

An old man's face appeared right in front of Ferrin's. His beard was short, a mix of grays and whites. His eyes sagged into soft skin and his lips were cracked. The nose of his face stuck out as far as a crow's beak. "I *knew* it was you, you filthy Mag." His dry lips turned up into a grin. "I could hear your footsteps coming down the tunnel. Scrip, scrap, scrip, scrap, your feet always go when you're exhausted. Just dragging yourself along. I've told you to put your feet up every once in a while!" He reached forward and pulled Ferrin's head into his chest.

Ferrin leaned into the jeweler's embrace, giving him a firm hug in return.

Naomi found herself smiling. So Ferrin was capable of accepting affection. Even if it was from a jeweler whom he had tried to steal from.

The jeweler stepped back from Ferrin and glanced out the doorway at the others. "Who the grave are they? You know the rule, Fin: no outsiders *or* insiders in my shop. Ever."

Again, Naomi caught herself suppressing a smile. *Fin?* She would have to remember that for later. Fuel for their fake fire.

Ferrin stepped back, lightly bumping into her. "This is a different situation, Brahm. We need your expertise desperately."

Brahm lingered on Naomi for a moment before flicking his eyes to Hux, then Vira. "Millicent's mother?" He shot his focus back to Ferrin. "What have you gotten yourself into?"

Ferrin held his hand out to Naomi. "Give me the necklace."

She drew it out and placed it in his hand. It glowed against his palm, extra vibrant in the dim tunnel.

Brahm's entire face lifted. "A capsule pendant."

"You know what this is?" Ferrin's voice perked.

Brahm looked down the tunnel before waving everyone inside. "Come in. All of you."

They spilled into the workshop. The room was squished already, and the extra bodies made it seem like it could combust. Metal pieces hovered in the air in disarray, shelved in the open air. Wood tables sat in no particular linear fashion and took up almost every inch of space. They were covered with springs and screws and strange vials filled with cloudy material. The room smelled of metal and rainwater.

Brahm took the necklace to a table with a gigantic magnifying glass hinged on a tripod. He set the necklace on the table and lowered the magnifying glass to hover above it. "A pearl inside a crescent moon," he said. "A symbol of prosperity within the universe."

Naomi nudged past Ferrin and stepped up to the edge of the table, looking through the glass at her necklace. "Prosperity? I was never rich."

His droopy eyelids lifted to her. "This is yours?"

"A family piece," she confirmed.

Ferrin stepped up behind her, leaning over her shoulder. "Is the symbol significant?"

Vira and Hux joined around the table. All five heads ducked together, gazing down at the glowing pearl.

"The symbol is just a symbol." Brahm poked the moon with metal tweezers. "But the glow. That's what makes this a capsule pendant."

Naomi's heart quickened. "Capsule, as in, it holds something?"

Brahm grunted, moving the tweezer tips to the pearl. "Yes. Why do you think it glows?"

She shifted, unsure. Even Ferrin didn't speak.

"It's because the pearl holds something within," the jeweler whispered, focused on the piece. "The glow is from a liquid. Something enchanted."

Naomi eyed the cloudy vials on Brahm's many tables. "Like what you have here?"

He nodded. "Yes. But my serums are held in lockets or mixed with liquid gold and then cooled. I could never accomplish filling a pearl. In fact, I don't know anyone who can." He straightened. "Where did you get this necklace?"

"I got it as a gift from my parents when I was four," Naomi said.

"And where did they get it from?"

She looked down, a wave of longing pressing on her chest. "I'm not sure. I lost them before I ever thought to ask them."

Ferrin put a gentle hand on her arm. "Brahm, what else can you tell us about the necklace?"

"Well." He picked up the piece and placed it back in Naomi's hand, curling her fingers around it. "Capsule pendants are meant to remain with their keepers. Otherwise, they don't work. And they can only be opened with a key. This glow you're seeing means one thing: the key is near."

Naomi's limbs thrummed. *The quill.* The key had to be the quill. Why else would the quill be glowing as well?

Brahm read her eyes. "Do you have another item?"

"No," she said, quick and short. "Just the necklace, as far as I'm aware." She could sense the tension floating between her companions. To share or not to share. Even though Brahm was proving to be helpful and safe, she couldn't risk it. Not when Vira put her entire life on hold to uncover the mystery surrounding the Massoud name. And Hux had abandoned the only life he knew by treason to keep the quill safe. And Ferrin? He was putting himself in the position to fail again. To see a Massoud die again. "But I'll be on the lookout." She bowed her head in thanks. "At least I know more now than I did."

The jeweler sighed and squeezed Ferrin's shoulder. "I understand the need for secrecy in pressing times. I'm no stranger to that. Why do you think my shop is underground?" He smiled, a relieved look. "You're supposed to be old, Fin."

Ferrin placed his hand on the old man's. "I'm a Magnificent. You know logic doesn't apply."

"Logic," Brahm mumbled. "Your age isn't logical, even as a Magnificent. I knew you. You had fire and passion. There was a purpose out there for you to find when you left Mira Isla." His whiskers sagged. "What happened? Why are you still here?"

Naomi stepped back to stand between Hux and Vira. She

watched Ferrin droop under Brahm's touch. He looked defeated, but even more tired.

"I made a horrible mistake," Ferrin said softly. "So I'm here to try again."

Brahm pulled him into an embrace. "You're still in there, Fin." His lips moved close to Ferrin's ear. "There's still fire behind your eyes. Find it. Claw it back to the surface." He stepped back, facing him. "And don't stay away so long this time. You think you're alone, but I'm never leaving." His last words ended in a whisper and his body faded away, leaving the workshop empty.

Ferrin stood alone, staring at the space where Brahm had just been.

Hux frowned, looking around the room.

Naomi nudged Vira. "Where'd he go?"

"Back to his resting place," Vira said quietly. "Brahm has been long dead. Think about it. Ferrin was fifteen when he knew him."

Ferrin moved his fingers through the air slowly, as if feeling if Brahm was really gone. "I knew he'd come if I needed him. Even in death we have purpose." He stepped back toward the group.

Naomi moved over so he could join. He nudged up next to her.

"Should we have told him about the quill?" she questioned. "If he's dead, he isn't a threat."

"That's not true." Ferrin turned away, heading back to the door. "The realm of death can have an influence on our world just as well. Better to be cautious." He stepped through the door, leaving the three in the shop. His footsteps echoed up the tunnel.

Naomi went to follow but stopped and turned to Hux. "Do you think he's okay? He seemed close to Brahm."

Hux nodded and waved Naomi forward. "In this life we lose people we love. It's a part of life. But not everyone gets to see their loved ones again. I'd say Ferrin is lucky."

She looked down at her feet as she made her way back up the tunnel. Ferrin was already out of sight. But Hux was right. She'd give anything to see her mother and father again. If only for a second. To hear their voices. Feel their embrace. She hadn't felt someone wrap their arms around her in years. She had forgotten what it felt like, but she knew she missed it. And she accepted that she would probably never feel it again. At least Ferrin had the chance at one more embrace from Brahm. Even if the jeweler was a dead man.

CHAPTER THIRTY-NINE

King Tal sat on the back ledge of the bell tower, his feet dangling. The night was quiet. The gargoyles remained frozen. Only a sliver of moon sat above the mountains. Towering over the city, King Tal could see the shape of the mountains. He never took to the roofs. He'd always been wary of getting so close to the gargoyles. He knew they saw things others didn't. But this moment was an exception.

There had been no sign of Saul and the other Riders in days. No message. He hoped to spot them striding down the mountainside, but to his dismay, the trees were inky black and alone. Did the ranger kill his men? It was possible. After all, Ferrin did try to kill the golden witch, Estell, on that dreadful night years ago. That was the story, anyway.

Tal rubbed his face, dragging his fingers through his beard. Why did he feel twisted? Unsettled? It was like he didn't know who he was. It was something he had felt before, but he always fixed it by going behind the curtain in the throne room, just like his family before him had. It was a secret ritual that kept them grounded. A ritual given to them by Calamity. A gift. Yet, every time he stepped behind the curtain, his hands would shake and cold sweat would line his neck and forehead. Calamity had chosen to uphold their royal bloodline as long as they served it. So Tal knew he couldn't be the one to break the cycle. It would mean death to his wife and three children and the end of his family's reign. He simply had to endure.

A shrill cry echoed from the mountains, snapping Tal back to reality. But it was only a mountain lion's call. Not Saul. Not his Riders.

A thump sounded below his feet and a head popped out from the window that held the bells. "Sir?"

Tal looked down at the young man, Adler, his top servant. "Yes? What is it?"

Adler hesitated. A single raindrop leaked from the sky and landed on his nose. "It's your father, sir."

———

Tal and Adler rushed side by side through the cathedral's west wing where the living quarters were located. The arched ceilings and raging torches made Tal feel like the hallway could swallow him up. His throat shrank, heart racing.

"Sir." Adler tried to slow him. "You need to prepare yourself. It's not a pretty sight."

"How long has he been dead?" Tal wheezed.

"I watched it happen, sir. I was at his bedside during my usual caretaker shift. I immediately came to find you."

"You didn't summon the doctor?"

Adler stopped at the thick, bedroom door. "I'm unaware of who knows your family's dealings. His death would give you away."

Tal hung his head, squeezing his eyes shut, cursing tears away. "Show me."

Hesitantly, Adler pushed open the door.

From the doorway, Tal could see his father's body lying in the bed with a sheet over his face. The curtains were drawn and the lanterns had been dimmed. He stepped forward, sensing Adler right behind. When he reached the edge of the bed, he couldn't lift a finger. Every good memory of his childhood washed over him. His father was a loving man. But just like everyone else in their bloodline, he was tainted by service to Calamity. It was all suddenly clear before him: his children would view him the same. A tainted father figure. Cursed.

Adler hovered his hand over the sheet on his father's face. "May I?"

Tal nodded.

When Adler drew the material back, the face of the body was ashen, as if he had died hours ago.

"He looks as a dead body should," Tal whispered. "Distressing, but not frightening."

Adler moved the sheet down, revealing his father's hands.

Tal staggered back. His father's hands were black. As if frostbite had taken over.

"It happened fast," Adler said. "One minute his hands were fine and the next they were filling up with black."

"You watched it happen?"

"I did. Your father requested to write you a letter, so I gave him paper, ink and a quill. While he was writing, his breathing became labored and suddenly the ink bottle fell to the floor."

Tal glanced down at the rug under the bed. A wet, black stain was next to the empty bottle.

Adler touched his father's fingers. "His hands started convulsing and turning into this. He thrust the letter into my chest before he took his last breath." He pulled the paper out from his inner pocket. "Here, sir."

Tal took it, hands shaking, as he held it close to his face and read. *Insert the key but warn Le'Gar. Ring the bell. Let*—He looked up. "He didn't get to finish it."

Adler looked down, shaking his head. "No, sir. Death came fast."

"Calamity didn't want my father to finish it. His hands are a symbol. Dark hands, Adler. My father belonged to The Dark Hand."

"So your father tried to defy Calamity in his last moments?" Adler pulled the sheet back over the body, pausing to stare at the eyes that he had shut with his own fingers. "Do you think that's why he died?"

"He was murdered." Tal dug his fingernails into his palms, crushing the letter. "Calamity murdered him. It will *always* murder."

Adler stood with his head sagging between his shoulders. "What are you going to do, sir?"

Tal sat on the edge of the bed, staring at the crumpled note. "I will still serve Calamity."

Adler nodded, silent.

Tal looked up. "I have three daughters. The eldest will be queen. If I defy Calamity, I'm condemning them all to death. If I keep my standing with it, only my eldest will have to carry the same burden I do now. Which is better, Adler?"

He only shook his head.

Tal stood, shouting. "I said which is better!"

"I don't know, sir!" he screamed back. "You live with death already!"

Tal dropped to his knees, covered his eyes and began to sob. "The grave take me before I have to decide."

CHAPTER FORTY

Late afternoon in Mira Isla came with dark clouds and nipping wind. Even so, the city below the turret remained lively with torches and the smell of evening meals roasting in the hearths. The mix of the smell and the autumn air comforted Naomi as she led the two horses away from the creek and back to the turret. The others had insisted on joining her, but she craved alone time. Living by herself for years hadn't prepared her for this constant company. As much as she was thankful for the companionship, the quiet of the woods refilled her. Besides, Ferrin seemed so tired that he may have fallen asleep in the middle of the trees if he had come.

The turret appeared and Naomi broke through the tree line and let the horses free to roam the grass surrounding the tower. She ambled to the edge of the cliff and stared down. She wished Mira Isla could keep her forever. It was meant for those with powers, after all.

She thought back to how she had commanded a mountain to appear and willed a basin to fill up and turn into a portal. It seemed like a dream now. But nonetheless, she lowered herself to her knees and placed her palms on the patchy moss covering the stone ground. Closing her eyes, she reached into her mind. *Make wildflowers grow.* When she opened her eyes and looked down, nothing under her hands had changed. The moss remained the same.

She tried again. *Make wildflowers grow.*

The ground didn't even budge.

"How?" she whispered. "How do I control it?"

She stood and headed for the turret's front door. Fresh footprints in the dirt told her that Hux had left, probably to get more wood for the hearth before the rain came. She put her palm on the splintery door and was about to push it open when Vira's voice from inside stopped her.

"Let me see, Ferrin." Vira's voice sounded demanding, yet worried.

Naomi pressed her ear against the door and heard soft shuffling around.

Vira's voice came again after a long pause. "You need to hold off on using your powers with such intensity. You haven't used them in years. Your body isn't fit for this amount. Not until you retrain it."

Ferrin's voice was sour. "I'd rather die than fail again. I'll use my powers however I see fit."

"And what if it really does kill you?" she asked hotly.

"Then you three keep going without me."

Naomi drew back. Why were his powers harming him? And how?

Vira's voice dropped, almost inaudible. "Naomi needs you."

Silence.

"She doesn't need me," he grumbled.

"She trusts you."

The snap of a twig made Naomi's head turn. She gazed into the forest, but all was still. Turning her head back to the door, she fought to hear what Ferrin was saying, but a rustling of leaves drew her away again. She hesitated for a moment, considering the options before her. She could ignore her instincts and head inside, hoping the noise was just an animal scampering across the forest floor. She could tell Vira and Ferrin about it and drag them out into the woods only to find nothing. Or she could inspect it herself.

Walking cautiously, she crossed the mossed-over rock to the tree line. The dark clouds above tinted the forest, but night hadn't fallen yet, giving Naomi enough reassurance to head into the trees. The turret shrunk from view as she crept forward. Wet leaves rotted the air, penetrating her nose. She didn't remember smelling it that strongly when she had led the horses to the creek.

The treetops clicked together in a sudden wind. She tilted her head back.

The sun was gone.

A voice slid past her ear. "*Omi.*"

Spinning around, she swung a fist. No one was there.

"Omi, why do you run from me?"

The forest whirred around her, blurred by her panicked vision. "Don't touch me!" she screamed, backpedaling, head thrashing. The tree above her shook as its leaves turned black and fell like heavy snow. One landed on her hand, leaving behind a black smear as it fluttered to the ground. She cried out, wiping the top of her hand against the stomach of her shirt.

"The dark worries you," the voice hissed, like spider legs over crusted leaves. "But only in the darkness can you survive."

"That's false!" She stumbled backward, hoping she was still heading in the direction of the turret. "I know what you are."

A tornado of brown leaves swirled up from the ground and dissolved into a shadow in the shape of a man. Red eyes were the only discernible feature. Even when it spoke, there was no mouth. "I've been searching for you."

"Of course you have," said Naomi, pulse rapping, anger building. "Surprise me with something else." She stopped moving, facing the being. Facing Calamity.

"Do you know why?" it crooned.

She ground her teeth together. "Because I can finish you."

Its head tilted, red eyes gleaming. "Darling, you're a part of me."

Her veins stiffened. "I know a lie when I hear one. I've *been* a lie." But acid churned in her gut. "You can't call me to you. I won't come."

"Which is why I've come to you instead."

Taking a single step back, she looked at it. "Why?"

"Because you were created for me, yet you wish to defy me."

She took another step back, praying that by now Ferrin would realize she's been gone too long. "Then why don't you just take me?"

Calamity rose, its feet levitating off the ground. It screamed. A sound that could split a ribcage in half.

Naomi covered her ears and dropped to her knees.

Thousands of flies burst forth, taking the place of the shadowed figure. They dove as a mass toward her.

She held her forearm up and waited for impact. When they hit her, she pierced the air with a shriek. The flies tumbled backward as if caught in the waves of her shout. She stood and sprinted. The flies didn't follow. Calamity didn't reappear. But she kept screaming. Trees splintered as she ran by. Roots shot up from the ground and flailed like eels out of water. She tripped on one, slamming to the ground. Her ankle twisted beneath her and cracked, swelling instantly.

"No!" she cried, waving her hands above her head to ward off flies. But they weren't there. The only thing she felt was rain. She was alone again.

She let her body drop to the now soaked forest floor and let the tears come. Calamity's words slurred around inside her drunken thoughts: *Darling, you're a part of me.* She sobbed harder.

A voice shouted from a distance. "Naomi!"

She didn't lift her head. The forest could have her. Swallow her up. *Take me*, she thought. *I command you to take me.*

"Naomi." A firm hand and the support of a forearm yanked her upward. "Naomi, look at me."

She did look, tears streaking through the caked-on dirt on her cheeks. "Hux." Thrashing, she tried pulling away from him. "Don't touch me! I'm going to hurt you!"

He squeezed her bicep, holding her close. "What?" The wind seemed to call his attention away and he glanced around the forest. Trees were cracked in half. Roots stuck out of the dirt like jagged swords. "Calamity was here," he said.

A sob gurgled from her throat. "Let me go, Hux! I'm going to *hurt* you!"

The realization in his eyes settled on her. "You did this."

"Please," she said, mouth hanging open and tears running over her lips. "I'm dangerous. Let me go." A desperate wail overtook her. "Let me go!"

He pulled her into himself, pressing her head against his chest. "Breathe, Naomi."

She sagged against him, crying into his clothes, feeling his heartbeat against her cheek. Her ankle throbbed and gave out. Hux tightened his hold, keeping her upright. She wrapped her arms around him, realizing he wasn't going to let go, and that she needed him.

"Can you walk at all?" he spoke calmly.

When she applied weight to her ankle, pain shot up through her shin. "Maybe. If you help me."

He propped her on his side and she draped her arm over his shoulders.

"We can go slow," he said, taking the first step.

She hobbled alongside him, shaking. Every ounce of her struggled to remain calm. She would never forgive herself if she lost control of her emotions and caused Hux harm.

Hux staggered for a moment, catching both himself and her. "Lean on me," he instructed. "You're pulling away."

"I'm afraid to hurt you," her voice slipped back into alarm.

"I'm not scared of you." He forced her closer. "What caused your power to flare?"

She gripped his cloak. "Calamity."

"So it found you again."

The turret appeared through the trees and Naomi's stomach plummeted. She was going to have to tell Ferrin that she had a connection with Calamity. That she might not be a saving grace, but a sickening threat.

"I don't think I'm innocent," she whispered.

"Naomi." Hux thumped toward the turret door, sloshing the muddied ground from the new rain. "None of us are."

CHAPTER FORTY-ONE

It was a whirlwind when Hux crashed through the door with Naomi at his hip. Vira and Ferrin sprang up from the kitchen table. The back of Ferrin's knees sent his chair clambering to the floor. He tripped on the table's leg as he darted to the door.

Vira reached them first, taking Naomi's other side. "What happened?"

They brought her to the chair by the fire and lowered her down.

Ferrin snagged the chair he had knocked over and placed it in front of her, propping her ankle up. He felt around her purple skin with quick but gentle fingers. "Not broken. Thank *Protection*."

Naomi's eyes swam with the threat of more tears. "I'm fine."

He leaned over her, his eyes wildly searching for any more injuries. "What happened?"

She wiped her nose with the back of her hand. "I said I'm *fine*."

"No you're not." He bent to be eye level. "You're terrified."

"Give her space, perhaps," Hux suggested, soft.

Ferrin turned toward him. "Did you see what happened?"

Hux held Naomi's eyes for a moment. She looked down, knowing she couldn't keep what happened a secret.

"She was startled by Calamity." Hux rocked back on his heels. "And it caused her to use her powers uncontrollably. Right, Naomi?"

She kept her vision focused on her hands in her lap, but nodded.

Vira went rigid. "So Calamity *is* here."

"It was," said Naomi, barely able to force it out. "But it fled. I just don't know where. Or why."

"Why would Calamity visit Mira Isla and not destroy it?" Vira paced the length of the room, her hair swishing just like the leaping flames in the hearth.

Hux watched her move. "And why wouldn't it take Naomi?"

Naomi gripped the sides of her chair, knowing full well why. Because she was a part of Calamity. It wouldn't destroy a part of itself. But how was she to explain that to them without believing they would turn and kill her? That thought brought her chin up. Maybe she should let them kill her. She'd rather lie beneath the decaying ground than serve Calamity. "I tore the forest to shreds," she said with shaking breaths. "I screamed away Calamity's flies. The Dark Hand fled from me." She stared right at Ferrin. "Because I'm a part of it."

Ferrin stood in front of her, the orange of the fire's flames flicking behind him. She expected shock and disgust to rule his expression, but instead it melted to warmth. "A part of it?"

Hux cleared his throat from behind. "She was afraid to touch me. I don't know what she saw, but—"

"I didn't just see." She exhaled. "I heard. Calamity spoke to me and said I was a part of it. Then I destroyed the woods." She remained trained on Ferrin's watchful eyes. "I'm sorry," she whispered. "I thought I was here to help. I didn't know."

Ferrin lowered himself to a knee, never removing his gaze from her. He reached for her lap and took both of her hands in his. "Since when has Calamity been a truthful voice?"

She shook ferociously in his grasp. "You don't believe it?"

"I don't."

"But I destroyed the woods," she choked.

He pulled her hands closer to his chest. "It was the result of panic," he explained. "I've destroyed things, too. When you can't control your emotions, you can't control your powers. Do you understand?"

She nodded, her forehead almost touching his.

"And you are not Calamity's masterpiece," he said with a fierce bite. "You are a threat to The Dark Hand. Of course it will try to persuade you to join its purpose. You are the only true obstacle in its way."

She let out a fluttering breath. "What am I supposed to do now?" She leaned forward, this time letting her forehead meet his. And he didn't pull away. He leaned right back, as if he needed the support as much as she.

His words came out tender. "You need to rest for the night. Let your emotions settle back down."

She shut her eyes, taking in deep, controlled breaths through her nose. "And tomorrow?"

"We can test the connection between the quill and the necklace," he said. "But your ankle needs to be better before we make a serious move." He wrapped a light hand around the swelling. "Here, I can—"

"Ferrin." Vira grabbed his shoulder. "*You* need to rest."

He looked like he could wallop her. "She needs to be healed."

"Give yourself at least a day," Vira begged. "Let your own body recover. We can bandage her ankle and apply lavender oil tonight."

Hux was already on the move toward the door. "I'll go into the city and get what we need."

Vira shot to his side. "I'll go with you. With Calamity prowling, none of us can be alone." She pierced Ferrin with a stare. "I swear it, Ferrin. Don't do any healing. Not today."

He waved her off with an irritated hand. "Yes, I hear you. Now go. I've got her."

Hux and Vira left, letting in a cold draft as the door opened into the storm. The fire next to Naomi's chair wavered. But the air calmed when the door closed again.

Ferrin sagged to the floor, hanging his head between his knees.

Naomi sat forward. "What are you hiding from me?"

"Huh?" He looked up, dark circles smudging the skin beneath his lower lashes.

She winced as she sat taller. "You've been slugging around since we got to Mira Isla. You slept all night yet you're barely able to keep your eyes open." She hesitated, deciding if she should admit she overheard Vira scolding him for using his powers too much. No one likes an eavesdrop.

"I'm tired, that's all." He stood. "Now do you think we can get you up the stairs? You should lie down."

She crossed her arms. "I'm not ill."

"You seem to think *I* am." He crossed his arms right back, staring down at her.

Pushing off the chair, she rose. Her ankle thudded to the ground and she grimaced. She tipped to the side, but held steady while glaring directly into his face. "How am I supposed to trust you if you won't trust me?"

He grabbed her arms when she wobbled again. "You're going to further hurt yourself. Sit down."

"I'm supposed to learn from you," she kept on. "If you push yourself to harm, why shouldn't I?"

His nostrils flared, but his lips fell in defeat. "Let me take you upstairs, Naomi. Then—"

She opened her mouth to further argue, but he held a finger over her lips.

"*Then*," he continued, "I'll show you." His gaze fell to the floor.

Considering his downcast look, she worried that perhaps she was asking him to reveal too much, but she deserved to know. If they were partners, she *must* know.

They managed to make it up the stairs where she collapsed onto the bed. He propped the pillows behind her to keep her upright and shoved his cloak under her ankle to elevate it. He touched it once again, his fingers lightly pressing on the swelling.

Naomi swatted at him. "Vira said no."

He withdrew his hand and sat on the edge of the bed. "It really grinds me inside that she thinks she knows what's best."

"Well, does she?" Naomi leaned back, finally feeling her shoulders truly relax.

His hunched posture told her the answer was yes. He could barely hold his head up with his own hands.

She frowned. Whatever was happening to him suddenly felt serious. "Tell me what's wrong," she coaxed. "Come on. I can't be the only one who is falling apart."

He side-eyed her. "You're not falling apart. You're just discovering what you're capable of." He rubbed his eyes. "I'm— I'm okay. But I haven't used my powers to this extent for a long time. I had no reason to. Until I met you." The corner of his mouth turned up. "I'm happy to protect you and the others, but my body isn't handling the sudden use well."

She watched him. "It's draining you."

"It's not just draining me." He grabbed the bottom of his shirt and hesitated. "The fatigue turns into physical wounds if exhaustion isn't enough." He yanked his shirt over his head, revealing all the sharp edges of his upper body muscles.

Naomi's core churned when she saw his back. With his shirt a heap in his lap, nothing could hide the gash now. It started at his upper back and slanted across his spine to end below his scapula. It was open and red. Deep. But it wasn't bloodied like a normal injury would be. This was the result of his magic. His body unfolding on itself.

"Ferrin." She held a hand over her mouth. "How could you let it get this bad?"

His face hung over his lap, shoulders rounded forward. "I couldn't stop it." When he turned to look at her, she thought she saw moisture over his pupils. "I stopped using my powers after Oliver was murdered. As a ranger I dealt with business between humans, so I didn't need to use my powers. They lay dormant for years. Until I suddenly decided to unleash it." Trying to sit up straight made him wince. "But what was I supposed to do? I have the ability to help us. I'm not going to cave because of a small cut."

"A *small cut*?" Naomi sat forward. "It looks like a ravine."

Their eyes met.

"I can't stop using my powers just because I'm uncomfortable," he said in a hushed tone. "Not when there's so much at stake."

They sat quietly, avoiding the obvious conversation of Ferrin's horrific gash until Vira appeared in the open doorway, holding two jars and a brown sack. Her eyebrows rose at the sight of the two. She lingered on Ferrin for a heavy minute, seeming to calculate what she made of his decision to show Naomi what was ailing him. But her shoulders dropped, as if relieved that he decided to come out with it.

She strode forward. "I have a bottle of lavender oil and wrap for that ankle of yours. How is it feeling?" Placing the items next to Naomi, she turned to examine the injury that was a little less swollen now that it was elevated.

"Okay right now," Naomi answered honestly.

Vira held another jar in her hand. A larger one. This one had strips of wet, white bandages inside. She held it out to Ferrin. "For your back. They're medicated."

He took the jar from her, nodding in thanks. "I appreciate it, Vira."

She stepped back, darting a look between them, then settled on him again. "I can wrap her ankle, but I understand that healing is in your nature. If you feel you need to—"

"I can do it," he said, nodding. "If I can't heal it with my hands, at least let me bandage it."

Vira laced her fingers over her stomach. "And your back?"

Naomi waved. "I can help him."

His entire body tensed.

"Alright." Vira looked between them one last time. "Hux and I will be downstairs."

When she left, Ferrin leapt off the bed. He kept his face down as he grabbed the bandages and lavender oil from Naomi's hands. "I'll have to wrap it with a good amount of pressure. It will hurt a bit."

She sat forward, watching him dab the lavender oil onto her bruising skin. "My mother used lavender oil for everything. She swore it was a miracle substance." A smile crept onto her face as she remembered. "The smell is comforting, but also sad."

He lifted her ankle into his hands and began to wrap. Still he kept his head bowed, but he nodded. "I know the feeling. To love a memory but feel sorrow because you can't get it back."

Following his hands with her eyes, she admired how gracefully he administered the wrap. As if he had done this thousands of times. But he was gentle too, not just diligent.

"Do this often?" she asked.

Pausing, he looked up, amusement flashing at the corners of his lips. "Pick-up lines like that are meant to be used in dingy taverns. And even then they're stale."

"If my ankle wasn't throbbing, I'd kick you for saying that. It wasn't a pick-up line, you vain soul."

He grinned and looked back down.

Her heart jumped. "You're just good at it. That's all."

"I know." He laughed quietly. "Or is it vain of me to admit?"

She rolled her eyes.

"My mother was a healer," he explained, tucking the end of the wrap within the already wound pieces. "A natural one, since she was human. I helped with a lot of her patients. Paid off, I suppose."

"I suppose." She twitched her ankle back and forth. "That feels stable. Well done."

He set the bottle of oil on the floor and sat on the edge of the bed again. "Well, you should probably get some sleep." Without glancing at her, he picked up his shirt and went to shrug it back on.

She reached forward and grabbed his bare arm. "Wait."

He stopped. She could feel the way his muscles froze beneath her touch. When she first met him, she thought it was because he hated her, but the more time she spent with him the more she realized he felt uncomfortable with any sort of affection.

"You're not leaving without me tending to that gash on your back," she demanded.

Slowly, he pulled away from her grasp. "I can do it myself."

"No." She pointed to the space in front of her. "Sit."

He raised an eyebrow.

"I mean it," she insisted. "Get over the pride or whatever it is that makes you act so foolish sometimes. The sooner you heal, the sooner you can use your powers again."

Tapping his toe on the ground, he actually seemed to consider bolting. Until finally he sighed.

He tossed the bottle of medicated bandages into her lap and crawled across the bed to sit directly in front of her. Her injured leg sat out straight, next to him, and his back was close to her chest. She saw the way his back rose and fell with heavy breathing as if he was nervous.

"It's not gonna kill you," she reassured. "Just sting."

When he didn't answer, she unscrewed the lid off the jar and straightened to begin. The gash was slanted, and he was too close. She needed to come at it at a slightly different angle. She placed her hand on his bare side to scoot him sideways and a laugh erupted from his lips. No, it erupted from his entire being. It was a frilly laugh. The kind that makes other people laugh.

The fluttering sound of it caused her to yank her hand away, a grin taking up her whole mouth. "What was *that*?"

He turned and looked at her, his face bright red, lips still beaming. "Don't *do* that, Naomi."

"Are you *ticklish*?" She exploded with laughter.

"Stuff it, Massoud." He lightly shoved her in the chest, but his smile hadn't disappeared yet.

"I'm sorry." She wiped a tear from her eye then pulled a bandage from the jar. "But that laugh of yours is just too good. Why don't you laugh more often? You'd seem kinder, you know." She placed the first bandage at the top of his wound and smoothed it out.

He gripped the bed sheets in pain. "I am kind."

"Well *I* know that," she said, laying another bandage.

"Good graves this is torture," he groaned. "And what do you mean you know that? You hardly know me at all."

She shrugged. "It's not hard to read kindness. You either have it or you don't."

"And what makes you believe I have it?"

She stuck the last strip onto the gash. "You're here."

He tilted his chin over his shoulder at her. "That's it?"

"It's enough."

He nodded and looked forward again.

She placed a hand on his shoulder. "Do the bandages feel all right?"

There was no reply.

"Ferrin?"

Suddenly his palm was on her fingers, holding her hand against his skin.

Her heart ramped up.

"Thank you," he said with an airy breath. "You don't know how it feels to have someone else take care of you when you've been doing it for yourself for over one hundred years."

She bowed her head, squeezing his shoulder. "I may not be 187, but I understand the feeling fully well."

Almost absentmindedly, he laced his fingers into hers and slid her hand down to his chest.

Now her heart *really* flew.

"You say I'm kind," he murmured. "But it's your kindness that has awoken the goodness in me again." He let go of her hand, letting it fall down his side to hang at her own.

"I don't think your goodness was ever gone," she said. "You just thought so."

CHAPTER FORTY-TWO

Maya and her Riders entered the village of Blaire as the last light of day slipped away. The windows of the timber cottages leading into town glowed warm with firelight and the chimneys breathed out musky smelling smoke. Light rain from earlier in the day had left the dirt road murky. Dirt flicked up to dot Maya's legs as the horses clomped through. Estell still sat behind her, quiet during most of the day's journey. The mountain that erupted in front of their targets had startled them both. A golden witch, Estell had revealed, couldn't create land masses. Which meant the mountain was created by someone else. Namely, the Massoud. As Blaire hummed with the beginning of night life, the Riders entered the main square. People lingered into the streets, greeting friends before dodging inside a tavern that sat lopsided next to the city's well.

One of Maya's Riders, Dorian, nudged his horse up next to her. He had a wonky cheek from a fight he lost two years ago and eyes with no light. "The people look happy," he said, aghast.

Maya felt her heart tighten, but she forced the feeling away and only nodded. "Blaire's queen is a good one. She truly has the people's well-being in the forefront of her mind."

Dorian frowned at her. "As if our king doesn't?"

"I didn't say that," she grunted. "King Leeland has built the most prestigious military force known to this side of the Desarian Sea. His strong suit is protection. Blaire's military is brittle. But their queen is a compassionate ruler. One who seeks to give her people a gentle life."

Estell tilted her head at Dorian. "You prefer military power?"

"Of course I prefer power over compassion." He drew his eyes from Estell's shoes to the top of her head. "And you seem to think the same. Otherwise you wouldn't be here."

She scoffed, casting a flirtatious glance at him. "I prefer lording over myself."

Maya sunk her teeth into her bottom lip. Something about the woman's persona put her on edge. She was a wild spirit cast out into the air and somehow landed in Zul's lap, with the strange knowledge of a supposed sacred bloodline. Not for the first time, Maya had a wave of regret for allowing Estell to join her company. But she calmed herself with a single breath. They wouldn't have made it this far without Estell. The golden witch could sense the presence of the souls they were in pursuit of. And that was an advantage Maya could not give up. Not if she wanted to successfully retrieve Hux and deliver him to her king.

"Do you still feel them?" Maya asked.

Estell stared into the village, searching the dirt streets. "I feel that they are closer than they have been. Perhaps they've passed through here."

She exhaled. "Good. Let's hit the tavern and replenish our bodies. Be vague if anyone asks about our business. I'm unaware of any other allies that Hux may have."

Most of Blaire's residents were inside the tavern. The bar

was circular, taking up the middle of the establishment, and tables and chairs littered the rest of the floor. Some of the Riders lined up at the bar and ordered food, joining in with the locals' conversation and banter. Maya thought Estell was doing the same thing until the golden witch turned back around with a mug of ale in each hand.

Estell shoved one toward her. "Let's sit."

Maya took the mug, eyeing it, pondering if the woman had slipped something in her drink.

"Relax." Estell rolled her eyes. "Woman to woman, let's have a chat."

They sat at a table in the corner of the tavern. Maya placed her back at the wall so she could watch her Riders. Estell sat across from her, drinking her ale like water.

"Why do you care what the Massoud girl does to Thãen anyway?" Maya pried. "You seem to only care for yourself. The wellbeing of Thãen shouldn't even be a speck in your thoughts."

Estell set her mug down and grinned. "Do you want to die?"

"Die?" Maya leaned forward. "Of course I don't want to die. Are you threatening me?"

"Of course I'm not threatening you," she mimicked. "But if the girl does what she's destined to do, everyone in Thãen will hardly stand a chance. A Massoud can challenge Calamity. That means open war. The Dark Hand won't stand to be asked to duel. It will only destroy us."

Maya dipped her head in even closer to Estell. "You're saying this Massoud has a sort of power over The Dark Hand?"

For a flicker of a moment, Estell's eyes wavered, as if she revealed something she didn't mean to. "Yes."

"Yet you want to stop her?" Maya's face crumpled with questioning forehead lines. "Do you *want* Calamity to rule?"

Estell sat back, bringing her ale to her lips again, drinking slowly. "I want to live."

"You won't live if Calamity wins. We will fall from Protection's hand." Maya slammed her finger into the table. "I'm here to live. You're going to eliminate a chance at that if you ruin this girl. I'm seeking Hux and the quill to save Thãen. You're seeking this girl to save Calamity." She narrowed her eyes. "I want you gone."

Estell shoved her mug to the side, the liquid sloshing over the edge. "Then good luck finding them." She pointed to her temple. "I can feel them. You can not."

"I want life and you want death," she snapped. "I'll take my chances."

A hand dropped down on Maya's shoulder. She drew her sword and had it underneath the man's chin before she was fully standing.

The man stepped back, hands raised. He had on Le'Garian armor, the crest of the lead Rider embedded into his chest plate.

She lowered the sword. "What do you want?"

Estell looked up, eyes glittering and curious.

"We're both here," the man said, hands still raised. "In Blaire. Why?"

"What does it matter?" Maya sheathed her sword back into its scabbard, not wanting to draw attention.

"Because we are both lead Riders," he said quietly, bowing his head to hers. "You and I both know we don't travel this far unless we have to."

Estell stood.

The man blinked, examining her. "Who is she?"

Maya's fingers twitched over the hilt of her weapon. "Who are *you*?"

He dragged his eyes away from Estell and back to Maya. "I'm Saul. Lead Rider of Le'Gar."

"Are you seeking something?" Maya tilted her head. "My

Riders and I are on mission. We don't have time to divert. If you're seeking help, I can't give it."

"I'm seeking a man," Saul said. "A ranger by the name of Ferrin."

Estell fluttered her eyelashes upward. "I know him."

Saul snapped his head to her. "You've seen him?"

She nodded. "In fact, he's with the company we are seeking."

Maya gave a wicked glare to Estell but didn't silence her.

"Is this true?" He gave his attention to Maya again.

Maya glowered. "What do you want him for?"

"Suspicious activity. Why is it your concern?"

"Because I'm leading a retrieval mission," she spat. "I'm not aiding in murder unless the situation is life or death."

Saul crossed his arms and dropped his chin. "We've set out to retrieve the ranger and deliver him to King Tal of Le'Gar."

Maya tipped her head toward Estell. "You know this woman, Rider? She seems to think she knows Le'Gar."

Saul and Estell shared a stare.

He broke the silence. "What's your name?"

"E."

Again, Maya didn't offer any kind of retort. If Estell wanted to keep her name hidden from this man, it wasn't her place to expose her. Respect goes two ways.

"I'm afraid I don't recognize you," he said. "Are you from Le'Gar?"

"Once," she admitted.

He narrowed his eyes. "Who are you after?"

She smiled, snake-like. "A Massoud."

His shoulders rose. "From Le'Gar?"

"I don't know, is she?"

Saul looked between the two women. "What is your connection?"

Maya gave a haughty huff. "Nothing anymore. We are no longer traveling together."

Estell sagged slightly, as if the comment pierced her just a tad. "She doesn't understand my motives."

"What is your plan of action once you find this Massoud?" Saul stepped toward her. "Hm?"

"To prevent her from destroying Thãen," Estell said through bared teeth. "Because I want to live."

Saul quizzed Maya. "And you'd rather die?"

"I'd rather leave the plan of action to my king," she grumbled. "Perhaps *you* two could join together on a perilous mission. I'm off to retrieve my treasonist."

At that, Saul's body jolted. "Treasonist?"

Maya rolled her eyes upward. "Is all my business yours to know?"

He shifted. "Your treasonist doesn't happen to be named Hux?"

Now *she* tensed. "Your king is spying on ours."

"No." He held his hands up. "I can't explain how I know of him. Or, I could, but it wouldn't make sense."

Estell brushed shoulders with Maya as she crept toward him. "Saul."

He stared down at her, mouth sagging. "Yes?"

She tapped her own chest. "It was me."

Maya frowned.

Saul was a few inches taller than Estell and stood right against her, staring down. He looked to be studying her, a question plastered on his expression. "You're the golden witch."

"I am." She didn't step away from his presence. "I had to let someone know of Hux's retrieval."

Maya grabbed her arm. "You helped him?"

Estell shrugged, stripping her arm away from Maya's grasp. "See? I think of people other than myself."

Maya glowered. "Why Le'Gar's Riders? Hux was from Raina."

"Le'Gar is as embedded into this as you are," Estell said. "You weren't the only ones who knew of the quill."

Maya stared back at her Riders who were now noticing Saul's Riders entering the tavern. She darted a stare back to Saul. "You said you wanted the ranger, not the quill."

"Either will do. I need to get something. For grave's sake, the quill can not come into contact with a Massoud."

Maya's lungs clenched. "A Massoud is riding with them. They're all together. Four total."

Saul held a fist above his head, as if he were about to throw a punch, but he slowly lowered it back down. "This is far worse than I thought."

Maya squinted, an idea seeping into her mind. "Do you have any leads on Ferrin's location?"

"No. And we've been out here for days." He rubbed his face. "There is only one place we haven't looked, and that's only because we can't."

"And where is that?" Maya asked.

Saul rested his stare on Estell. "Mira Isla."

Estell's face stood unwavering. "Mira Isla is a myth."

He recoiled. "A myth? You're a golden witch and you haven't been to Mira Isla?"

She scowled. "I'm not a loved witch."

"You cause trouble?" He raised an eyebrow. "Good. All the best golden witches do." He paused. "Le'Gar had a golden witch once. One that aided the throne." A shadow fell over his eyes. "Only she was betrayed and eventually fled the city."

Estell's lip twitched, but she remained stiff as straw. "How unfortunate for your golden witch."

"Unfortunate indeed," Saul agreed. "There aren't any like her anymore."

"Maybe there are," Estell said gently. "I'll help you. I sense an understanding between us."

Maya leveled her shoulders. "You want what, Rider? The quill or the ranger?"

"I sought the ranger, but the Massoud is the end goal." He huffed, looking around. "How many Riders do you have?"

"Sixteen including me," she said. "What are you suggesting? Riding together?"

He pointed a thick finger at Estell. "She can get us into Mira Isla. If that's where our criminals lie, that's where we must go. I need her. And so do you, Maya."

Maya narrowed her eyes, leaning closer to him. "I know what I need. I need my treasonist and I need that quill."

They stood nose to nose, eye to eye, for a few stale moments.

"Take both," Saul breathed. "I'll escort E and the Massoud back to Le'Gar."

Maya's eyes flicked to Estell, who nodded.

"She wants the Massoud dead," Maya warned him. "Promise me you'll keep the girl alive until you hand her over to your king for him to deal with."

He hesitated.

Maya moved forward, closing the gap between them, bumping into his chest plate. "Deal or you'll be back down to your own Riders."

He clenched his teeth. "Deal."

CHAPTER FORTY-THREE

Ferrin slunk down the turret's stairs to the first floor. His eyelids drooped, but the medicated bandages were soothing to his wound and his shirt no longer rubbed against it. It was a comforting feeling, but that wasn't why his heart was steady. The feeling of Naomi's hands on his skin lingered. Her hands in his. The tenderness of someone who cared about him. It put a lump in his throat and a knot in his chest. Estell had touched him before, and it felt similar to how he felt now. But Estell's touch turned a different shade with time. A darker shade. A possessive one. One of gray hues and muddled browns. She was fog. What he felt now was warmth. A slow sunrise.

It terrified him.

Hux looked up from the ground where he sat cross-legged. Two dice lay near his shins. The fire was roaring and Vira was gone.

Ferrin ran a hand through his hair and collapsed next to him, snagging the dice. "What are you playing?"

"Stars and Prophecies." Hux chuckled.

Ferrin shook the cubes. "What the devil is that?"

Hux signaled to have the dice back. Ferrin placed them in his palm. He held them out so Ferrin could see. "The number you roll determines what constellation you'll use to tell your prophecy."

"A fortune telling game?" Ferrin snickered. "Did you already give it a go?"

Hux nodded, staring into the flames. "I rolled a two and a one. So my constellation has three stars. Do you know which one that is?

Ferrin didn't even have to think. "The Trail of Blood." The constellation was a line of three stars, said to represent blood droplets from the ankle of a wounded warrior.

"What do you think that could mean for me?" Hux asked.

Furrowing his brows, Ferrin sighed, but gave in to the game. "You were lead Rider. That naturally makes you a warrior. Could mean there is danger in your future." He pulled a knee into his chest. "Or it could mean you've already suffered something and you're still bleeding." His voice caught and he swallowed.

Hux stared down at his hands. "Sounds like the prophecy could fit for both you and me."

"You know my past pain," he said through a tight throat. "I already know I'm still bleeding." Swallowing again, he gripped his pant leg. "But I think...I think something is starting to heal."

Hux raised a thick eyebrow. "Why do you think so?"

He shrugged, then closed his eyes. "I feel a stirring. That's all."

"Good." He placed the dice back into Ferrin's hands. "Roll 'em. See what your prophecy says."

Ferrin closed his fingers over them, then stopped. "What about you? What are you bleeding from?"

Hux glanced away. "I let Vira suffer alone for years. And only now am I admitting to her how much I love her."

Ferrin let out a long, whooshing breath. "You're passionate about her?"

"It doesn't have to be passion," he said. "I just love her. As a friend. As a part of me. Maybe in another life she could have been something more, but now it's murky." He waved a hand above his head. "It's a mist in the wind. I waited too long and I did things wrong."

"I'm sorry." Ferrin shook the dice in his hand. "Regrets are suffocating."

"That they are," Hux grunted. "Now would you roll those?"

He glanced in Hux's direction before tossing the cubes on the floor. A six and a five. "Eleven."

Hux looked up at the ceiling, thinking. "Eleven. You got the Snowdrop."

Ferrin drew the shape of the constellation on the ground with his finger. Four stars for the straight part of the stem and a fifth that curved to make the bent shape of a snowdrop plant. The remaining six made two drooping petals. "It's a plant that appears when spring is on the verge, but snow still sticks to the ground." He looked up. "Beauty in desolate places? Or a symbol of perseverance?"

"Or promise of a better season ahead," Hux said, giving a faint smile. "It's your prophecy. Think of it how you will."

The door behind them swung open and Vira slipped in. Night air blew in with her, flickering the hearth's flames.

She removed her cloak and draped it over one of the table's chairs. "Is Naomi resting?"

Ferrin nodded, remaining on the floor. "She fell asleep fast. Using her power took a lot out of her."

Vira strode to the hearth and sat with them. She eyed the dice then glanced at Ferrin. "And you?"

"What about me?"

"Did the bandages help?"

He readjusted his legs, suddenly feeling antsy. "Yes. Yes, I feel loads better already."

She kept her focus on him, watching him squirm. "You showed her."

"Yes, I showed her."

She smirked, looking away.

He scowled, but a strange pressure built in his stomach. The way Vira said it made him want to smile. "She deserved to know," he justified. "I had to have an explanation for why I couldn't heal her ankle on the spot."

"Of course," Vira said, eyes wide. "I'm not questioning your reasoning." Another flat smile.

"You can be slightly infuriating," he grumbled. "The way you try to read me."

"Only slightly?"

Hux looked down, hiding a grin of his own.

Ferrin hesitated, then huffed. "Yes. Slightly. Because you aren't as awful as I originally assumed." Now it was his turn for his lips to twitch upward. "You aren't a beast. Well done."

She grew serious, studying him. "Well, ranger. I'd say you aren't so bad yourself."

He rested his palms on his thighs. "Wonderful. Now we can both eliminate an enemy from our list."

She waved him away and scooted next to Hux. "I never saw you as an enemy, Ferrin."

He snickered. "I most definitely saw you as one."

"I know." She leaned against Hux's shoulder and closed her eyes. "But it's okay. I forgive you."

CHAPTER FORTY-FOUR

Naomi stood in King Tal's throne room again. It was the same dream as before. Tal had tumbled through the door, throat spilling blood. The Dark Hand towered above her. She shrieked, covering her head with her arms.

"Naomi!" a voice shouted.

Whipping her head to the side, she saw the face again. Blurred features, as if made of watercolor.

She jolted awake. The room was dark, the sheets twisted around her thrashing limbs. Night still sat outside the turret window. She threw the covers aside and landed on the floor, collapsing when the pain in her ankle shot upward.

"For goodness sake," she mumbled, massaging the tender joint.

"Naomi?" Ferrin's voice floated up the stairs. "Was that you?"

She ground her teeth and pulled herself up. "Yes. I'm fine."

But he was already at the top of the stairs, his face clouded from lack of sleep. "Did you fall?"

"I'm fine. I just forgot about my ankle. A dream woke me up."

He crossed the room and held an arm out to her. "Sit down."

"Ferrin." She lifted her hands away from his touch. "Stop fussing over me."

The sound of the downstairs door slamming open caught their attention.

"Mama!" Millicent's voice screamed.

Without thinking of the pain anymore, Naomi ran to the top of the stairs with Ferrin at her side. Below, Millicent tore through the room, grabbing Vira's side.

Vira spun away from her conversation with Hux and grabbed her daughter. "What is it, love?"

Millicent's face was pinched and pale. "Mama, we need you at the gates! Amani is dead. There's been an invasion!"

Vira leapt forward. "Hux! Now. Grab your sword."

Naomi limped down the stairs, wincing and hopping on her good leg. "Vira! We're going too."

She swung her head around. "Not with that ankle. You're staying here."

"Vira, please." She stumbled on the last step.

Ferrin caught her elbow, steadying her. "Vira's right."

"Pack our things, Naomi," Vira ordered. "Get ready to leave." She shoved her daughter toward her. "And keep her safe."

"Mama," Millicent cried. "Don't leave me!"

Naomi grabbed the sobbing girl and held her close to her side. "I've got her, Vira."

Vira brisked over to her and pressed the quill into her hands. "You have both items now. *Stay hidden.*" She bent down and kissed Millicent on the head. "I mean it, Naomi. Get ready to leave." She spun away and grabbed Hux's shoulder, guiding him out the door.

Ferrin went to follow, then turned around to look at Naomi

one last time. "Oh *graves*," he grumbled. He moved over to her. Dropping to his knees, he wrapped his hands around her ankle.

Naomi tried pulling away. "You haven't recovered yet!"

He only tightened his grip. "I've recovered enough for this. You will not be left behind with a disadvantage."

The pain in her joint turned from an ache to a warmth. A light tingle moved around under her skin as he let go. There was no more swelling or bruising. She could comfortably put all of her weight on it again.

He stood, squeezing Millicent's shoulder, but he bore his stare into Naomi. "I'll be back."

She nodded. "I'll be ready."

And he was gone.

Naomi gripped Millicent's arm. "Stick close to me."

She led the little girl back upstairs where she grabbed Ferrin's satchel and began stuffing in every piece of clothing and any leftover lavender and bandages. She kept the quill in her hand, afraid to carelessly stuff it away and lose it. The necklace was in her pocket. A safe place temporarily, but only around her neck would the jewelry truly be secured. She reached into her pocket and grasped it. As she pulled her hand out, the turret rumbled. The floors quivered and Millicent clung to Naomi to keep steady. The little girl's body knocked into hers, sending her stumbling to the side. The shaking turret didn't make the stumble easy to stop, and Naomi dropped to her knees. The quill slammed to the ground under the fist that caught her fall and the necklace in her other hand bounced to the floor. It rolled toward the quill and touched the tip.

Millicent reached for her. "Miss Naomi, are you alright?"

Naomi didn't answer. She just stared at the quill. When the tip of it touched the necklace's pearl, the glow inside the pearl swirled. The liquid had been activated, and it moved outside of the piece of jewelry and onto the golden feather. Where the quill was once glowing too, now it beamed brighter than a star. The tip was the shiniest, so thick with light that it looked like it could drip. Just like ink on a real quill.

"That's it," Naomi whispered. "The necklace held the ink for the quill."

"What are you talking about?" Millicent tried to pull her up. "Hurry. It's getting dark."

Naomi looked up. It was the middle of the night already. But Millicent was right. It *was* getting darker.

She stood, clasped the dimming necklace around her neck and stuffed the quill inside Ferrin's bag in an attempt to hide its glow. A holler from outside grabbed her attention. She ran to the open window and looked down at Mira Isla. Firelight from torches snaked through the streets. Either from the invaders or Mira Isla's guard.

Millicent appeared behind her. "Who are they?"

Naomi turned. "I don't know, but I have a few guesses."

"Who?"

She turned Millicent around by the shoulders. "It doesn't matter. Are you a fast runner?"

Millicent picked up the bottom of her dress. "Not when I'm wearing this."

Naomi squatted and grabbed the flowy material, tying it in a knot at Millicent's thigh. It was a sloppy job, but it was bustled enough to allow for sprinting.

"Where will we run?" Millicent asked, anxiousness sneaking into her attempted calm tone.

Naomi went to reply, but the turret shook again. The room flooded with darkness, as if the air itself took on the color. The only thing she could make out in the dark was the faded outline of the window, because the night sky was brighter than what now surrounded them.

"Millicent!" Naomi thrashed around. "Grab hold of me."

The girl's shaking fingers found her hand and squeezed tight.

"Just follow me," Naomi ordered, gripping the bag with the quill. "To the stairs, and then I'll guide us down."

Millicent was silent, hardly breathing.

Naomi's heart raced. "Millie?"

"Naomi," Millicent whispered. "Behind you."

CHAPTER FORTY-FIVE

Naomi spun. A set of red eyes sat above her shoulder. She reeled back. The shadowed body with the eyes morphed, billowing up and out like a fast-blooming flower. The eyes melted inward and disappeared when five dark fingers stretched out of the body, expanding to fill the room.

"Millie, the forest!" Naomi shouted while shoving her to the stairs. "Go!"

Millicent tripped and fell to her knees. Naomi dropped the bag, grabbed the back of Millie's dress and lifted her to her feet. She sent the girl down the stairs as The Dark Hand finished growing, bulging against the ceiling of the turret, its fingers hanging down like a weeping willow. A finger swiped downward, reaching for Naomi's legs. She leapt to the side and grabbed Ferrin's satchel. Fumbling, she searched the inside, praying he had an extra weapon.

He did.

She withdrew a dagger. Wind from Calamity's movements threw her hair around her face, making it difficult to see, but a heavy pressure told her that The Dark Hand was lowering, attempting to grab her. She slashed the dagger through the shadow. It made no impact. Worldly weapons against the outer forces were useless.

Dropping the dagger, she flopped to her belly and rolled to the top of the stairs. The Hand slammed down against the ground, cracking the floorboards. She swung her leg back into the room, snagged the strap of Ferrin's satchel with her foot and pulled it to her.

Calamity shrunk back down to a shadowed man as she thundered down the steps and darted to the front door. Cold fingers wrapped around her wrist, holding her back. Shock pierced her chest. Calamity's touch erupted her buried emotions. Fear, hate, the want for revenge. For a split second, she wanted to kill Ferrin for betraying her ancestor. But that thought startled her all the more, jerking her back to reality. She drove her free hand into the satchel and revealed the quill. It dripped with golden ink, yet a drop never truly fell. Its beam cast walls of light around the turret.

The Dark Hand released its grip on Naomi's wrist and shifted back. It swept through the kitchen table like a ghost would. Dying flames in the hearth illuminated its shadow, burning it with light. That alone sent Calamity raging. It hollered like a wounded lion, an open black mouth releasing flies.

Naomi took The Dark Hand's moment of rage and fled.

The night was welcoming. Her bare feet gripped the damp ground. Stones and sticks struck her soles, but she propelled into the forest. Ferrin's satchel bounced on her hip. Trees blurred by. Distant shouting from the center of Mira Isla drifted up the cliff, sending Naomi sprinting even harder.

To enter Mira Isla, a golden witch or Magnificent had to be with the invaders. The only golden witch who had a reason to lead an invasion was Estell. And the thought of Estell having power over anything sent a panic through Naomi.

She skirted to the path that led down the cliff into the city. Millicent was nowhere in sight. Spikes of fear stabbed Naomi's stomach. She prayed Millicent knew enough to flee in the other direction of the city to avoid the commotion of the invasion. But she, on the other hand, would gladly head into it. A fire had been ignited inside of her. Words in her head and heart screamed, *Not my people! Not my world! They will not be touched.*

When she reached the bottom of the cliff, thickets of ivy and winding streams swam in front of her. She plowed her way through them to the dirt path that led into the city. But as soon as she set her feet on the path, she saw a group of Riders up ahead, riding on horseback away from the city. They were headed toward her. Their torches warbled in the night, revealing their glinting armor with every stride of their horses.

She dove back into the thick of the ivy, crouching low, staying hidden. Her chest thrummed the closer they got. Especially when she could identify the front rider as the lead Rider of Raina, who Hux had called Maya. And Estell sitting directly behind.

One of the Riders at the back of the pack let out a short shriek and toppled to the ground. Maya tugged her horse around. The Rider lay on the ground with an arrow sticking out of his back.

"Weapons up!" Maya shouted.

Naomi shook, trying to remain still.

Another arrow flew from somewhere within the dark of the surrounding trees. It struck Maya's bicep. She flinched, but her armor deflected it. "Fire into the trees!" she ordered.

The two remaining Riders behind her obeyed, sending their own arrows into the forest.

A shuffle sounded behind Naomi and suddenly Ferrin was right upon her. She almost yelped, but he shoved a hand over her mouth, screaming with his eyes to keep quiet. He stayed at her level, letting the ivy swallow them both.

Estell dropped to the ground, wading over to the ivy thicket. She bent down and laid a hand atop the greenery. She sneered. "I feel them."

Maya kept looking from the trees to the ivy. "Where? Arrows are coming from the trees."

"But their energy is coming from the ivy," Estell said, beginning to wade in.

Ferrin pressed a hand into Naomi's back, forcing her down completely. She surrendered, lying flat on her stomach. Estell's feet were treading closer, and Naomi couldn't see anything except twigs and leaves in her face. But she could hear the thrashing—the angry pursuit of the golden witch who would probably kill them.

When Estell's feet were close enough, Ferrin shot up, raising his bow. He was inches from her, but he didn't release the arrow.

Naomi glanced up at him from her hidden place. Why wasn't he ending her?

"How many of you are there?" Ferrin demanded.

Estell stopped moving. "Are you going to kill me?"

Naomi could hear Maya ordering her other two Riders to stay on the path before she crashed through the twigs to join Estell.

"I don't want to," Ferrin answered. "But I will."

Estell stepped forward, letting the tip of his arrow touch her chest. "I'll tell you what you want if you hand her over."

He didn't even twitch. "She's already gone."

"You lie," Estell said like squealing steam. "I *feel* her, darling."

"I told her to run," he continued, steady. "I knew you'd come for her."

Her gaze fell. "Why do you think so low of me, Fin?"

There was silence.

Ferrin breathed, haggard. "Because I witnessed you murder a boy."

"It was a job."

"One you could have said no to!" he shouted.

"You weren't raised as low as I was!" she screamed right back. "The king saved my life!"

His voice erupted into the night. "And you took one in return! *Curse* you, Estell. I won't let you take another."

She snarled. "We'll see." She grabbed his arrow and aimed it upward. With a single wave of her hand, she shoved him back with a ripple of power.

Ferrin lifted an arm and threw energy back at her, but she deflected it by shielding herself with her forearm. His power didn't seem to phase her.

Estell reached down into the ivy and yanked Naomi up by the back of her shirt.

Naomi swiped at her with wild claws, but Estell pulled her into her chest. Naomi's back was pressed against the golden witch and a knife was at her throat.

Ferrin lifted his bow again, this time aiming at Estell's forehead. "Release her or I'll send the arrow through your skull."

Maya tugged on Estell's arm. "Retrieval, Estell! The girl is a hostage, not a criminal."

"*I* determine what she is!" Estell shouted, face reddening with every word. "Your Riders got me here, I don't need you anymore. Go find your treasonist."

Maya's gaze went to Ferrin's. He kept his focus trained on the dead center of Estell's forehead. Naomi tried to read both of their expressions, but all she could focus on was the blade against the thin skin of her throat.

"I said release her," Ferrin thundered again. "Or I'll let the arrow go and use my powers to shove it deeper."

Naomi felt Estell's heart speed up.

"Don't do this to me, Ferrin," Estell whispered. "I'm trying to protect Thãen. You aren't my enemy."

For a moment, Naomi saw his strength falter. But his knuckles tightened again, turning white. "Let her go," he said, calmer. "I don't want to kill you, Estell."

Maya pointed her sword at Estell's back. "You said you would deliver her to King Tal," she said with a tremble. "You promised this to Saul, too."

Ferrin gave a questioning look to Maya, seeming surprised at her sudden turn on Estell.

Naomi squirmed. She tried to calm her breathing, keep her vision clear, and hold her panic at bay. She had the power to change the situation. She knew that. If only she could regulate herself and drown her panic. *Let lightning strike Estell,* she wished. But nothing happened.

Ferrin's words rang out in her head. *When you can't control your emotions, you can't control your powers.*

Naomi's mind reeled. She was going to die. Estell was going to slice her throat. She was panicking, and she couldn't calm herself.

She tried again, though her focus was scattered. *Let the ground swallow her up.*

Nothing happened.

She scrambled to think back to the moment she caused the mountain to erupt from the ground. What had she felt at that moment? Desperation, yes, but also fear. How had she controlled her emotions then?

Maya nudged her sword forward to tap Estell's shoulder blade. "Place the girl on my horse. We are taking her to Le'Gar's king."

"Over my dead body you are," Ferrin steamed. He dropped his bow and threw his hand up, slamming his palm out straight, sending Estell flailing backward from his invisible force.

Naomi rocketed backward with her. The dagger beneath her chin sliced her jaw.

Maya crashed to the ground first. Estell landed on top of her. Both Maya's sword and Estell's dagger went skittering across the path. The two Riders on the path jerked to action, aiming their bows at Naomi as she rolled sideways and leapt up.

A body dropped out of an overhanging tree. Hux. His massive frame slammed into one of the Riders and they both hit the ground.

The last Rider standing let his arrow fly.

The swish of a person emerged from the trees, placing itself between Naomi and the arrow. The arrow struck the person in the chest. Her black hair flailed backward as her neck arched in pain.

Then Vira fell.

CHAPTER FORTY-SIX

"Vira!" Hux screamed.

Ferrin lunged out of the ivy, tearing to their fallen witch.

Naomi dropped to her knees, holding her hand over her mouth.

Dirt spewed as Ferrin slid down to Vira's side, pulling her head into his lap. "Vira. Vira." He jostled her head, trying to keep her eyes open. "Look at me."

She choked and shook with shock. Her eyes rolled. Her breathing labored. The arrow stuck out from the right side of her chest.

"Stay with us." Ferrin pulled her into his arms.

The Rider lifted another arrow, aiming for Ferrin's back. Naomi caught the movement and leapt up. She skidded around Ferrin and stood in front of him, squeezing her eyes shut as she waited for the next arrow to hit her instead. But the sound of Hux's sword ended the Rider and the thump of his body told Naomi no arrow was going to fly.

Hux sprinted to Ferrin's side, sinking to his knees next to Vira's struggling body. "Ferrin, heal her. Save her. *Please,*

Ferrin." He dropped his forehead against hers. "Keep breathing, Vira. I've got you. Ferrin's got you."

Naomi remained standing in front of the others, watching Estell and Maya squirm and start to rise up from the ground. She glanced back, hoping life still lingered behind Vira's eyes. For now, she held on. For now.

Estell pushed herself upright and trudged toward Naomi. "Look what you've done. You wouldn't surrender to me and now your golden witch lies dead."

Naomi's breathing stuttered. "She's not dead. We have a healer."

"Ah, yes." Estell stopped right in front of her. "The Magnificent. Though he's powerful, he can't undo death."

"Death hasn't made its claim yet," she said with spite in her teeth.

"Come with me," Estell whispered, shimmering with a grin. "And no more death will come."

Naomi hesitated, then stepped forward. "Alright. But let me leave Ferrin's belongings with him."

Estell glanced down at the satchel at Naomi's hip.

Maya stepped up behind Estell's shoulder. "The quill. You have it in there."

Naomi opened the flap of the bag to let the two see inside. "It's just healing items. Now let me get it to him before Vira loses her fight or you won't have me."

Maya shoved Naomi toward her friends. "Go. You have thirty seconds."

She ran over to them. Ferrin hadn't pulled the arrow out so as not to cause major bleeding, but he kept his hands pressed around the wounded area. Vira's breathing was slow. Watery. Her eyes were closed. Hux remained low to the ground, close to Vira's ear, begging her to hold on.

Naomi bent down, setting the satchel at Ferrin's side. In the same motion, she pulled the quill out from the breast of her shirt. Her body blocked it from Maya and Estell and she slid it into Ferrin's trousers.

He fluttered his eyes upward at her. "What are you doing?" he whispered.

"Just trust me."

Maya, growing suspicious, appeared behind them. With noticeable hesitation, she held her sword at the back of Hux's neck. "Hux. You are under arrest for treason to King Leeland."

Hux gripped Vira's shirt sleeve, a sign that he wasn't going anywhere. "You don't know the weight of it!" he exploded.

Maya's hand trembled.

"You don't know the weight!" he roared. "Maya, please."

"It's my duty to retrieve you." Her voice shook. "I'm doing what I know is right."

"Please," he said again, bowing his head. "I wouldn't have gone my own way if I didn't think it right either."

Estell plowed forward. "No more delays. I want the Massoud *now*."

Naomi went to rise.

Ferrin grabbed her arm. "*Do something*," he spoke low. "Concentrate." He let her go.

Naomi stood, facing Estell. Maya was two feet away, still aiming her sword at Hux. It could be easy. All she had to do was control her emotions.

With a deep inhale, she closed her eyes and thought about the moment she created the mountain. She had been afraid then, but she had also felt safe. Because at that time she was surrounded by Hux, Ferrin, and Vira. Now it was different, though. Vira was dying. Hux was in despair. Ferrin was trying to keep Vira alive. Naomi was alone, and that was the most terrifying feeling of all. Even so, she stood tall and envisioned herself standing alone in nothing but vast open space. She put the vision of Vira fighting for her life out of her mind. She shoved away the pain of seeing Hux so distraught. And with one final breath, she swallowed the dread she felt at the thought of leaving Ferrin behind. For one perfect moment her emotions were calm and still, and a sense of control took over her chest.

Estell reached for her in an angry swipe.

Naomi stepped back. *The ground swallow you up,* she thought.

The soil quaked. Estell threw her arms out to the sides, an attempt to remain standing, but her knees buckled. The dirt beneath her quivered and caved in like a pit of sand. Estell sunk with it, her bottom half disappearing. Her face changed then. A look of terror. It was enough to make Naomi's heart squeeze with guilt as the rest of Estell disappeared, her arms flailing to remain above ground. But she was gone before a scream could erupt from her throat.

Maya leapt away from Hux, but Naomi had already moved on to her. The guilt of sending Estell beneath the dirt lingered in her stomach. She couldn't summon the same words for Maya.

The trees take her.

Overhanging branches swept low like arms, curling around Maya and lifting her off the path. She shouted and thrashed, but the trees continued on, securing her in their branches and holding her captive. Her shouting faded as the trees lifted her higher into the canopy.

Release her when the sun rises, Naomi thought reluctantly. *Don't hurt her.*

Ferrin looked over his shoulder, his face white and twisted. He glanced at Naomi before focusing back on Vira who was fading in his hands.

Naomi turned and bolted back to them, her stored emotions

now flooding back. She squatted in front of Ferrin. His head was bent over Vira in a stance of defeat.

"Tell me you can heal her," Naomi begged.

He looked up. "I don't have enough in me. I can try. Maybe I can stall the process. But I can't fix her right this minute."

Hux clamped a firm hand on his shoulder. "You need more time."

He nodded. "I need more time. I saw Saul in the city with the Riders. He'll come for us next. We have to get out of the city, but I don't know how long Vira can hold on. I need to get her somewhere safe where I can do some healing or we'll have to leave her here." He shook his head. "And I'm not going to leave her."

Vira took in a single gasp. The sound struck Naomi with a sickening feeling of sorrow.

"We can give you more time," Naomi claimed.

Ferrin kept his hands over Vira's wound, but held Naomi's gaze. "How?"

"Hux and I will leave. We'll go alone to draw Saul and Maya away. I ordered the trees to release Maya when the sun rises, so she'll try to find Hux again and arrest him for treason. Saul wants me because I'm a Massoud. Maya won't come after you if Hux isn't with you and Saul will continue to hunt for me. If we leave, you'll have enough time to get Vira somewhere safe without having to defend yourself."

Vira gasped again. Ferrin tilted her head up to alleviate her struggle. "Good graves, Naomi, I know you're right," he choked. "What about Estell? Is she gone for good?"

Naomi eyed the ground where Estell had disappeared. "Nothing seems more final than being buried beneath the soil. I think she's gone."

Ferrin nodded. "Go, Naomi."

Her insides twisted. "You have the quill. Best to keep it

separated from me. The necklace is the source of ink for the quill."

"What?" His breath caught, trying to focus on Vira and the new information all at once. "Ink?"

She nodded. "Yes, Ferrin. Listen to me. Keep the quill and I'll keep the necklace. The quill won't work without me. If either of us get caught, no one will be able to make a move against Calamity."

"Alright," he said. "Good *graves*. What if I can't save her?"

Hux hung his head. "Then this is her fate."

Naomi stared at Ferrin through the hair falling in front of his face. His cheeks trembled like he was trying not to cry.

"You listen to me," she said softly.

He managed to look at her, worry clouding the gentle features of his face.

"No matter what happens here, you need to find us again." She gripped his shoulders. "Do you understand? If Vira dies, we still need you. We still want you."

He nodded, his entire body trembling.

She leaned forward and wrapped her arms around him. His face pressed into her collarbone. She held back her own tears and kissed the top of his head.

He spoke against her ear. "You trust Hux with your life. And you protect him with just as much vigor."

"I will," she promised.

They withdrew, but he lifted a hand to her cheek. "There's an oak tree marked with five knots. It will lead you out of Mira Isla. An emergency portal. No golden witch or Magnificent needed."

She placed her hand on his, holding it against her cheek a moment longer. "Thank you." She sniffed. "I wish it didn't have to be this way."

"So do I." He swallowed a sob. "But I'll find you again and I will help you bring an end to the world's darkness. As you've already done to my own darkness."

Shouts from the city drifted through the air, the invasion still raging. But soon Naomi and Hux would be gone, leaving the Riders with nothing to pursue. Ferrin could take Vira somewhere safe and Mira Isla would be left alone.

Hux helped Naomi up. "We need to go."

She nodded.

"Ferrin," Hux strained.

"I know." Ferrin shifted Vira over his shoulder. "I will do everything in my power."

"I know you will," Hux said, aiding Ferrin as he rose with Vira in his arms. "But she did this to save Naomi. She knew what she was doing. If she dies, it won't be your fault." He took a moment to collect himself. "And keep yourself safe. We want to see you again."

"You will," Ferrin grunted, trudging into the dark treeline. "Calamity has no idea of the rage it just released in me."

Naomi watched him go, understanding his words and feeling them as her own. Calamity had no idea of the force she vowed to become.

Hux tore away into the dark in the direction Ferrin had pointed them. Naomi sprinted behind. Her lungs burned, her throat closed. The trembling of her lips let out a small, desperate cry. *Protect him*, she thought, bringing Ferrin's face to her mind. *In Protection's name, keep him safe. For me, keep him safe.*

As she ran, she noticed a new feeling in her chest. It felt like a door. With enough willpower, she could shut the door, slamming away all of her heightened emotions. But as soon as she willed the door to open again, all of the horrible feelings would come running back. She practiced controlling that door over and over, knowing that her powers relied on her ability to open and shut that door.

A strong wind ripped through the trees, twirling around her and Hux. A damp, orange leaf blew up from the ground. It smacked her in the arm, sticking to her as she ran. A tremor and an itch penetrated her skin beneath the leaf. When she plucked the leaf from her skin, red light flashed behind her eyes. Just like it had when she touched The Rooted Lady. A voice inside her head screamed. No hushed tone like before.

It must flow! It screamed. *Let it flow! You must retreat to Le'Gar! Le'Gar! GO HOME, NAOMI MASSOUD!*

Naomi dropped the leaf, gasping for breath.

Hux zipped to her side. "What is it? Is it your ankle? I'll carry you."

"No," she said, sharp. "No." Rubbing her eyes, she focused on the woods around her, able to see their blurry shapes. The red light was gone. Her mind free again. "I need to go home." She looked up at him, her face shriveled in worry.

"What do you mean?" he asked softly. "Beezus has long been destroyed. We need to get out of *here*."

"Not Beezus," she said. "Le'Gar. For Protection's sake, Hux, I need to get back to Le'Gar." She breathed through her nose, willing away nausea.

"Okay," he soothed. "I hear you. But why? They want you dead."

"I know," she exclaimed with dread. "But something is there for me. I need to go back to my gargoyles."

CHAPTER FORTY-SEVEN

Sweat dripped down Ferrin's face as he finally made it out of the hills and into Mira Isla's streets. The streets were empty and dark. The invaders had already passed through here, and the residents of Mira Isla were no doubt hiding behind locked doors.

Ferrin readjusted Vira on his shoulder. She felt awfully limp. He wasn't sure if she was still alive. But even though his legs shook with fatigue, he carried on, hauling Vira through the winding streets to a place he knew would be safe. To Brahm's underground jewelry shop.

He was almost to the dingy alleyway when a small figure came tearing toward him. He jumped back, ready to throw energy to protect him and Vira, but he stopped when the figure was right in front of him. It was Millicent.

Her face was streaked with tears and her dress was ripped and soiled with dirt.

"Millicent," Ferrin said, taking a step toward her.

The little girl pointed to Vira hanging over Ferrin's shoulder. "Is that—"

Ferrin gently grabbed Millicent's arm and pulled her along with him. "Come on. I'm taking your mother somewhere safe. Are you hurt?"

Millicent's sobs echoed through the streets. "No. But I saw The Dark Hand and I think it's going to kill Naomi."

"It won't kill her," Ferrin said. "She's strong." He stood in front of the alley wall and let go of Millicent to swipe open the invisible door within the rock.

He struggled on his way down the stone steps. It was dark and Vira was dead weight. Her blood dripped down his chest and he fought back a lump in his throat. *Please don't let her be dead. Please. For her daughter's sake, please.*

Millicent followed behind and Ferrin kept his free hand on her, forcing her to keep up as she cried.

"We're going to help your mother," he promised. "I'm going to do everything I can."

When they reached Brahm's wooden door, Ferrin didn't even knock. He waved a force of energy over the lock and the door swung open. He stepped inside and in a swish of vapor, Brahm materialized. He stood in front of Ferrin with watery eyes and a foreboding look.

"What's happened?" Brahm asked. He looked sadly at Vira hanging helplessly over Ferrin's exhausted body. "Oh no."

"The arrow's still in her," Ferrin informed quickly. "I need a safe place to heal."

Without a second thought, Brahm spun and swept an arm across a long table, clearing it of all tools and spare metal. Ferrin lay Vira on the table on her back. Her breathing was almost unnoticeable, but Ferrin could see the small sips of breath she was still taking.

Brahm swished around the shop, grabbing anything he could use to mop up her blood.

Ferrin placed both hands around the arrow sticking out of

Vira. He would have to pull it out, but he needed to feel for a pathway of healing first. Vira would have little time once the arrow was removed. But to Ferrin's dismay, he couldn't sense any strong pathways of healing within her body. There were fragments of life still coursing through her, but the fragments were weak. He could hardly grasp onto them. Nevertheless, he had to try.

Turning, he saw Millicent watching. Her little face was in shock and her whole body trembled. Ferrin removed his hands from Vira and pulled Millicent into himself, pressing her face into the front of his shirt.

"Don't look," he ordered. "Cover your ears."

Millicent obeyed, covering her ears and keeping her face buried in his chest.

Brahm put both hands on the arrow. "I feel her passing into my realm of death. You must start the healing process or you'll lose her if you haven't already."

Ferrin pressed his hands around Vira's wound again. "Pull out the arrow."

Brahm removed the arrow and Ferrin quickly bore down on the gaping hole where blood rushed out faster now.

Vira squirmed in pain and Millicent lifted her head.

"Don't look, Millie," Ferrin snapped. "Keep your head down."

Brahm held a wet washcloth over Vira's forehead. "Why was she struck?"

Ferrin focused on his breathing as he sent waves of healing energy into the wound. "Grab the item that's in my pocket."

Brahm frowned but moved around the table and pulled out the quill. He stared at it and moved his fingers slowly over the feather, watching it move effortlessly like a real feather would, even though it was cased in gold.

"What is this?" Brahm whispered.

Ferrin's eyes were closed and his arms began to shake as the healing process became more difficult. "You tell me."

Brahm laid a hand on Ferrin's shoulder. "Your arms are ripping open, my friend."

Ferrin glanced at his arms where fresh cuts were opening. The result of his powers attacking his body.

"I don't care," Ferrin said, gasping for breath. "Brahm, what is this quill? I have to know. The quill is the reason Vira is hurt."

Brahm watched Vira, the quill lying in his open palm. "Just the quill?"

Ferrin looked up. "No."

"Did the quill work with the capsule necklace you brought to me?"

"Yes."

Vira took a deep breath and Ferrin pressed his hands down harder. "Come on," he mumbled. "Come on, Vira."

"Capsule pendants are often passed down through royal families," Brahm explained, stealing glances at Vira every time she so much as twitched. "But I have the feeling you're about to tell me you haven't been riding with royalty."

"I haven't," Ferrin agreed. He moved his hands away from Vira's wound and to her neck, resting them over her airway.

"And you're right," Brahm said. "You haven't been riding with royalty. You've been riding with a god."

Ferrin's blood ran cold. He looked up, taking in Brahm's serious face. "What do you mean?"

Brahm trailed his finger over the quill. "This isn't made from any material from Thãen. This was crafted in the Outer Void. In the realm of the higher beings. This was created to be used by a god."

Ferrin looked down at Vira, wishing she were conscious. Not only because he feared she might die in front of her daughter, but because he trusted that Vira could back up Brahm's claim.

"Naomi isn't a god," Ferrin whispered. "She's—"

"A Massoud," Brahm said softly.

"Yes," he admitted with a heavy breath. "How did you know?"

"I reside in the realm of death," Brahm said. "We are closer to the Outer Void than the living. We know things. We hear things. A Massoud is rumored to be the savior of Thãen, and rumored to be a god, just like Protection. Just like Calamity."

"Naomi is not like Calamity," Ferrin retorted.

Brahm gave Ferrin a sad look. "Not every god is good. Not every god is bad. Some of them are both."

"Not Naomi," Ferrin argued. "She is light."

Vira let out a cry and Ferrin threw a hand over her wound again. Her breathing that had been growing steady plummeted again. He was losing her.

Millicent sniffed into Ferrin's shirt. "Is my mum okay? Is she coming back?"

"I'm doing everything I can," Ferrin choked.

Brahm moved back to Vira's head and replaced the washcloth on her skin. He set the quill down beside her on the table. "You shouldn't have let your Massoud out of your sight."

"It wasn't my choice," he said. "She left so I would have time to heal Vira."

"That could have been a grave mistake," Brahm said sadly. "A god who can't control their powers can easily fall. They either fall into evil or fall into the arms of death just by pure lack of experience. She needs someone like you to help her learn her powers."

Ferrin closed his eyes. "Please don't, Brahm. I'm already worried for her."

Brahm nodded and looked down into Vira's face. "What if

you can't save this golden witch?" he whispered so Millicent couldn't hear.

"I will still continue the fight," Ferrin said through a shaky breath. "I will find Naomi and I will push her to be the god you say she is. It's what Vira would want, whether dead or alive. And it's what I want. I want to see Naomi through to the end."

CHAPTER FORTY-EIGHT

Eli the Magnificent crept across the roof, nearing the window of the abandoned room above the city. The room that Naomi Massoud used to occupy. The stone beast still sat on the ledge, guarding. But it gave the old man a glance.

Eli paused when he saw his own reflection in the window glass. Because his body wasn't the only one there. Next to his reflection was another person. Someone inside the room. Just as he predicted.

He pushed open the window. The woman inside faced him calmly. Her arms were crossed and shoulders poised as if she expected him.

"I must admit," he said, stepping down into the room. "I never assumed you were the one I kept feeling."

She scoffed, but smiled. "I'm surprised. I let her rent the room above my library for goodness sake."

He trailed his eyes around the room, examining Naomi's old home. "How did you know about her, Deirdre? Not even royalty knew. It strikes me odd that a librarian would have the knowledge of a Massoud. And you let her stay here. Why?"

"I know a lot of things," she whispered. "And I know that she is not the force of destruction that many believe Massouds to be. She is meant for good."

Eli furrowed his brows and cocked his head. Deirdre hadn't been in Le'Gar as long as he had been and she wasn't a Magnificent. So there was no way she lived to see and experience what had happened to Oliver Massoud. But he kept feeling the presence of magic in the city. That feeling had guided him here. "You're a golden witch?" he asked.

She shook her head. As she did so, her eyes faded and glassed over to match that of the gargoyles. Solid colored. Absent. Stone.

Eli stepped back, his heart speeding.

"Don't be frightened," she begged. "I can explain. And I will."

He sensed no danger in her. Not even an ounce. "Do you see the full picture?" He dared to move toward her. "Do you know how it ends?"

"Not fully," she shuttered, looking down. When she glanced up again, her eyes had returned to their human state. "But I know how it began."

Eli's fingers twitched at his sides. "Can you help the cause?"

She nodded, slow. "I can help. But Naomi must be willing to fight."

"She's willing," Eli confirmed. "I've seen her in my mind recently. She's changed." He gave a little smile. "She's ready to fight."

ALSO BY KEIRA F. JACOBS

Daughter of Destiny

Keeper of the Light

Other

The Testimony of Bendigo Fletcher

ABOUT THE AUTHOR

Keira F. Jacobs grew up in the gorgeous state of Michigan, then planted new roots in sunny South Carolina with her husband. She spends most of her time raising her two boys, exercising, cooking, reading, leading worship at her local church, and writing. Those closest to her know that she loves Harry Potter, the Shire, coffee, gluten free oreos, and almost every genre of music.